Beloved
of
Ishmael

by

V M Steele

author of

The Scarred Wrists,
Hunters of Humans,
The Yellow Shadow.

Published 1937 by

Stanley Paul & Co., Ltd.
Paternoster Row - London - E.C.4

Originally printed in Great Britain at the
Anchor Press, Tiptree, Essex

Library and Archives Canada Cataloguing in Publication

Steele, V. M., author
    Beloved of Ishmael / V. M. Steele

Originally published: 1937
ISBN 978-1-896238-22-7 (softcover)

    1. Title.

PR6011.172B45 2017   823'.912   C2017-907448-2

Twin Eagles Publishing

**Box 2031
Sechelt BC
V0N 3A0**

pblakey@telus.net

604 885 7503

twineaglespublishing.com

ACKNOWLEDGEMENTS

The publication of the four 'lost' novels of Dion Fortune (Violet Mary Firth) has been quite a journey and I would like to acknowledge the hard work, dedication and financial assistance of Richard Brzustowicz, without whom none of the books would have seen the light of day.

I would also like to thank Sara Greer for proofreading *Beloved of Ishmael*, and furthermore this poor page setter would like to take responsibility for any typos, 'scannos' or spacing errors that may remain.

Finally I would like to add a reader's caution and spoiler alert.

This novel was written in 1937, when conventions of speech were less politically correct, and may be construed by present day readers as insulting to non-white races. The foreword, written by Mr. Brzustowicz, goes into some detail regarding the circumstances of the times, and the influences affecting the author, but does so in such a way as to reveal the plot, so if you want to be surprised by some of the story's twists and turns, wait until you have finished the book before you read the foreword.

Paul Blakey
Roberts Creek, 2017

FOREWORD

Chaste in Martaban:

Beloved of Ishmael (1937)

If ... there is no capacity for response, the reader will probably classify the stories with Tarzan of the Apes. If there is a capacity for response, and at the same time repressions and dissociations of psychopathology corresponding to the thesis of the book the reader... will have the equivalent of a fairly sever psychic shock because the book has spoken to their subconsciousness words they do not desire to hear. ...One of these days I may be lucky enough to be reviewed by a reviewer with a complex, and then my fortune is made!

Dion Fortune, *"The Novels of Dion Fortune"* (reprinted in Dion Fortune's Rites of Isis and of Pan, Skylight Press, 2013)

As little as Violet Firth could have expected it, of all the V. M. Steele novels, or of the Dion Fortune novels, this is the one most likely to tread firmly and relentlessly on the complexes of the early 21st century reader. Furthermore, although she expected readers to be shocked for essentially Freudian reasons, due to her relative bluntness about sexual mores, readers of the early 21st century are more likely to be shocked for *Adlerian* reasons.

One of the popular approaches to reading nowadays has

been described as, "Skim until offended," and people given to this approach will not have to read very far into the novel before their complexes have been well and truly trod on. To explain why, however, I'll first have to describe the novel.

Power and the Land

The story begins with Nina, daughter of a country vicar, on her way by ship to Africa to meet her fiancé, who has insisted that they be married in Africa. During the voyage, she becomes acquainted with a woman missionary, whose strength of character she admires without finding her altogether congenial. She hears that Africa has a generally deleterious effect on whites, who become prey to disease and drink, and general demoralization. When she asks whether it is possible to avoid this effect, she hears that there are few people who manage to do so. There are for example some missionaries whose dedication and discipline carries them through. There is also a deplorable example, a renegade Briton, one Cassalis, who has engaged in a career of lawlessness—slaving, rum-running, gun-running, and so on. He has also "unified the Juju lodges" and established "African Tammany," an extensive network of crime and corruption that has worked to keep him safe from official retaliation. He has also, somehow, managed to keep himself healthy and vigorous—perhaps too vigorous, if it is true that he has half-breed children scattered along the coast.

When she finally arrives at the river settlement to which her fiancé has summoned her, Nina gradually discovers several things, none of them welcome. First, it becomes clear that her fiancé is falling apart. He has become an alcoholic wreck, and is barely able to function. Second, it seems that he is all too familiar with people like himself, or worse; the hotel he has arranged seems a very dubious establishment.

All the Europeans she encounters seem at best pathetic ruins, and often much worse. Nevertheless, she finds herself delighted and enthralled by Africa itself, feeling that she has finally awakened from a long, dreary dream.

Her fiancé takes her out for a bit, and is met by an old acquaintance, one Lewis, who is a vivid contrast to everyone else. He seems vigorous and healthy; he is dressed in a kind woolen garment that, he explains, is far more suitable to the climate than those worn by the Europeans, and he seems to have an acute and ironical turn of mind. During their conversation, she shares her sense of delight at the vitality that seems to well up from the very soil, and Lewis suddenly stops treating her as a negligible accessory to her fiancé, and begins to engage in a real conversation—about Africa, the difference between heaven-oriented religion and earth-oriented religion, and other matters. He also makes some remarks that lead Nina to think that he might be someone useful to know —and far more likely to be helpful than her fiancé.

In fact, when she and her fiancé return to the hotel, two other things become clear. All the material that he has asked her to buy and bring out to set up their new household is actually being sold off to raise money—and he has no intentions of marrying her at all, but (she suspects, and the general attitude of the hotel patrons suggests) is probably looking to sell her off as well.

She manages to get away from her fiancé, and meet up with Lewis, explain her situation, and throw herself on his self-interested and ironical mercy. He offers to get her out of town on his launch (with a very competent black African crew), and they manage to escape their pursuers and make off up the river. After some further conversation, Lewis proposes that they stop at a mission on the river and get married. She agrees. They do—but in the course of the proceedings she discovers that "Lewis" is not his surname, as she'd assumed—his full name is in fact "Lewis Cassalis". Difficulties ensue.

The story then proceeds on three main tracks.

First, the account of the vicissitudes of the relationship between Nina and Cassalis, which suffers a series of impediments and resolutions that have nothing to do with suspense about getting married or having sexual relations—rather reminiscent of the Edgar Rice Burroughs plots in many of the Tarzan novels, in which Lord Greystoke and his wife are always being separated by events and villainy, and have to struggle to be reunited.)

Second, the gradual elucidation of Cassalis' backstory —his fall from colonial grace, his adoption by Ibrahim, an Arab slave trader, his deep delight with the vitality of Africa and his initiation into the ways of African life, his acculturation to, and mastery of, the system, his complete alienation from "respectable" colonial life and avoidance of it when he is not preying on it, and his pleasure in being part of a counter-system that is African rather than colonial.

Third, there is the contemporary track—Cassalis' trading activities, their stay in his secret highland retreat, the recurrent attempts of the colonial authorities to capture and prosecute him, and several episodes of capture and escape.

The tangle of villainies and misunderstandings must be resolved by three parties: Nina, Cassalis, and a newly-appointed senior colonial official and his wife (who both know a surprising amount about what goes on, and are utterly unfazed by the gritty realities of life). In the end, the couple is reunited and their union strengthened, the legal tangles are resolved, the rebellion redirected, and Cassalis is offered a job tailored to his particular skills and quirks.

This story has several features that have probably caused more recent readers to squirm. First, the it takes the colonial situation more or less as a given, and does not offer any overt or explicit critique of it; in fact, the resolution involves a re-integration with it. Second, the story features not only stock characters and ethnic stereotypes, but a substantial vocabulary of casual ethnic disparagement (Portuguese traders are "dagoes"; black Africans are generally "niggers", or occasionally "bucks" or "mammies", although "picaninny" is also used at one point to refer to Lewis' and Nina's child). Third, the "Ju-ju lodge" subplot, in which Africans are manipulated through their belief in the cult of the ape messiah, seems to rely on an insulting view of African gullibility. (On the other hand, there is no use of the comedic stereotype of the eye-rolling, horrified, superstitious black; the black Africans of the novel are not figures of fun.) Fourth, the two main characters have very little interest in the proprieties —either of their time or of ours. For example, it is at one point mentioned in passing that Cassalis has stopped patronizing brothels after his marriage—but this is not mentioned in a way that suggests that there is any ethical weight in either course of action. When someone asserts to Nina, in the course of an attempt to alienate her from him, that Cassalis has half-breed offspring up and down the coast, it barely registers with her as an issue. In a setting that nowadays would be heavily moralized (or "politicized"), none of the characters indulges in moralizing reflection. Cassalis turns away from slave-trading because it displeases him; while he was involved with it, he tried to treat his chains of slaves fairly well because it made good business sense, and because it pleased him to do so. The main characters act from their energies; they enact their desires. They act on the basis of taste and distaste, alliance and enmity, honor and dishonor. Corruption is not immoral: it is weak, ignoble, distasteful—and occasionally useful enough. Except for the occasional righteous missionary, an explicit concern with proprieties and morality is usually an attribute of the degenerate and corrupt.

In many ways, the plausibility and motive force of the novel depend on the idea of individual reactions to the elemental force and energy of the African soil, presented in a way reminiscent of CG Jung's accounts of his own African experiences, and not unlike Charles Williams' novel *Shadows of Ecstasy* (1933), in which there is an incursion of African energy into sleepy England.

Three questions arise. First, what can a reader in the early 21st century make of this story? Second, what was the author intending to do? And third, how does it fit into the body of her work?

In the Foreign Country of the Past

In the English-speaking world of the early 21st century, there are several issues that are so embedded in a tissue of cultural contradictions that they are hard to examine, or discuss, dispassionately—and any attempt to do so is often felt to be itself illegitimate. One of these is the issue of race.

It is almost inevitable that a reader nowadays will read this book through the filter of the conflicting, even paradoxical, demands of these cultural contradictions. Modern publishers tend to vet carefully books that touch on issues of race, sexuality, cultural conflict, and so on, even trying them out on focus groups or consulting sensitivity committees before committing to publishing them. Encountering a book that has clearly not been through such a process can be at very least disconcerting, and for some people quite distressing.

Of course, no one is obliged to read this book. For those who undertake the adventure, however, it may be helpful to remember that it was written in a time when the modern complex fabric of anxiety, guilt and hostility was still to be woven, and before people had become to treating such issues with exquisite delicacy.

The book will, unavoidably, be at least a bit jarring. But that can be a positive, even instructive experience, if one reads mindfully, being aware of one's own reactions as the story unfolds. By an accident of history, this novel has come to achieve a kind of distancing effect that will tend to keep readers from naive immersion, and lead them to be instead to be aware of the interplay of the thriller-romance fantasy and their own reactions.

Most people who read this book will be doing so because they wish to know more of the author, rather than because they simply want to pass the time with a romance or adventure. For such readers, then, this distancing effect will be a positive feature, rather than a defect.

The Only Thing We Learn From History

Our author was not a denizen of the early 21st century: she was born toward the end of 1890, and died at the beginning of 1946. As far as anyone knows, the farthest she ever went from England was Wales; it is not clear that she ever reached Scotland. What, then, was she doing writing of Africa?

Africa featured frequently in the fiction and journalism of the early 20th century—Edgar Rice Burroughs and Edgar Wallace come to mind, along with Lawrence G. Green. Furthermore, at least two of the author's teachers, Dr. Lillias Hamilton (the unscrupulous "Warden" in *Psychic Self-Defense*) and Dr. Theodore Moriarty (the model for Dr. Taverner), had spent time in Africa before she knew them.

Despite this, it is important to remember that she was not writing about Africa as an ethnographic and historical reality. She was using the African setting to write about something else, and in doing so she makes certain assumptions that were part of the tradition (exoteric as well as esoteric) from which she wrote.

First, it is clear that "Africa" in the novel stands for energy and power: that those who thrive there are those for whom energy and power are congenial, and those who fail are those who are weak, or who cannot open themselves to the abundance of energy offered by the land. In the terms of the novel, virtue is, and comes from, strength; vice is, and comes, from weakness—as indeed the roots of the words suggest. The primary motivators for all characters are issues of strength and power: even sexuality is lived in terms of power and weakness, honor and dishonor. In psychological terms, the novel is cast Adlerian rather than Freudian or even Jungian, terms. Superiority and inferiority are the issues, not desire, or a quest for meaning. Cassalis, the hero, is bad and dangerous to know, and arguably a bit mad, and the heroine recognizes, and responds immediately to, the difference between the alpha male Cassalis and her less-than-beta fiancé. But "Africa" also means something in the esoteric context from which she was writing. Esotericists have often claimed to see beyond, or better than, the natural science of their day, using current natural science to interpret the esoteric tradition, and using the esoteric tradition to "correct" or re-vision those natural sciences. In the early to mid-20th century, one such process occurred with respect to the relationship that was posited to exist between the energy centers of the body (as depicted, for example, in Theosophical works, or in the Indian works from which they derived) and the endocrine glands, the functions of which were coming under scientific investigation at that time. Esotericists linked the endocrine glands to the "psychic centers" (whichever version they were inclined to use), and used the lore of the psychic centers to re-interpret the function of the endocrine glands.

At that time, the older idea of characteristic constitutional humoral balances (phlegmatic, choleric, and so on) became reinterpreted as characteristic types of constitutional endocrine balance: thus, Dr. Rupert Malcolm, in *Moon Magic*, spends time in the National Gallery reflecting on the endocrine balances of the nudes.

Beyond this, however, it was thought that races each had a characteristic endocrine balance or constitutional type. (See, for example, Ivor Geike Cobb's 1928 book, *The Glands of Destiny*). This is one of the sources of the idea that, since occult training works on the "energy centers" (endocrine glands), certain modes of training are better suited to one racial type (endocrine constitution) than another, and using the inappropriate mode of training could lead to serious disturbances—not just psychological, but physiological as well. Racial hybridization, too, was looked on as a source of physiological unbalance, as though well-established equilibria would be put into disarray by indiscriminate blending. As is always the case in medicine, every new discovery leads to a rush of excited speculation that is often treated as fact, until practical application reveals the shortcomings of the premature synthesis (when the shiny new tool you have is a hammer, the world presents a multitude of thumbs). By the early 21st century, the simplicities of the earlier synthesis have become untenable. Endocrinology, pharmacology, and genetics no longer much resemble what they were in the 1920s, and esoteric notions based in century-old biology have become more of a puzzle than a key.

A very full scholarly career could be devoted to tracing out the history of the interaction between esotericism and biomedicine; no doubt before the end of that career, new material would still be becoming available.

Final Overview

With the publication of the fourth V. M. Steele novel, all known works written under that name are available again.

What can be said of the whole body of work?

All four novels are quite congruent with the novels of Dion Fortune, in that they are explorations of the struggles of, and choices made by, people who are decidedly outcast and marginal. In three of the four, the male protagonist has been outcast and stigmatized; only in Hunters of Humans is the male protagonist a part of the respectable world—and even so, his position is a transitional one. In all four, the female protagonist is a young, displaced woman who chooses —or is led by circumstances to be almost forced to choose— inner truth over outer respectability, to make her own system lest she be enslaved by another's.

In all four, the authority of the conventional or respectable world is itself called into question not only by the choice of life over convention, but by the frequent ironical observations made by the narrative voice about the ways in which the conventional world itself is maintained by back-stage manipulations and accommodations. Finally, the reintegration at the end is achieved on the outcasts' own terms, and represents a partial surrender on the part of the forces of conventional authority (and the authority of convention).

However, there is a sharp break between first two, set in England and the last two, set in Africa and China. The world of the first two is English; in the last two, although the story involves an Englishwoman going into a strange land, that strange land also comes, in effect, to England, in the English imagination of the writer and readers.

The last two also suggest an uncompleted thematic pattern. In some occult lore, there are three major energies underlying reality, Power, Wisdom and Love, and these are associated with the religious systems of Africa, "the East" (Buddhism), and "the West" (Christianity). It is conceivable that the novel set in Africa was intended to exemplify the theme of Power, and that set in China was meant to exemplify the theme of Wisdom. If so, it may also be that the author's unexpected death prevented her from writing yet a third novel, one dealing with the energies of Love.

We have the author's own remarks about her aim in writing her occult novels; unfortunately, nothing survives about any larger aim in writing these seemingly non-occult novels. However, given her testimony about the initiatory agenda of the major occult novels, we might well speculate that these secular novels also contained an initiatory intent.

In the absence of evidence, such speculations are likely to be arbitrary at best. Still, the pattern in all four novels is that of a romance-thriller, a union of male and female, in the context of a reconciliation of the lower with the higher, the old with the new, individual energy and power with the world of convention, and, finally, the foreign with the domestic.

It would hardly be going too far to suppose that our perceptive and analytic author, aware of the transformations that her country and her world were undergoing, was hoping to provide certain seed ideas to the minds of her readers, and through them, to the 'group mind" of her nation. Her hope would have been that such seed ideas would enable her readers, and the people of her nation, to hold in a single image the integration of opposites, and thereby provide a pattern to resolve those conflicts on an inner level, so that they would not have to work themselves out more disastrously in the outer world.

Richard Brzustowicz, December 2017

CHAPTER 1

NINA BARNET leant over the steamer rail and counted the packages that lay on the quay. She had been advised by the agent to keep her packages small, as they would have to go up country on the backs of porters, and she had obeyed; in consequence they lay in an untidy little flock, completely overshadowed by the neighbouring packing-cases and Saratoga trunks of touring Americans.

She felt very lonely and melancholy at that moment. Her family had considered that, as they strongly disapproved of the whole affair, they had done all that could be expected of them in seeing her off at the local station, and she had been left to cross Liverpool and get down to the docks and get herself and her belongings on board the *S.S. Benin* as best she might. This enterprise had presented no especial difficulties, but all the same she felt scared and forlorn as she stood alone on the deck of the steamer watching the bustle on the quay as the derricks swung the last of the luggage on board and the Blue Peter flip-flipped over her head and a haze of grey smoke rose out of the funnels.

She saw telegraph-boys come on board with handfuls of telegrams for departing travellers; and special messengers with great bunches of flowers; and in the purser's office there were parcels for all sorts of folk; but for her there was nothing, save a bundle of well-worn letters in her bag and a man's signet ring on her third finger. She was embarking on a woman's greatest adventure entirely alone, and the courage that had sustained her through the year and a half of her bitterly contested engagement was beginning to flag, leaving her defenceless against the world.

The skies were grey as steel; the wind that blew over the Liverpool dockhead was cold and keen, and the dirty water overside slapped at the steamer's rusty plates in a way that promised heavy weather once they were outside the shelter of the Mersey Heads.

The forward derrick picked up a great net full of grimy canvas mailbags and dropped it into the hold. The siren let off a shattering roar; a bugler took his stand at the head of the wide, rubber-carpeted stairs that led down to the saloon, and made ear-splitting noises; and stewards went up and down the alleyways crying: "All off for the shore!" A couple of dock-hands laid hold of the gangway and dragged it clear of the ship's side. The siren let off another bellow. First one of the great mooring-cables and then the other fell with a splash into the water. A tug, hitherto completely hidden from view by the towering sides of the ship, gave a squeal; its powerful twin screws began to kick up the Mersey mud, and, as the tow-rope tightened, the ship's head was gradually hauled clear of the quay; then a shudder ran through her frame, and a steady thumpety-thud began to beat like a great heart. Slowly the big ship gathered steerage-way; the tug slipped to one side, the hawser was cast off, the Blue Peter was hauled down from the fore and the Red Ensign broken out from the flagstaff at the stem—the voyage began.

Acting on the advice of a fatherly steward, Nina did not remain on deck to watch the progress down the unlovely river, but went below to get unpacked while the ship was still within the shelter of the land. The steward had informed her that there would be "a bit of a popple outside", whatever that might be, and going past the dining-saloon she caught a glimpse of polished wooden frames being clamped on to the

16

long tables, and guessed that these were the fiddles. Evidently the bit of a popple would be sufficient to fling the crockery about.

In her cabin she found a small, dried-up little wisp of a woman, with a complexion like neglected wash-leather, very busy with a cabin trunk.

"Ah!" exclaimed the stranger at sight of her. "You have come down to unpack? How very wise! Do let us have everything put away before we get outside the Heads. It is such a nuisance if things break loose." She secured a medicine-bottle to the folding washstand with a skilful twist of a rubber band: evidently an experienced traveller.

Nina felt instantly cheered. The little woman was friendly and kindly without being obtrusive. She would be a pleasant travelling companion.

Nina gazed at her, and wondered whether her own complexion would get like wash-leather after a few years of West African suns. At any rate she need not screw her hair into a bun behind as if about to wash her ears. A glance at the cabin trunk over which the little woman was bending revealed that she was a Miss Leete, and that she was bound for the Okambu Mission station in Dahomey. That explained her style of hairdressing, and Nina took heart again. It might not be necessary for anyone who had not got a soul above cosmetics to get a skin like that. The little missionary lady was a competent and businesslike unpacker and had finished long before Nina had, and sat down on the settee under the porthole to chat to her companion.

"And where are you going to?" she inquired, looking like a dilapidated but cheerful sparrow.

"To a place called Okiki, at the mouth of the river Wari. Do you know that part?"

"No, I have never been as far south as that. I get off before you do."

Slowly the floor rose up like a lift on the Underground, hung poised for a moment, and then gently subsided into space. Nina took three running steps across the scanty floor-space and brought up all standing against the wash stand.

"A good job we got unpacked when we did," said Miss Leete. "And what is your fiancé?"—her eyes noting the ringed hand that was adjusting the oddments in the rack over the wash-stand that served as a dressing-table.

"He is in the Customs service," said Nina, and took three unexpected steps backwards and sat down on her bunk.

"I think I shall go to bed now," said Miss Leete, "and if I were you I should do the same; you evidently have not got your sea-legs."

The opening days of all voyages are alike to the bad sailor. Nina felt as if she would sell her hope of heaven for five minutes' cessation of the ceaseless pitch and toss. A cheerful young man in a very smart uniform, with a line of red braid between the two gold ones on his cuffs, came and looked at her, laughed, and told her to drink champagne till the cabin went round and round as well as up and down. Miss Leete ate four square meals a day, and munched biscuits at midnight, but nevertheless declined to leave her bunk until the Bay was passed.

Finally the stewardess very firmly put Nina into a few clothes and a big coat, led her up on deck, tucked her up in her rug, and left her to take the air, promising that she would be as fit as a fiddle in two tweaks, and that there was nothing like a good go of sea-sickness to clear you out. Nina believed her.

She lay back in the long chair, almost too weak to raise her head, watching the horizon moving slowly up and down as the ship rolled gently in the swell left behind by the storm. The sea was a brilliant blue with a sparkle on the crests of the rollers where they caught the sun, and there was a warm balminess in the air such as Nina had never felt before. Evidently they were getting south.

She lay back watching the swing of the horizon, and in a few minutes she dropped off to sleep. The deck steward came and looked at her presently, and went away again. The bugle calling to lunch blared close beside her, but still she slept. It was not till four o'clock in the afternoon that she was awakened by someone shaking her shoulder, and opened dazed eyes to find the deck steward balancing a heavily loaded tea-tray precariously on her knees. After tea she went down to her cabin and took her hair firmly in hand. That evening she put on her prettiest frock and made her first appearance in the saloon.

She was flattered to find that she was seated at the captain's table, at his right hand. Her *vis-a-vis* grinned and enlightened her, without troubling about preamble or introduction.

"The captain always keeps an eye on the brides in case they get snapped up by the wrong party. Women are scarce with us, and we appreciate 'em accordingly. I've been told off to look after you till he appears. We'll be making Las Palmas during the night, and he never leaves the bridge while we're in soundings."

Nina looked round the big saloon, and saw that the diners divided into two well-defined classes—the gay, tourist type of pleasure-seeker, who formed the majority; and a handful of hard-bitten, sun-dried men, with here and there a woman of Miss Leete's type.

That evening there was a dance. Nina took a turn or two with the young doctor, and then went weary to bed, for a week's solid sea-sickness is hard work. Nor did she arise till midday next morning, and then she found that the pleasure-seekers were gone, disembarked at Las Palmas, and that all that remained on board were the hard-bitten men and handful of dried-up women. The ranks in the saloon closed up to three tables, presided over respectively by the captain, the purser, and the doctor. Everybody seemed to know everybody else, and the captain appeared at last to take charge of his flock. There was only one other woman beside Nina at the captain's table, and she was down the far end, out of earshot.

The conversation related to matters entirely outside Nina's ken but nevertheless keenly interesting as concerning her new life. They argued about rainfall, boasting of the number of inches that had fallen in an hour in their respective localities, and the average humidity at midday and the height of the mercury at midnight. The figures meant nothing to her, it sounded as if they were discussing the suburbs of hell—a moist, steaming hell, in which the drop of water which Dives begged of Lazarus would have passed unnoticed in Abraham's perspiring bosom.

It suddenly occurred to her to wonder how the pile of organdie frocks she had made for her trousseau were going to stand this damp heat, and comforted herself with the remembrance that Okiki was on the coast, and therefore presumably enjoyed sea-breezes.

She was recalled to herself by the buzz of interest that ran round the table as the captain said something about "Cassalis's latest'!

" 'My God,' I said to him, 'what do you want a piano for?'

" 'To play hymn tunes on,' sez he.

" 'Well, you'd better fetch it away quick,' sez I. 'It's not my business to open it if the Customs have passed it, but I'll be glad to see the last of it.' And dashed if the blessed donkeyman didn't drop it out of the slings, and it burst open, and there were the barrels of rifles!

" 'Bless me soul,' sez Cassalis, 'they've sent me an organ instead of a piano!' "

"What did you do?" inquired a hard-featured Coaster as the laughter died down.

"Looked the other way," said the captain. "I'd no wish to fall foul of Cassalis."

"I don't blame you. Neither has anybody else who's tried it once," said the Coaster. "I was on board the *Biafra* when he fetched off a couple of cases of Brumma gem handcuffs that were invoiced through to him as large as life. Handcuffs aren't contraband like rifles, but of course it was obvious what they were wanted for; but nobody dared stop him."

"What were they wanted for?" demanded the interested but mystified Nina.

"Slave trade," said the Coaster. "Bringing the slaves down, handcuffed to a long chain. They start off with a hundred, and if they land in with fifty they consider it a good trip."

"But I thought slavery had been abolished."

"Then you thought wrong. There's any amount of it. And Cassalis and his old pal Sheik Ibrahim are at the bottom of most of it."

"But is it allowed?"

"Of course it isn't allowed. But how are you going to stop it? You can't police thousands of square miles of tropical forest. Cassalis and his fighting blacks pick up the niggers over a wide area. March 'em in chains up to the edge of the Sahara, taking months over the trip. Blacks can't turn on 'em because they all come from different tribes and can't speak each other's lingo, so they can't organize. That's where Cassalis is so cute. Then old Ibrahim meets him between the desert and the sown, picks up what's left of his blacks after the journey, and takes 'em on to one of those sacred cities which are too holy for any white man to enter. They're no more holy than I am. They're where the big slave markets

21

are held. But the League of Nations chirrups away about the sacredness of the black man's religion. Just as sacred to him as ours is to us. Mustn't interfere with it. Oh dear, no. Let him bow down to wood and stone if he wants. He has a perfect right to. But they never inquire what is behind the wood and stone that is too sacred for an unbeliever to look at, and that's where all the dealing in black ivory goes on."

"Do you suppose Cassalis ever gets into those sacred cities out in the desert?" asked the captain.

"Cassalis gets in everywhere. He's gone clean native, you know. He belongs to all the secret societies up and down the Coast. He's the Lord High Mumbo-Jumbo in his own parts. It's not a case of Cassalis getting in; it's a case of Cassalis convening the meeting."

"I hate to see a man go native," said the captain.

"I'll say this for Cassalis, though," said the Coaster. "He hasn't deteriorated. He has kept his end up remarkably. Been out ten years without going home, and as fit as a fiddle. How does he do it? The rest of us are dead to the wide at the end of three years."

"Doesn't drink, for one thing," chipped in another man. "I've never seen Cassalis even merry. Always the same cold-blooded, poker-faced blighter. He works as steadily at his slave-trading, and gun-running, and rum-dealing, and every-thing that destroys the nigger, body and soul, as a Scotch elder peddling Bibles. If Cassalis could be induced to turn his talents to better uses, he'd be a first-class chap. But as it is he's the most dangerous brute unhung down the entire Coast. Any decent man ought to shoot him on sight. But you never get any evidence against him, and never will."

"Surely the number of fellows he's quarrelled with, who've come to untimely ends, must begin to mount up into evidence?"

"They won't let you put it that way in a court of law. You

have to prove each case separately. And that is exactly what you can't do. But a chap's enemies don't die off so systematically without a reason."

"What do they die of?"

"Anything and everything. Canoe capsizes, and the feller gets eaten by crocodiles. That's his favourite gambit. Or the porters come in without their boss and say he died of sudden death miles from anywhere. You go to fetch in the body, and find they've buried it about six inches deep, and the bones are picked clean. What can you prove? What can you do? Do you remember that journalist chap, the editor of the Coast Times, who made a dead set at Cassalis and showed him up, and dared him to bring a libel action? What did Cassalis do? Bring a libel action? Not he. He just dropped round to the bar at the local hotel and told the Dago bar tender that he'd guarantee the chap's drink bill, and in three months they were putting up the tombstone. We've come to the conclusion that it is unlucky to meddle with Cassalis; but, to do him justice, Cassalis never meddles unless he's meddled with. But he's a dangerous brute, all the same."

" 'Face the wall, my darlings, as the gentlemen go by'," said the Coaster, who evidently had a taste for poetical quotation.

"How does he manage to keep fit when everyone else finds the climate so trying?" asked Nina, hoping for health tips.

"Ah, how does he? That's a problem that's often puzzled us. They say he's got some nigger herb that keeps him going. But I doubt it. Iron constitution, I suppose. And not drinking."

"Not drinking won't do it. You go under quicker if you drink, but that's all. The missionaries don't drink, and they don't last much longer than the rest of us."

Then followed an argument, concerning the respective

23

virtues of various well-advertised brands of health salts, that threatened to become very technical and intimate.

Nina slipped out of her revolving chair unnoticed and went up to walk the deck in the mellow evening air and watch the last of the sunset. There is something melancholy in the falling dusk, and especially in the swiftly falling tropical dusk, and as the lights were switched on, on the promenade deck, Nina drew from her under-arm bag a packet of letters and began to read them through for company.

She read them in chronological order. The first was on the notepaper of the *Biafra*, the sister ship to the *Benin*. A warm glow came over her as she read it. The next in series were on Customs-house paper, and they made her very happy, for they talked of the prospects of a home of their own, and a little headland the writer had observed, where a bungalow could be put up to catch all the breezes. Then there was a lamentable fall-off in the tone of the letters, and the paper on which they were written was dirty and smeared, and there were bitter complaints of the heat and humidity as the rainy season got in its work.

After that the letters picked up a bit, but somehow they never quite recovered their original tone. The earlier letters were the best—and the most comforting. He said in the later ones that he had been very busy, and was just sending her a line to go on with, and would write fully next week. But, somehow, he never did write fully. Then there was a gap, followed by a line to say he had had a nasty go of fever. Then another gap, and a line to say he had been very busy. Then another gap, and more fever. Then a shakily written letter full of maudlin sentiment, ending up with an accusation of infidelity. Finally there was the answer to the letter wherein she said an aunt had died and left her a small legacy, and should she use the money to come out to him and set up house keeping? This letter alarmed her, and yet

24

pleased her. It was like the cry of a lost soul going up from hell. Yes, for God's sake come, and come quickly. He was at the end of his tether. But if only he had her with him, every-thing should be all right. He promised her that.

So she had come, and here she was. The coast of Africa lay like a shadow to port as the ship slid silently through the phosphorescent water and she leant on the rail looking for-ward, listening to the tread of the watch officer on the bridge overhead keeping the ceaseless vigil.

Her fiancé had been the cousin of her father's curate, who had come down to join his relative in his country digs for a holiday before going out to take up an appointment on the West Coast. It had been a case of love at first sight on both sides. On his, because he thought her the loveliest thing he had ever seen, hidden away as she was in this re-mote moorland village. On her side, because he was the first presentable young man who had ever come her way. They were constantly together for the fortnight, and when Harold Morley went off to his post he left his signet ring behind on Nina's third finger, and promises of eternal fidelity in both their hearts. Paternal authority had at first been disposed to look with favour upon the young man, though distrusting the brief acquaintance, for his salary sounded princely to rural clerical ears; but a certain lack of enthusiasm on the part of the curate cousin had caused questions to be asked, and when the Missionary Society's speaker came round on his tour of the diocese, inquiries were made, and they learnt why it was so large a salary was being paid to so young a man; and, moreover, what manner of men they were who were willing to put up with the conditions under which that salary had to be earned.

Parental authority had put its foot down uncompromis-ingly, and therein it made a mistake. For love is a hunger; and as the starving man hungers for food, and the drowning

25

man craves for air, so the lovelorn wight demands love with an inexorable demand. There is no realization that love is only one of the ingredients in the mixed diet that the soul requires to keep it in health. It is useless to tell the starving man that he does not live by bread alone; or the drowning man that he cannot live on air.

If Mr. Barnet had had any sense, he would have left things alone, and allowed the young man to cook his own goose at his leisure, as he assuredly would do if all that was told were true. But, as it was, all Nina's idealism, all her loyalty, all her self-sacrifice, rallied to the defence of her chosen mate. The only effectual treatment would have been to chain her up in an outhouse and leave her to bark it off. But unfortunately that treatment cannot be applied to the female of the human species.

Mr. Barnet did the heavy father, and Mrs. Barnet did the worldly-wise mother, with tearful interludes, to the best of her limited ability; but Nina, who had a good deal of her father in her make-up, stuck to her guns the more firmly the more they tried to dislodge her; and, regardless of the fact that the young man would soon be due for leave and could come to fetch her, decided to use her aunt's legacy to go out to him.

All the cumulative frustrations of her twenty-two years of solitary youth came to the boil at once. The grey skies, the empty fields, the feeble flickers at the local cinema, all became unendurable simultaneously. She was reading a serial of African life, all about lovely, open-air maids and strong, lean, bronzed men under the Equator; and not realizing that Kenya and the West Coast have not got quite the same climate, and do not attract quite the same class of resident, she made herself a quantity of tropical frocks, and bought a sun-helmet and khaki shirts and shorts, set aside sufficient money for a lower deck berth, and invested the rest in dainty household goods. Everything, in fact, was planned from the pages of the serial in the ladies' paper, especially the shirts and shorts.

The little missionary woman, Miss Leete, was landing next morning at Georgetown, the principal port of that part, to take up her duties among the piccaninnies of Dahomey; and when Nina went down to her cabin she was called upon to sit on a cabin trunk, for Miss Leete believed in being ready in good time. When all was strapped, Miss Leete sent the steward for a pot of tea, and despite the heat in the cabin— to which she seemed serenely oblivious, though her face was cascading with perspiration after her packing—she insisted that Nina should carouse with her on that stimulating beverage as a kind of farewell binge; and Nina, who had come to like her in spite of her unprepossessing exterior, agreed to sacrifice herself in a good cause.

"My dear," said Miss Leete, handling the teapot artistically as the ship rolled to the swell, "make tea your standby, not lemon-squash; and never, never, under any circumstances, unless, of course you are really at death's door, touch alcohol."

"They were saying at the captain's table that a man with a grudge against another once guaranteed his drink bill as a revenge."

"Yes, I've heard that story. It's perfectly true. It was that dreadful man Cassalis."

"Yes. That was who they said it was. Have you ever come across Cassalis yourself? Is he really as bad as they say?"

Miss Leete gave a shudder; it was obvious she regretted that her religious denomination had nothing corresponding to crossing oneself.

"I actually saw him once. In the forest. With a slave gang," she whispered in a hushed voice, as if the Inquisition were after her.

"What's he like?"

"A big man with a beard, and very cruel eyes. He looked at me dreadfully. I think he did not like being seen by a white woman. The men are all afraid of him and won't give evidence against him. But I went to the magistrate and signed an affidavit and sent it straight home to the head office of our Society. But nothing came of it," she added, with a sigh.

"Do they treat the slaves very badly?" asked Nina.

"Yes, dreadfully. They drag them along by chains, and never unhandcuff them for weeks on end."

"Does Cassalis actually drive the slaves himself?"

"He was doing so when I saw him. But that was a good many years ago. I think he mainly organizes the business now. He is supposed to be very, very wealthy."

"How did he make all his money? By slave trading?"

"Partly. And partly by selling gin to the natives. It is simply dreadful, up our way. Whole villages wiped out."

"They were saying at the captain's table that he ought to be shot on sight."

"He certainly ought," said Miss Leete viciously, "and I'd gladly do it."

"Oh, I don't know," said Nina. "I think I rather admire an adventurer. They call him the uncrowned king of the Coast. He reminds me of the Elizabethan sea-dogs."

"You would not have liked the buccaneers very much, my dear, if you had been a nun in Panama. I have seen Cassalis's handiwork with my own eyes, and I think that shooting is too good for him. These scoundrels are not at all romantic at close quarters, believe me."

They turned in, for Miss Leete had to be up betimes in case they arrived at the roadstead earlier than they expected, for there was no harbour for them to put into, and ships cannot hang about in the open sea.

Nina dreamed of bearded adventurers climbing on board with cutlasses in their teeth and chasing her round and round the decks, pistols in their hands. Then the pistols changed into soda-water siphons, and the cheerful young doctor came along and advised her to drink champagne until the world went round and round instead of up and down, the champagne apparently being served in siphons.

Next morning there came alongside a surf-boat full of huge black men with next to nothing on. Miss Leete swathed herself from head to heel in a travelling-rug in spite of the heat, toddled placidly down the accommodation ladder, ignoring the hand held out to her by the second officer, and fell skilfully on to the broad, bare chest of an enormous buck nigger, who fielded her equally skilfully. The darky crew gave way with a yell, and Miss Leete passed out of Nina's life for ever.

"Cute old bird," said the hard-bitten Coaster, who was leaning his elbows on the rail at Nina's side. "She knows what's what. Now you young ladies go about in muslin dresses in the sun, but she goes about in a steamer-rug. Cassalis taught us that trick. He learnt it from the Arabs. What keeps the heat in in a cold climate will keep the heat out in a hot climate."

"Is that how Cassalis keeps his health when everybody else loses theirs?"

"One of the reasons, probably. And living native fashion. The natives know what suits the climate. But I believe myself that he has his headquarters at a high altitude, and goes almost up to the snow line to recuperate after his expeditions."

"Up to the what ?"

"The snow line. Didn't you know we had snow in Africa?"

"Good heavens, no! What do you mean?"

"Well, if you start going up a big mountain, even right on the Equator, you go through all the climates, tropical, sub-tropical, temperate, as you go higher and higher, till finally you get an alpine climate. You get snow in the gullies on Kilimanjaro all the year round. I think myself that Cassalis hangs out high up on one of the peaks that lie back of the coastal ranges. But how he gets there is a secret that's well kept. You see, Cassalis never associates with white men, and the niggers fear him as if he were the devil."

"What makes them fear him so much?"

"He is absolutely ruthless. Shoots on sight, and shoots to kill. He models his manners on those of the Arab slave-traders he's so thick with. A most unmitigated ruffian. It is his boast that no man has ever crossed him and got away with it. The niggers believe that implicitly, and he makes it his business to live up to his reputation. It is his most valuable stock-in-trade. He only has to go into a village and the niggers just lie down and die, and he takes up a collection of the best specimens for his string."

"What is it that makes everyone hate him so much?"

"Well, you see, he's such a callous brute. And absolutely unscrupulous. What Cassalis wants he takes. If anyone interferes with him, he lays for that fellow till he gets him. He's the terror of the Coast. You've been going to the pictures too much, Miss Barnet. Cassalis isn't any Douglas Fairbanks, you know. He's a pretty sordid sort of ruffian at close quarters."

"But why doesn't the Government tackle him?"

"It probably will, one day. The difficulty is to get definite evidence on which to act. There isn't a nigger on the Coast that will give Cassalis away."

"But why not, if they hate and fear him so much?"

"I didn't say they hated him. I only said they feared him.

30

Cassalis has got a way with niggers. Besides, there's nothing a nigger loves so much as the thing he fears. Seems to be part of their religion. And Cassalis never lets his niggers down. If anyone does the dirty on one of his niggers, he goes after the fellow just the same as if it had been done to him. The niggers know it, and they stand by him to a man. You see, the kind of whites we get out here are given to doing the dirty a good deal and the niggers get a pretty thin time of it with them. But Cassalis's niggers always get a square deal because they've got Cassalis's brains behind them. Every chief on the Coast wants to sign on with Cassalis's secret societies because they know then that they're safe from slave-raiding, for nobody dares meddle with them because Cassalis would be on their track one-time."

"Do you think I shall meet Cassalis at Okiki?"

"Yes, I expect you will. It's by way of being a port. And your prospective husband is in the Customs, isn't he? Yes, you're sure to run across Cassalis sooner or later. And, when you do, avoid him like the plague. That's my advice. If he took a fancy to you, you'd come off badly."

Another Coaster came and joined them.

"I say, Jenkins," said the first, "do you know whether Cassalis frequents Okiki?"

"Couldn't say. He's always changing his port of call as he makes places too hot to hold him. He's corrupted the Customs and harbour officials up and down the Coast from end to end. He's got the whole lot squared. All the native police, too, are in his pay. African Tammany, I call it. I tell you, he's made a dirty mess of this coast."

31

CHAPTER II

TWO days later it was Nina's turn to disembark. She remembered Miss Leete and the steamer-rug, but could not bring herself to envelop the billowing crispness of her white organdie in its stifling folds. She contented her self with a wide-brimmed sun-helmet and a light wrap to protect her frock. With a beating heart she watched the accommodation ladder being lowered as a surf-boat manned by Kroo-boys came alongside. A man all in white drill waved to her from the stem-sheets; she guessed he must be Harold, although she could not see his face clearly in the shadow of his big pith helmet amid all the sun-glare. The whole crew gathered at the rail to give the bride a cheer, and she went down the accommodation ladder on the arm of no less a person than the captain himself. But, alas, she did not time her transit from rolling ship to tossing boat as neatly as did Miss Leete, and she and her intended would have gone over board to the sharks together if an immense Kroo-boy had not gathered them both impartially to his musky-smelling bosom.

The rowers, with their usual yell, gave way with a will, and the boat began to ride the long rollers towards the shore. The ship's siren gave a benedictory toot as her bows swung slowly round for the open sea. Then the long, steady rollers gave place to an alarming tumble of broken water that scared the life out of Nina as they crossed the bar, and they found themselves working into a wide estuary between two low, palm-crowned heads. The freshness of the open sea was left behind, and the steam of a perpetual washing-day struck Nina in the face. The reek of rank, rotting vegetation, like hot cabbage water poured down a defective sink, came to them from the mud banks, for it was low tide, and now that there was no breeze save that made by their own passage through the water the Kroo-boys were very noticeable.

It was not a prepossessing entry upon her new life. But she was very anxious to be pleased, and the grinning faces of the delighted crew, throwing a terrific amount of style into it as they brought home the bride, cheered her considerably. How could one help liking such magnificent specimens of humanity?

Now that she was no longer watching the sickening slope of the waves, she turned and looked at her companion. She saw that his face under his sun-helmet was much fatter than it used to be; but as it was burnt a brick red, she could not tell whether he was looking well or not. His eyes she could not see, for he was wearing sun-glasses against the glare. She slipped her hand through his arm as she sat beside him, and he gave it a squeeze against his side that was very reassuring.

The surrounding shores were low and flat with a scanty sprinkle of palms growing on them. The township of Okiki appeared to consist of a small cluster of white washed, single-storeyed houses gathered about a large, substantial, two-storey building that flew the Union Jack. A stone-built quay flanked one side of the river for some distance and a number of row-boats, canoes and launches swung at their moorings in the slow current of the mud coloured stream.

They drew in under the shadow of the quay. High above their heads hung great iron rings to which ships of a considerable size could be moored. Passing this part of the harbour, which was evidently intended for the accommodation of ocean-going vessels, they came to a low, shelf-like structure that sloped up in a cart-track to the same height as the rest of the quay and formed a jetty at which small boats could land. Bounding the quay at this point was a low wall, and it was completely lined with heads. Evidently the entire population of Okiki was there to see the bride arrive. It was an embarrassing moment, and Nina devoutly hoped that she would acquit herself better at leaving the boat than she had done at boarding it.

The problem was solved for her by the Kroo-boys, one of whom leapt ashore, seized her hand, and gave her a pull, while another shoved behind; and up she went, in a billow of organdie skirts, without a single mark from the slime en-crusted walls. Then they applied the same method to Har-old, and up he went too, like a sack of potatoes, and the Kroo-boys gave a valedictory yell as they backed water.

Nina shook out her ruffled skirts under the watching eyes of all the loungers, and involuntarily glanced upwards at the row of heads above her. They were not a very prepossess-ing crowd, leaning their elbows on the low wall, with their shoulders hunched about their ears by their attitude. All their faces were tinted to various shades of sunburn, from a sickly and liverish yellow to a real, ripe mahogany. They looked a rough and rather dejected party, and Nina saw at once that there was no one there who could meet her on a social equality. They bore not the remotest resemblance to the illustrations of the serial story which had finally clinched her resolution.

Feeling a little cast-down by this disillusionment, she com-menced to climb the sloping path leading to the upper quay, and, as she did so, came face to face with the man at the end of the line of watching heads. In some curious way he re-minded her of a basking lizard on a wall. His clean-shaven, aquiline face was more leathery and less roasting-red than most of the others. His eyes were light grey, and gazed at her unblinkingly under drooping lids. His bare arms, sinewy under his short-sleeved khaki mesh shirt, were burnt a vivid red-brown, as was his bare chest. A gold wrist-watch decorated his left wrist. A voluminous cloak of roughly woven camel-hair, with a tasselled hood like a monk's cowl, was caught about his throat by a loosely-tied cord and effectually protected his back from the blazing sun which beat down unchecked upon the spines of the others.

There was something about this man, an air of vigour, it might be, that set him completely apart from the down-at-heel, drooping collection of longshore loafers.

Their eyes met and held each other's with a curious, almost hypnotic regard; and as Nina advanced up the sloping footway she slowly turned her head, unable to withdraw her gaze. Then, suddenly realizing what she was doing, she hastily looked away, her lowered head effectually concealing her face under its sun-helmet from the watcher on the quay. A sudden realization came to her that if she were to live happily with Harold she would have to avoid this man.

At the top of the steps that led on to the quay Nina's fiancé drew level with her and slipped his arm through hers.

"Splendid to have you," he whispered huskily under her sun-helmet. She suddenly realized these were the first words he had spoken to her. All he had done so far had been to smile at her rather inanely. But, then, allowances must be made for men who are in love.

They turned off the path from the jetty and found themselves on the quay itself, and face to face with them was the man in the camel-hair cloak, who had evidently placed himself at that strategic point to await them, knowing that they must pass by him.

"Hullo, Lewis," said Harold with a nervous laugh.

The stranger's impassive countenance relaxed into a slow

smile, as if its leathery skin bent with difficulty.

"Hullo, lad," he said. "Allow me to wish your bride luck."

He held out his hand, and Nina put hers in it. He took it, and looked at her with a curious expression in his eyes. It suddenly struck Nina that this hard-featured stranger was frightfully sorry for her. She could not imagine why. The unblinking grey eyes under the drooping lids that sheltered them from the sun-glare seemed to be gazing into her very soul without allowing her to look back into his. She knew at once by his voice that he was an educated man, very different from the rest of the loungers, who were more of the seaman type.

She could not find a word to say for herself as the man stood there, holding her hand and looking into her eyes. She felt the impact of a very strong but very secretive and aloof personality; and again came the warning prick that she would have to avoid this man's society if she were to live in peace with her husband. He was so extraordinarily magnetic, was this stranger. He seemed to be drawing all the life in her body out towards him. She had never met anyone quite so fascinating. And then, with a hasty movement, she withdrew her hand and turned towards the man at her side, who stood grinning inanely under his sun-helmet, also apparently unable to find a word to say for himself in the presence of the stranger.

The man who had been addressed as Lewis drew back to let them pass, but his deep-set eyes still continued to hold Nina's. She felt instinctively that this man was lawless, and that the thing he wanted he would take. And suddenly she knew, deep down in her instinctive self, that he wanted her. She remembered what the captain had said about white women being rare and precious on the Coast. She, whose flower-like prettiness was not uncommon at home, suddenly

36

realized that in the eyes of these sun-dried men she was a raving beauty. All round her she felt the eyes of desire gazing at her; a goodly proportion of the longshore loungers were Portuguese, and they made no secret whatever of their inclinations.

She stepped forward hastily, anywhere to get away from all these starers. Harold moved with her, and arm in arm they crossed the broad sun-baked quay and he guided her into the open door of a mean-looking hotel that stood facing the harbour.

Nina found herself in a large room like a barn that appeared to be a kind of lounge, furnished with dilapidated cane chairs and steamer-chairs and small, glass topped tables. Across one end was a bar, with a Dago bar-tender in a dingy white jacket. On the bar stood a magnum of champagne; round its neck was a bow of white satin ribbon, the only clean thing in the place.

"Ayee, Mistah Morley," exclaimed the Dago. "Come and 'ave one on the 'ouse!"

Harold led her up to the bar.

"Senhor Pedro Garcias—my wife," he said formally, indicating Nina with a lordly wave of his hand. Nina thought his remarks a little premature and his theatrical gesture not in the best of taste.

The barman uncorked the bottle of champagne and poured out three foaming glasses, gave them one each and took one himself, and, with a graceful gesture and a ravishing smile, toasted the bride, his large, dark eyes gazing at her languishingly over the brim of his glass, her Dresden-china daintiness being very much to his Latin taste. It surprised Nina that the presence of her fiancé seemed to put no check on the shameless ogling to which she was being subjected on all hands.

Two of the rougher specimens of the longshore loafers

came in, to be greeted with bows and glass-wavings by the bar-tender and supplied with glasses of champagne, in which they drank her health with gusto. Then more men came in, and long whisky pegs began to mingle with the glasses of champagne on the counter.

Nina began to feel more and more uneasy as the room got fuller and fuller of the rough crowd. Harold leant his elbows on the counter and appeared to be staring into space under his sun-helmet, which he had omitted to remove on entering the house, apparently lost in thought, a glass of champagne before him.

Someone touched her on the arm, and she looked round, startled, to find a dark-skinned, greasy-haired Portuguese woman, with a coarse but not unkindly face, standing beside her.

"You come alonga me," she said in a low voice, and Nina followed her, Harold paying no attention.

She followed the woman in her gaudy, dirty cotton overall that lavishly revealed an overflowing figure, down a passage that was screened from the lounge by a bead curtain; at the end of the passage she opened a door, and led Nina into a large room in the centre of which stood an enormous, frowzy double bed, with Isabella coloured mosquito-curtains looped back from it.

The room was littered with a man's clothing; trousers lay on the floor; jackets hung disconsolately on the backs of chairs; dirty underwear was everywhere, as if its owner had just stepped out of it and left it to lie. A most unsavoury apartment. And dominating it all stood a whisky-bottle three parts full, two whisky-bottles entirely empty, and her own photograph.

"You lika have a leedle wash?" demanded the Portuguese woman, who appeared to be the landlady of the hotel.

"Yes-yes, please," said Nina nervously, "but I think I will

have it in my own room. You see, we are not married yet."

The woman shook her head slowly.

"Senhor Morley, 'e say nutting about anozzer room."

"Oh," said Nina, very embarrassed. "Then I expect we are going to be married this afternoon."

"I nod know," said the Portuguese woman, eyeing her curiously; and, turning on the heel of her sloppy shoes, she walked with her slow, gliding walk out of the room, leaving the girl alone.

Nina seated herself in a broken-down cane lounge-chair, after turning an armful of soiled underwear out of it. She felt almost sick with nervousness. She was entirely at a loss to understand Harold's curious manner towards her, and the lustful starings of the low-down loungers filled her with fear. Unless Harold were able to afford her effectual protection, she was going to have a very unpleasant time with all these over-gallant Dagos.

She sat and waited, listening to the buzzing of the flies round the battered kerosene lamp that hung from the ceiling and the bursts of rough laughter from the bar, growing gradually more boisterous as the time went by. Her wrist-watch told her that it was three o'clock, and she had had no lunch. She did not dare to venture out into the bar, full of that crowd of half-drunken ruffians, to seek her fiancé, but in a fever of anxiety and impatience sat awaiting him in the sordid bedroom. She had an idea that after three o'clock one could not legally get married.

At length her anxiety was relieved by the sound of footsteps coming down the passage. They paused outside the door. Then the door opened, and Harold stood on the threshold. He had discarded his sun-helmet at last, and for the first time she could see his face. There was no doubt whatever as to what was the matter with him. He was dead drunk.

He stood holding on by the door and swaying as if he

39

were on board ship in a storm. He swung with the door till she thought it would come off its hinges. Then he lurched forward, and came staggering across the dirty matting to a long steamer-chair that stood beside the table bearing her photo and the whisky-bottles, and pitched into it with a crash, by some miracle arriving right side up. He lay staring at the ceiling for a few minutes, entirely oblivious of her presence; then he slowly heaved himself up on to his elbow and very carefully, and with much rattling of the edge of the glass on the neck of the bottle, poured himself out nearly a quarter of a tumbler of whisky. Carefully holding the glass at one side of the siphon, he pressed the handle down and shot a stream of soda-water all over the table, not one drop of which entered the glass; then he raised the tumbler to his lips and tossed down the neat whisky at one gulp, heaved a deep sigh of satisfaction and closed his eyes.

Nina watched this performance as if paralysed, unable to move or speak. She studied the face of the oblivious man in the chair, and saw by the puffiness of the eyes that this was no accidental inebriation of a bridegroom made drunk for a joke by his friends. The face of the man in the chair was that of a heavy and habitual drinker. All her love, all her hopes, all her loyalty, were centred about this man—and there he was, a sodden wreck!

She gazed at him intently, asking herself if it were possible that he could be redeemed. And something in her replied that it was not. If his self-control and his self-respect were so far gone that he could not keep sober to receive his bride, there was no hope for him. Definitely, finally, the resolution crystallized in her that she would not go through with the marriage. To do so would be to bind herself to utter degradation.

But if she did not go through with it, what then? She had a little money with her, but not very much. Certainly not

40

enough for a passage home. And she very definitely did not want to go home. Anything was better than to return with her tail between her legs, to hear, "I told you so."

She thought that it ought not to be difficult to get a job on the Coast if white women were at a premium. Surely some trader's wife would be glad of her as home help? Her whole soul revolted at the idea of returning to leaden Northern skies now that she had felt this glorious tropical light and heat. Fresh out from England, the terrible enervation of the Coast had not yet had time to get in its work.

If she got a job in some nice type of home, she told herself, women being at a premium instead of a discount, as they were in England, where there was not a single eligible man in the whole countryside so far as she knew, she might meet some man whom she could care for and with whom she could make a home.

For the greatest shock of this revelation of her fiancé's condition had not been the degradation of the man she loved, but the loss of the eagerly longed-for home. Her acquaintance with Harold Morley had been so slight that the thing she was in love with was not the man himself, but the image of him she had built up in her imagination, in which the pictures that illustrated the serial in the ladies' paper had played an ever-increasing part as actual memory began to fade.

But, even so, she had had a severe shock; for it is not a pleasant thing to see even a complete stranger in the condition to which her fiancé had been reduced. All the eagerness of affection and loyalty that she had come prepared to pour out on him so whole-heartedly, and that should have brought them such happiness and comradeship, had suddenly collapsed on her hands, and she could only gaze ruefully upon the handful of bitter dust which was all that was left to her of her Dead Sea fruit.

But Nina was of a gallant and adventurous turn of mind; and the dourness of Mr. Barnet in her became a stiff upper lip. Moreover, her acquaintance with Harold Morley being so slight, although her feelings had all the intensity of first love, they had not that depth and strong twining into the very fibres of the being that only comes with time and nearness. She looked at the sodden wreck in the chair, and was able to turn her face away.

All the same, she could not blind herself to the fact that she was in a very tight corner. Deprived of the protection of her prospective husband, she would be exposed to the advances of all the Dago loafers in that unsavoury port. She guessed now why their eyes had been so bold. They knew well enough to what manner of man she had given herself. She also knew why there had been that queer expression of pity in the eyes of the man in the camel-hair cloak.

With the memory of that look, a sudden resolution came to her. Go through with this marriage she would not, and she must have some sort of protection from some decent man until plans could be made for her future. The Portuguese hotel proprietor would obviously be a good deal worse than useless to appeal to. There was only one possible man in this whole port, and that was the man whom her husband had addressed as Lewis, and who had held her hand and wished her luck. His eyes had told her plainly enough, had she had the knowledge to interpret his look, that he knew what she had let herself in for, and was exceedingly sorry for her. Perhaps his act in placing himself right in her path as she landed had not been over bold, as she at first had thought, but might have been a means of getting himself introduced to her in order that she might have someone to turn to when disillusionment burst on her like a bomb, as he had probably known it must.

And then it occurred to her that she was idealizing a man

42

who, from the looks of him, probably was burdened with very little indeed in the way of ideals. His eyes had contained the same bold lustfulness as the others; not quite so bold, perhaps, because the man was a gentleman, but her feminine instinct knew it was there.

But, all the same, she had to have the protection of someone, and this man was obviously the strongest personality there. It is a very deep-rooted instinct, quite apart from any active need of protection, for a woman to turn to the most vigorous male by choice, and in Nina's overwrought mind there leapt up the image of the man Lewis who had looked at her as if he wanted her, and who was, most distinctly, a personality. Her first reaction to him had been to regard him as a temptation that must be resisted for the sake of Harold; but now that Harold was out of the reckoning he ceased to be a temptation and became a prospect.

She realized that, in view of the way the man had looked at her, she was running a distinct risk in throwing herself upon his mercy for protection. He would doubtless be perfectly willing to protect her from all the pawing Dagos, but would he be equally willing to protect her from himself, and play the stainless knight-errant to her maidenhood? Or would he regard her need as his opportunity and expect to be paid in kind for his protection?

On the other hand, on this terrible coast, where white women were at a premium, would he regard her as a choice prize, eagerly to be bound to him by marriage? And if so, what manner of man would she find this grimfaced adventurer to be if she were married to him? Then there was always the possibility that he might not be free to offer her marriage owing to some previously contracted alliance, and yet might desire her. What, then, would be her line of action? Once in his clutches, she might find considerable difficulty in getting out of them again. She had a suspicion that in this demoral-

43

izing climate chivalry might prove a minus quantity.

A deep snore came from Harold, and he stirred restlessly in his chair. Nina rose to her feet. It was inadvisable for her to linger if she meant to go. Any moment he might wake from his uneasy slumber, and it would be a very difficult and stormy matter to depart then. She had best go while the going was good.

She suspected that, after having lined the quay to see the bride arrive, which was evidently an event of the first importance in this dead-alive hole, all the men of the place had adjourned to the hotel for drinks and jokes presumably at Harold's expense. She guessed that Lewis would not be far to seek, and that if she went up to him boldly, formidable as he was, she would not appeal in vain. At any rate, it was better to have one man who was at least a gentleman to deal with, than to be passed from hand to hand and quarrelled over by the Dagos.

With her heart beating so loudly that she thought everyone must hear it, she put aside the bead curtain and stepped out into the now crowded lounge. As she had expected, Lewis was standing beside the bar, leaning his elbow on it with the negligent, lounging attitude that seemed to be habitual with him, and his eyes met hers with the same steady, droop-lidded gaze as they had done at their first encounter. The buzz of talk hushed at her entrance, and all the men stared at her, knowing the disillusionment that had awaited her, and eager to see how she had taken it; the Anglo-Saxons pitying her with a rough sympathy, and the Dagos licking their lips in anticipation of the opportunities that might await them. Nina took her courage in both hands, and with a beating heart walked straight up to Lewis.

"I am in rather a difficulty," she said in a low voice that everybody strained their ears to hear. "I wonder if I might speak to you? Perhaps you could advise me."

44

"Certainly," replied the man in the same low tones. "Shall we come outside?"

They moved together towards the doors, the loungers giving back in a dead silence before them. Lewis took his sun-helmet and camel-hair cloak from a hook on the wall and held the door open for her, and Nina passed through, only to recoil with a cry as the intense heat of the tropical sun struck at her through her thin, sleeveless frock, for she had forgotten her wrap.

"Here, take this," said her companion, and she felt the soft, light camel-hair cloak thrown over her shoulders. Thankfully she wrapped its protecting folds about her as she felt a hand on her arm piloting her across the wide stretch of dusty quay that lay between the hotel and the harbour. Lewis guided her down the same sloping track by which she had come up from the boat. Halfway down there was a stone seat recessed in the wall, in deep shade, and invisible to all eyes save those on the boats out in the harbour.

"Shall we sit here?" he said.

They sat down, one at each end of the seat, facing each other. Nina clutched her bag to her heart, the bag containing all poor Harold's letters, quite unable to speak. This man gazing at her out of his heavy-lidded eyes was proving even more formidable at close quarters than she had anticipated. He saw her embarrassment, and considerately turned his eyes away and looked out across the harbour, giving her time to recover herself.

She gazed at the keen, hawk's profile presented to her, and wondered what manner of man she had to deal with. Something very potent for good or evil, she felt, lurked in this man. His was no ordinary personality. She judged him to be in the early thirties, younger than she had taken him for at first sight.

At length she mastered herself sufficiently to break the

45

silence.

"I think you know the kind of difficulty I am in," she said.

"Do I?" said the man, withdrawing his eyes from the horizon and turning them on her again with the same unblinking stare that she found so disconcerting.

"I—I can't go through with the marriage."

"No, I don't suppose you can."

"Is he—is he often like this?"

"I don't live here, I only come and go; but I have never seen him any different."

"I can't possibly marry him. It would be utter degradation. A drunkard is no use to anybody."

"No, you certainly can't marry him, even if there were anyone here to marry you, which there isn't."

"No one here to marry us? Then what did he propose to do with me?"

"That is what we have all been wondering."

"I can't possibly stop on at that hotel. There will be a terrible scene when he wakes up and finds I won't marry him. Is there anywhere else where I can go to?"

"That is the problem! The only thing I can suggest is that I put you in an empty hut and set a guard over you. The Portuguese woman at the hotel is the only woman in the town, and she is no earthly use to you. That might solve the problem for one night, but what after that? You can't live here under a guard indefinitely. It will be a fortnight before the next boat calls, and if it is heavy weather you won't be able to get on board in the open roadstead, and will have to wait for the following one, and I cannot stop on here to look after you for very long."

"I am not at all keen on going back to England. I am wondering whether I could not get a job of some sort out here."

"No, you certainly couldn't. There isn't another white woman nearer than Georgetown. It is no place out here for a woman on her own, with all these Dagos about."

"Then—then what can I do?"

"The only thing I can think of is that I should take you in my launch up the river with me, and drop you at the mission station at Waigonda as I pass. I don't fancy there is a woman there, though these missionary women do get into the most extraordinary places; but there is a white padre, and he would probably look after you and treat you decently till he could arrange to get you sent home safely. There is a launch that goes round calling at all the mission stations periodically, taking them supplies. I expect he will send you out on that. It ought to be due somewhere about now."

"Yes," said Nina wistfully.

"Don't you want to go home?"

She looked up, and saw that for the first time the man had opened his eyes widely and was smiling, and the change was extraordinary. He was no longer sinister, but very charming.

"No," she said, "I don't want to go a bit. It is so wonderful out here. Everything seems so very much alive. Back in England we are only half alive."

"They think just the opposite out here. They think that they are only half alive."

"I didn't mean the people. I meant the place. Africa is so much more alive than England. I can't describe it any other way. Perhaps it is the strong light. Perhaps it is that everything grows so strongly. I don't know. Life seems to be pushing out of the earth with tremendous force here."

"Oh, so you have felt that, have you?" said the man slowly. "You have felt the tremendous life of Africa, the elemental force?"

"I have felt something. I don't know what it is. It seems to wrap me round and take hold of me and draw me in. I am

47

different already to what I was when I landed."

"Are you better or worse?"

"I think my people would think I was worse, that I was heading straight for the dogs. But I think that I am better because I am so much more truly myself. I am doing the thing I want to do, not the thing I ought to do. I suppose I ought to stick to Harold, for better or for worse, and try and save him; but I don't want to, and I'm not going to!"

The man smiled, and a very curious expression came into his eyes that she could not fathom. He seemed to be calculating something, and keeping the results of his calculations to himself.

"I perceive that you are not on the side of the missionaries," he said.

"I don't know anything about the missionaries. The only one I have met is Miss Leete, and I liked her."

"Oh, Miss Leete?"

"Yes, do you know her?"

"I know of her. Up Dahomey way, isn't she?"

"Yes, I believe so. But what do you mean when you say that I am not on the side of the missionaries?"

"I mean that you would not like to see Africa Christianized, and all its wild life put to sit on benches in a tin chapel."

"No, I certainly wouldn't. I can't imagine Africa being Christianized, can you?"

"Personally, no. I think it would disagree with it very actively. After all, the best thing in Africa is its overflowing pagan life. Stamp that out, and what have you got left? Nothing. Africa does not run to brains. It is fullness of life we have here, and nothing else. I think its own religion suits it best, if you ask me."

"What is its own religion?"

"The worship of the forces you feel rising up so strongly

48

out of the earth. Most primitive peoples worship the sun; but the negroes don't. They worship the earth and its forces."

"I think it is simply too fascinating for words. How does one get in touch with it?"

He looked at her curiously.

"I shouldn't try to, if I were you," he said.

"But I have!"

"How do you know ?"

"Because I can feel the life of Africa all around me, and I know it likes me. Africa has taken me. You can say what you like."

The man looked out over the muddy harbour. "Has it?" he said at length, after a long pause. He turned to her suddenly.

"Come, now, we must be practical," he said. "Would you care to tell me how you are placed financially? How are you off for funds?"

"I have got about twenty pounds on me," she said.

"That is not going to take you very far. Is that the limit of your resources?"

"Well, I have got a lot of household things in my boxes that ought to fetch something if sold. They might as well be sold. I shan't need them now."

As she spoke there rose before her all the hopes and dreams that had been hers as she had sewn and embroidered and chosen all the pretty things that were to have made her home, and an overwhelming wave of emotion swept over her. She bowed her head under her sun-helmet so that the man might not see her face, and pressed her handkerchief hard to her lips.

With tear-filled eyes she stared out over the muddy harbour, and to recover her self-control forced herself to count the boats lying there at the mooring-buoys. There were a number of native craft; a few surf-boats, such as she had

49

come ashore in; a couple of small launches; and, further out, a big launch with fine lines and a portholed cabin. This was the only craft on which there were any signs of life. A nigger in engineer's overalls appeared and disappeared in a hatchway, evidently attending to the engine, for the faint clink of a spanner on steel came to her across the water. She watched his bullet head bobbing up and down as he worked, and tried to think of Africa, and not of what might have been.

She recovered herself and turned back to her companion, and saw that he was watching her with a strangely softened expression on his hard face.

"Rotten luck," he said quietly.

"Yes, rotten," said Nina, "but it is no use thinking about it."

"Well, now, shall I run you up to Waigonda and hand you over to the padre ?"

"I can't think of anything better, can you? And when I get there, I may be able to get hold of a job of some sort, and stop on."

"I don't fancy that, with your views, you will get a job at the mission station."

"No, and I don't fancy that I should keep it very long if I did. But what about Georgetown? Wouldn't there be any chance of a job for me there?"

"I doubt it. All the work is done by niggers, and no one attempts to raise kids there."

Nina said no more; but, all the same, she was not lightly to be put off. She felt that she had established relations with Africa, and the life of the place would make room for her.

"Well, have you made up your mind to come with me to Waigonda?"

"Yes, if you will be so kind as to take me."

"Will you tell me something? What makes you think you can trust me? Do I impress you as being a good man?"

Nina looked at him quizzically.

"Well, I wouldn't go so far as to say I would choose you for superintendent of a Sunday-school, but I think you would be a good friend to your friends; and if I trust you I don't think you will let me down."

"I'll try not," said Lewis quietly. "Now, what about getting on board the launch? I fancy those are your goods on the jetty, that haven't been carried up yet."

He pointed to a pile of packages, topped by a suit-case, just below them.

"Yes, those are mine. How very fortunate!"

"Yes, your luck has begun to turn. It would have been very awkward getting them out of the hotel under Pedro's nose. I don't fancy he would have let them go very easily."

He rose, inserted his hand inside the open bosom of his shirt, and drew out a small silver whistle hung on a lanyard. He blew it, and it gave out a faint, high note, like a prolonged bat's squeak, so high as to be almost inaudible to civilized ears; but the primitive ears of the negro working on the big launch heard it, and he popped up his bullet head, responded with a wave of his arm, and the sound of an engine starting up came to them across the water. The big launch swung in a graceful curve and came gently alongside the jetty at their feet. The tide had risen since Nina's arrival, and embarking was an easier matter than disembarking had been. Lewis, with one foot on the jetty and one on the thwarts, pulled the boat in and held out a hand to her. She placed hers in it, and stepped easily down on to a cushioned seat, ducked under an awning, and found herself in the undecked forward part of the launch.

Lockers ran all round it, and on those nearest the cabin lay cushions, transforming them into comfortable seats. Lewis did not follow her, but went aft, and she heard him talking to the nigger engineer in his own language. Nina sat down on one of the seats and looked round her, rather startled by her own daring.

The launch was much bigger than she had expected. Behind the open cockpit in the fore part was a good-sized cabin whose double doors were folded back flat against the walls, so that cabin and cockpit were practically continuous, thus making the cabin exceptionally airy. She peeped inside and guessed that anyone sleeping on the leather-covered settees that formed bunks on either hand would be pretty comfortable.

The panelling and fitments were all of birds-eye maple. Above one of the bunks was a rack of books, small pocket editions of the classics and well worn. Everything was very neat. There was none of the demoralized disorder here that had characterized Harold's slovenly apartment.

Everything was polished and bright and sparkling, shining with elbow-grease, as if whoever tended it found it a labour of love. In contrast, the outside of the launch was drab. Clean and well cared for, but drab. There was no sparkling brass to look smart. Everything was covered over with tan-coloured paint, the exact shade of the muddy water overside. Even the awning was of khaki canvas.

Lewis, too, Nina observed, was all khaki-coloured from head to heel. His sun-helmet was tan, not white; his shirt was of tan cellular material. His tan boots were soled with crepe rubber, and he moved as quietly along the quay as his barefooted nigger engineer. She could imagine that a hundred yards out from the shore he and his launch would be almost invisible. And then there was the high-toned dog-whistle that could only be heard by negroes and not by civilized men. She wondered who and what Lewis might be, and suspected that there was something lawless and rebellious about him.

His puttee-covered legs suddenly appeared on the seat, to be followed immediately by the rest of him.

"Ngumba has gone off to round up the crew. Like to see round the establishment while we are waiting?"

Nina acquiesced.

"Here is the saloon. I hope you will be comfortable on one of those bunks with a rug. I am afraid we don't run to sheets. I generally sleep outside in the cockpit, myself. Through that door is a wash-place, where you can beautify yourself. I am afraid the drawers are full of all my junk, but I dare say you can manage with your suit-case and the pegs until we arrive at Waigonda."

"When do you expect to get there?"

"The day after tomorrow. Early, probably. It is a fair distance, you know."

"Am I taking you a great deal out of your way?"

"Not a great deal."

He led her through a door at the far end of the little saloon, and she found herself on the decked-over waist of the boat towards the stern. A hatch in the middle of the deck-space showed where goods could be stored in a miniature hold, and the raised poop at the stern held a galley and quarters for the crew. The launch must have measured some forty feet over all, and was a very perfectly equipped craft of her kind. Evidently money had been no object when she was built.

On top of the cabin was a kind of miniature conning-tower where the wheel and the controls were housed. In front of it a big car-headlight was mounted on a tripod. Evidently the steersman was perched up here to get a good view of the river and all its hidden snags and sandbanks; and it only needed to furl the awning to make the launch a handy sea-going craft in which to run down the coast. The launch, with her exquisite fittings, was not merely a rich man's toy, but admirably adapted for her work among the African rivers and roadsteads.

Nina felt a profound sense of relief and thankfulness at being taken in hand and looked after by a man of the type of Lewis, after her father's cheese-paring repressiveness and Harold's slovenly inadequacy. Here in Africa it was obvious that a woman could not fend for herself. She could only exist as the appendage of some male; it seemed to Nina that she had chosen her male well. Lewis was far and away the pick of the bunch, among some not very keen competition.

CHAPTER III

"**WELL**, there you are. You've seen all there is to see," said Lewis, surveying his little craft with pride. "And what do you think of her?"

"She's rather lovely, isn't she?" said Nina. "But why does she hide her light under a bushel ?"

"What do you mean?"

"Well, so very smart inside, and so very sober outside."

"The only thing to do with your light in Africa is to put it under a bushel. That's the only safe place for it. If you set it on a candlestick, someone invariably starts shooting at it. Now may I escort you back to the cockpit, where you can take your ease while we get your dunnage stowed below?"

Nina had a feeling that he did not wish to be questioned as to why he and his launch desired to avoid notice. Left alone in the cockpit, she began to do some serious thinking. What was she doing, and whither was she going? She considered critically her own attitude towards Lewis, and it seemed curious, even to herself. She knew here on the Coast, where white women were scarce, and such as there were, were so soon rendered unlovely by the climate, that her girlish freshness was exceedingly attractive to all the males. She knew that at the first touch of flirtatiousness Lewis would be all over her, and that she was only keeping him in check at the moment by her dignity and a calm refusal to react to him. A male, however over-gallant, finds it exceedingly difficult to get past the guard of a woman who won't react, but remains politely pleasant and conventional.

She knew that she was stranded here in Africa; that she had not the remotest chance of getting any employment by which she could maintain herself, and would sooner buy a broom and sweep a crossing than go home with her tail between her legs. Lewis was decidedly attractive and obviously prosperous. If she dangled her feminine bait before him, she was certain he would snap at it. But then, supposing he turned out to be already appropriated and could not offer her honourable marriage, she might have a very great deal of difficulty in getting him off her hook. He was very obviously not a man to be trifled with, and would probably prove a very awkward handful if he were crossed. Once she put a match to the kindling she would have no further control over the flames, and she needed to be sure that they were burning safely in the grate of holy matrimony, or her second state was likely to be worse than her first.

She had a feeling that in trusting Lewis and putting him on his honour she had made an appeal to all that was best in the man, and he was responding gladly. He would put her ashore at the mission station in perfect safety so long as she made it quite clear that this was what she desired. But one unguarded look, she felt sure, would set the furze afire.

All her training and traditions were in favour of caution with this man; but the fundamental adventuress that lay concealed under her demure exterior was awake and demanding its rights. There was nothing she wanted so much as to crook her little finger and see Lewis leap to her, as she felt certain he would.

But she censured herself severely. All her better nature told her that there was so much more in love than the mere call of the senses. There was comradeship, and sympathy, and an ideal held in common. If the elemental female in her

56

responded to the call of this fine male animal, she might bitterly regret it.

Lewis and his crew were busy aft getting her belongings stowed below, and she saw how wise had been the agent's advice to have the packages small and handy. She went into the little washing-place, hardly big enough for a doll's house, and noted Lewis's shaving-tackle and talcum, all neatly bestowed and of the very best quality. She removed her sun-helmet and got to work on her hair. Luckily for her, it had a natural wave, and clung about her head in a satiny gold cap with little frills over the ears; and the damper it was, the tighter it curled. Her transparent pink and white, fresh out from grey skies and wet winds, needed nothing save the shine removing. Her organdie dress had wilted, however, and, finding her suit case on the cabin floor, she got out a fresh one, in palest pink. Sheer silk stockings and a pair of white suede sandals that showed her toes replaced the canvas deck shoes she had used for coming ashore. A little dab of flower-scent behind each ear, and Nina was ready for the conquest of Lewis, whatever the risk might be.

She went forward into the cockpit and arranged herself on one of the seats, her back against the cabin bulkhead, her feet laid along the cushions, silken ankles demurely crossed and just peeping out from under her billowing skirts. The launch lay in the deep shade of the quay wall, and it was cool and pleasant, the flowing tide masking for the time being the harbour smells. Nina formed the opinion that the horrors of the climate were greatly over-rated. The clinking of tin-cans and a whiff of petrol reached her, and she knew that the launch was being fuelled for its long journey up the river.

Suddenly it occurred to her that she had never given a single thought to the jilted Harold since she had set foot on Lewis's launch. She tossed her head. Africa had taken her to its heart. She had gone primitive, and meekness and long-

57

suffering were not for her. She took the bundle of tired letters out of her bag, viewed them with distaste, and began to tear them small, one by one, without reading them. Lewis, seeing the scraps of torn-up paper going past on the tide as he worked at the stern, chuckled to himself, guessing what they were.

Nina gave herself a final preening, considered as much of herself as was visible in the mirror of her vanity case, and came to the conclusion that things were at last beginning to look a bit more like the illustrations to the serial story in the ladies' paper.

She suddenly looked up to find Lewis standing over her, gazing down at her with a curious expression in his eyes, and knew that the pink organdie had done its work. She had not heard him come; he must have moved as silently as a cat. She was seized with inexplicable panic. She had had no experience of men except Harold, and her father's curate, who believed in celibacy. Theoretically, she pined for a flirtation, but in actual practice she shrank away panic-stricken from the forces she felt to be simmering below the surface in Lewis and that a look might unleash.

Lewis sat down on the opposite locker without a word, reached for his hip pocket, and produced a monogrammed gold cigarette-case.

"May I offer you a cigarette?" he said.

Nina tried to see what his initials were, so that she might guess at his Christian name, but the monogram was an elaborate example of the engraver's art, and quite illegible.

She accepted a cigarette, and he proceeded to give her a light from a gold lighter. Evidently he had a taste for unobtrusive luxury, carefully hidden from the casual eye. His launch was drab outside, but bird's-eye maple within. Lewis himself wore khaki shirt and shorts like the rest of the men in the mangy little port, but eighteen-carat smoking-tackle was in the pocket of his shorts. She noted that the hand that held the little flame at arm's length to her cigarette was absolutely steady; one whiff, and she was alight.

At a yell from the stern he arose and, picking up a boat-hook that lay along the floor, thrust the bows of the launch clear of the quay wall. The engine began to sputter, and then to throb, and the little craft swept out into the open water, turned about, and headed upstream.

A negro youth clad in singlet and shorts came through the cabin with a tea-tray in his hand, all arrayed with shining silver and fine china. The edibles, however, consisted of a plate of fancy biscuits.

Lewis pulled a folding table from behind a locker and fitted its feet into holes in the floor, where they held firmly.

"I am trying to think how long it is since a woman poured out tea for me," he said.

Nina heaved a sigh of relief and relaxed. That disposed of one of her anxieties, anyway.

She took her feet off the cushions, smoothed down the miniature crinoline of pink organdie that stood out around her like the feathers of a fluffy bird, and gave her attention to the tea-tray.

Lewis did not seem to have much to say for himself, but she knew he was watching every move she made, though she never caught his eye.

Silence fell between them; and, prompted by she knew not what devil, she suddenly drew her engagement ring off her third finger and held it out to him lying upon her small pink palm.

"What shall I do with this?" she said.

Without a word Lewis leant forward, picked up the ring, and flung it far out into the river. Then he looked into her eyes and laughed. Nina felt that things were beginning to move, but, like a beginner on a toboggan run, tried to reduce the pace by digging in her heels.

"Shall I give you some more tea?" she inquired nervously. ·

"Thanks," said Lewis, handing her his cup.

"When do you think we shall get into Waigonda?"

"We shall get in some time tomorrow, instead of the day after; I am going to travel all night. There is the dickens of a confuffle at the hotel. Morley has wakened up; Pedro has taken up the cudgels on his behalf, and they are accusing me of kidnapping you. I want to get in ahead of the runners or the padre may not be very affable."

"I am so frightfully sorry to let you in for all this unpleasantness."

"Doesn't matter. All in the day's work. I am not *persona grata* in this part of the world, anyway."

Nina was somewhat perturbed by this change in his plans. She had counted on having at least forty-eight hours in which to observe Lewis before she crooked the finger that should call him to her.

"Have you heard when the missionary launch is expected?" she asked.

"Any day, I believe."

Silence fell between them again. Lewis's second cup of tea stood forgotten on the locker beside him while he stared at the toes of his boots. Suddenly he raised his head and looked fixedly at Nina.

"I have got a proposition to put before you," he said.

Nina turned and looked at him, startled by the intensity of his voice.

"There are two courses open to you. I can land you at Waigonda tomorrow morning, as originally suggested, and the padre will pack you safely home to your people; or, landing at Waigonda as before, we can ask the padre to marry us, and you can come home with me. I don't ask for a decision

60

now, but think it over, and tell me your decision tomorrow morning when we get to Waigonda."

Nina was so startled by this sudden proposal, despite the fact that her own mind had been working along these lines but a few moments previously, that she sat up amid her billowing pink skirts, looking like a frightened child.

"Have another cigarette?" he said, holding out his case towards her. "You have no need to be frightened of me. I'll land you at Waigonda as arranged if you say the word."

But she saw that the hand that held the lighter this time was not quite steady.

"I—I appreciate your offer," she said, "and I'll think it over."

"I am sorry I can't give you a longer time in which to think it over," said the man, "but we can neither of us afford to hang about in this district. You, because the padre won't want you on his hands longer than he can help, and I—for other reasons."

"I—I like you very much," said Nina, "but it is taking an awful risk to marry a person one knows as little as I know you."

"Risks have got to be taken for anything in life that is worth having. It is my trade to take risks. And, anyway, I am taking a jolly sight bigger risk in marrying you than you are in marrying me."

"What do you mean?"

"Well, if you don't like me, you can always leave me. But I have got to take you right into the centre of my affairs if I marry you, and if you don't fit in you are going to disorganize them pretty badly. If you hadn't told me that you liked Africa, I shouldn't have risked it."

"If I marry you, I will stand by you. I won't take you on and let you down. I think Ruth had the right idea about marriage when she said: 'Thy people shall be my people, and thy God my God.' "

Lewis stared at her for a long time in silence. At length he said : "Do you realize who my people and my gods are?"

"African?" said Nina.

"Yes," said Lewis.

"That is one of the chief attractions to me, you know," said Nina with a mischievous smile.

The entry of the darky youth to remove the tea-tray created a diversion for which Nina was truly thankful. Lewis in this mood, simmering like a kettle that is just going to boil over, was an anxious handful. She had no idea what he might choose to do next. They were literally aboard the lugger, and the maid was very much his if he chose to take her.

A marvellous sunset lit up the broad waters of the river, and the forest lay dark on either hand. The only sound was the soft purring of the motor aft and the rippling of the water under the sharp bows of the launch as it breasted the current.

The silence was becoming oppressive. Lewis seemed to be brooding darkly among his own thoughts, gazing out over the golden water. Nina felt she could bear no more, and must speak.

"Won't you tell me something about yourself?" she said. "I really feel we ought to make the most of our time to get acquainted."

Lewis came back to earth with a start, and looked at her sharply.

"You want my autobiography?" he asked.

"Excerpts," said Nina. "I'll give you mine in exchange. Daughter of poor but honest parents. Clergy, to be precise—"

"Both of 'em?" inquired Lewis.

"Well, not both, since you are so particular. Born in moorland parish near Ilkley. Brought up there, too. Been to

London once for twenty-first birthday. That is all."

"You don't appear to have had much chance to get into mischief, so I suppose you will be making up for arrears at the first opportunity."

"Well, what about you?"

"What about me? Son of the manse, same as yourself. Father a rural dean. Didn't like me. I didn't like him. Wanted to make a parson of me. I wanted to be a soldier. We compromised on engineering. Went to Cambridge. Father teetotal crank. I'd never tasted alcohol. Tried it for the first time. Miscalculated. Came into hall tight. Wanted to fight everybody. Not because I'd had such an awful lot, but because I'd never had any experience of alcohol and didn't know how to manage it. Insisted on fighting the dean. Made quite a mess of him, too, before I could be stopped. Sent down. Arrived home. Chucked out. Drink the old man's bug bear. Treated my one and only unlucky binge as if it were chronic alcoholism. Walked to Southampton. Ten bob in pocket. Got job as trimmer on tramp bound for Gold Coast. Appalling conditions. Deserted at first port. Captured by native constable. Swotted said constable on boko. Took to the bush. Fell in with Arab trader. Decently treated. Given a job. Stuck to him ever since. That's my history. I don't know what you think, but I don't think I'd have handled a youngster the way they handled me."

"And you like the life out here?"

"Love it. Wouldn't go back on any terms. There's only one thing lacking."

"What's that?"

"You!" Lewis's eyes seemed to pierce her through and through.

Nina moved uneasily.

"Are we going to have some supper?" she said. "I'm getting awfully hungry. I've had nothing but the sugar biscuits

63

since breakfast. Harold forgot to give me any lunch."

"I say, I'm frightfully sorry. It never occurred to me you hadn't been fed. I'll go and bustle them up in the galley."

Lewis disappeared through the open doors of the cabin, and Nina heaved a sigh of relief. His intense method of love-making contrasted rather startlingly with the more tepid approaches of Harold, of which alone she had had previous experience. She felt as if she were driving a car without brakes; if she allowed it to get up speed at all, it would be out of control.

Lewis returned, followed by the darky youth who acted as steward. Everything had obviously come out of tins, and the place of bread was taken by Thin Captain biscuits; but to Nina, as yet new to tinned stuff and very hungry, it tasted excellent.

"I don't live on tins when I'm at home," said Lewis. "I eat native food cooked native fashion, to a great extent. I think it helps to keep you fit. All this tinned stuff is darned bad for your inside. I think that's half of what's the matter with the chaps out here. It's by no manner of means all the climate."

"Are you interested in native art?" asked Nina.

"Yes, very. I've got quite a collection of it up at my place. There's some wonderful stuff comes out of Benin. It's all the rage in Paris now, isn't it?"

"How do you know?"

"I take in the magazines."

"Don't you ever want to come back to civilization on a holiday?"

"I get a spasm of it occasionally. But nothing ever comes of it. Mine is the sort of business that, if I went away and left it, I mightn't find there when I came back. You have given me a particularly bad spasm just at the moment. I feel as if I want to chuck everything and go home."

His voice suddenly rang out over the dark water:

"Is London what it used to be?
Is the Strand still there?
Do the boys still go down the West with its light and
    glare?
Are the girls still beautiful?
Are my friends all right?
Oh, what would I give to be with them in the old town
    tonight!"

A voice over their heads from the miniature conning tower took up the refrain in a kind of chanting chorus with no words to it. Other voices joined in from aft, where the crew were gathered, and the old-time music hall ditty floated across the water to be returned as an echo from the hollow banks.

It was strangely impressive. The wailing negro voices took up the white man's song of exile without knowing its meaning and expressed all Africa through it.

Lewis rose and opened the locker he had been sitting on, and took out a small African war-drum. Bending his hand back sharply at the wrist, he began to beat upon the stretched skin alternately with the heel of his hand and the knuckles, evoking two notes of different pitch. He paused, and in the silence they heard a drum reply from the bank. Then, farther off, came the sound of another drum, and in the intervals between the two a still farther drumming that was no louder than a heart-beat. Then the other bank began to answer, and they could hear the drums talking to each other all up and down the forest.

"Those are my people," said Lewis. "Why should I go back to London to be a stranger and an outcast? Nobody wants me there. Here I am welcome, and they like me and understand me. I shall never go back, Nina."

They rounded a bluff that was hiding the newly risen

moon, and found themselves in a flood of silver. Nina's dress, bleached by the moonlight, looked ghostly white. Lewis's hawk-like features were exaggerated into harsh crags and hollows, making him look like a grotesque Florentine mask, a caricature of himself. It was all strange and unreal, like some stage piece, and Nina was half frightened, half excited, by the exotic weirdness of it all.

She turned in her seat and, leaning on the thwart, gazed out over the moon-silvered water, trying to penetrate the velvety darkness of the trees, to which they were drawing near on the bend. Her back was to the boat, and she did not hear Lewis move, but suddenly she felt his arms round her. His cheek was against hers, and his voice whispering breathlessly in her ear:

"Say you'll come home with me, Nina? I'm simply desperately in love with you. You've got to come home with me! I'll never let you go. So it's no use saying you won't."

Nina twisted round in his arms, and his lips were on hers. It seemed to her as if she lost consciousness during that long, passionate kiss in which all the man's starvation for his kind welled up and broke forth.

He released her, thrust her from him roughly, and caught her by the wrists.

"Well, will you come?"

"Have I any choice?"

"No, none. But say you'll come!"

Nina laughed softly.

"Yes, I'll come," she said. Then she was kissed again.

She pushed him from her gently, and he let her do it. Standing with her hand on his breast to hold him off, she said:

"Do you know when this thing began? This thing between us, I mean?"

"No, when did it?"

66

"The moment I set foot on Africa, when I looked up and caught your eye. I said to myself then that I'd have to avoid you if I were to have any peace with Harold."

"You felt it?"

"Yes."

"So did I. That was why I came and spoke to you at the top of the jetty. It was a good thing you chucked Morley of your own accord. I'd never have let him have you, Nina."

"How would you have stopped him?"

"God knows. Knocked him on the head, if all else failed. But he'd never have had you."

"It seems to me that you are rather a dangerous person to be associated with."

"I'm all right if you take me the right way. I never meddle with anybody unless they meddle with me. Nobody can say I ever picked a quarrel with them; but if anybody goes about looking for trouble, I hate to see him disappointed."

"I wonder how I am going to manage you if I marry you. Are you a wife-beater in addition to your other crimes?"

"Nina, I'll be a perfect fool over you. You'll be able to put me round your little finger. But for God's sake don't ever make me jealous, for I won't be responsible for what happens if you do."

"I think I'd better go to bed," said Nina. "I am very tired, and you mightn't like the way I was looking at the man in the moon."

"Yes, I think you had. I'll make a hole in my manners if I talk to you by moonlight any longer."

CHAPTER IV

NINA slept wrapped up in Lewis's camel-hair cloak, and slept soundly, to the lullaby of purring engine and rippling water. The sun was high in the heavens before she presented herself to Lewis's company under the awning in the cockpit, and found him looking exceedingly smart in white ducks, with dark crimson tie and cummerbund.

"My wedding day," he said, when he saw her gazing at his glory, and laughed when she blushed and tossed her head.

He sat down on the locker at her feet, and began to play with her toes, that showed through the transparent silk of her sheer stockings and pierced open-work sandals. He reminded her of a young father enchanted with his firstborn. There was nothing this morning of last night's stormy passion. Lewis was in the highest spirits, laughing and chaffing her, and joking with his crew in their own language till it seemed as if the darky youth's face would split clean in half with his grin. Altogether, it was a very joyous bridal boatload that drew in at the little wooden jetty of the mission station.

"You had better wait a bit, Nina, while I go on and break it gently to the padre what we want of him. And for goodness' sake put on some more substantial shoes than these, or you will scandalize the good man, and possibly get something in your foot you won't fancy, into the bargain. This isn't England."

Nina, sitting on the cabin bunk changing her shoes,

watched him through the porthole with pride as he went across the open space between the jetty and the mission house, contrasting his well-set-up, athletic figure with that of the pot-bellied missionary with his drooping shoulders clad in rusty black alpaca.

She noticed that Lewis greeted the padre by raising his hand to his sun-helmet, but the padre was at no pains to return the salute, nor did the two men shake hands.

There seemed to be an argument, decidedly acrimonious, going on between them. Finally the missionary shrugged his shoulders and, turning on his heel, entered the whitewashed tin church, and Lewis came towards the launch over the dusty bare ground. His face was an enigmatic mask. Nothing could be read from it. It was only from the padre's gestures and expression that Nina had learnt that all was not of the most amiable.

"Ready, Nina?" asked Lewis, holding out a hand to help her on to the jetty. She stepped lightly out and stood beside him, all in spotless white from head to heel.

They went hand in hand up to the mean tin church, Nina's heart beating quickly and unevenly and her breath coming with difficulty. She would not, dared not, let herself think. She had made her choice and she must abide by it.

Lewis was not on good terms with the padre, she could see that, and so she would evidently be denied the comfort and support of any kindliness from him.

The padre had lit a couple of candles on the bare altar, and had there as witnesses two members of his household: a consumptive-looking negro lay preacher, who stared at Lewis as if he were a dangerous piece of machinery, and a coal-black mammy who rolled her eyes till she looked like an ebony Pekinese. Nina and Lewis took their places as directed, and the service began, the padre reading in a rapid gabble. He evidently thoroughly disapproved of the whole proceeding, and eyed Lewis over his book as if he hated the sight of him but dared not defy him.

The service went on, with its solemn adjuration that as they should answer at the Day of Judgment they should disclose whether there was any lawful impediment to their being made man and wife in the sight of God.

Then, instructed by the padre, Lewis took Nina's hand in his and, looking steadily into her eyes, said :

"I, Lewis Cassalis, take thee, Nina Barnet, to be my wedded wife . . ."

Nina felt everything go round and darken, and if Lewis had not had firm hold of her hand she would have fallen. Somehow, prompted by the padre, she got out the words:

"I, Nina Barnet, take thee, Lewis Cassalis, to be my wedded husband."

As from a very long distance she heard :

"With this ring I thee wed. With my body I thee worship."

Then came the voice of the padre:

"Whom God hath joined, let no man put asunder."

Then she and Cassalis rose from their knees and went out into the blazing sunshine, man and wife, the padre gazing after them glumly.

Nina dropped down on to the cushioned locker, too shocked and dazed to know what she was doing, and Cassalis stood staring down at her white face in perplexity.

"What's the matter, Nina?" he asked anxiously.

"I thought your name was Lewis," said Nina brokenly, through dry lips. .

"So it is—my Christian name. But my surname is Cassalis. Didn't you know that?"

"No."

The man's face darkened ominously.

"Would it have made any difference if you had?"

70

"I—I don't know."

"I suppose you have been hearing stories about me."

"Yes. Are they true?"

"How do I know? I don't know what you've heard."

"About the slave trade. And selling drink to the natives. And—and a lot of murders."

Cassalis's face looked as black as evil. "Well, and what if they are?"

"I—I don't like it," said Nina, struggling to sit up straight and keep a hold on her dignity.

"This is a primitive country. You mustn't judge by civilized standards. You'll be jolly glad to have my hand keep your head when there's trouble. You won't talk about murders then. I suppose that damned Leete woman has been talking to you."

"Not only her. The whole ship."

"What did they say?"

"They said you ought to be shot on sight."

Cassalis laughed shortly. "Then if they think that, why don't they do it? I'd do it to them if I felt that way about it."

"Why do you do these things?"

"What things?"

"The slave-trading—and ruining the natives with drink."

"Mind your own business. I did not ask your opinion. If you think you are going to reform me, you are very much mistaken."

"I wish I'd known you were Cassalis before I married you."

"I wish you had, too," said Cassalis savagely, and turned into the cabin, leaving her alone.

There is not much privacy to be obtained on a forty foot launch, and Cassalis obtained such as there was by turning

71

the nigger engineer out of the conning-tower and taking the wheel himself, spinning the spokes violently to avoid drifting logs that were coming down-stream after some cloudburst on the upper reaches. Nina heard them climbing up and down on to the cabin roof, and guessed from the wildness of the steering who was at the wheel, and what manner of temper he was in. She shuddered. She had heard on all hands what a dangerous man Cassalis was, and wondered what would be her fate if she crossed him.

It was plainly very risky to defy him and earn his ill-will, for she was completely at his mercy. But she was, as she had said, a daughter of the manse, and the way the twig is bent the tree will grow, unless violent traction is put upon it. Hard as she kicked against the pricks where her father's rigid ideas of righteousness were concerned, his unswerving uprightness and devotion to what he conceived to be his duty were graven deep in her heart as only childhood's impressions can be graven. What ever fanciful theosophies she might take up with in later life, the concept of a God of righteousness would remain.

She had sat beside her trembling mother on Easter Sunday, the day on which the offerings of the congregation are given to the incumbent and make all the difference for the ensuing year in poorly endowed parishes such as theirs, and heard her father inveigh against the housing conditions prevailing in the district, while the local magnate sat in his pew looking like the devil. There was no cheque in the bag that year, but her father was the local hero.

Those things make an impression on a child, an impression of a deep pride in the family integrity which must never be let down. It was ground into her very soul that she was her brother's keeper, and that God would require his blood at her hands.

Consequently when she realized that the man who had

fascinated her so much was the man who was responsible for African Tammany, and for the long strings of tortured and dying negroes dragged half across Africa to be sold into slavery, something in her rose up stiff and stark; and just as her father had elected to call the local magnate to the judgment of God for the state of his cottage property on the particular Sunday when the clergyman's collection was taken up—instead of waiting till next Sunday, when he would have had that gentleman's cheque safe in his banking account—so must Nina refuse to accept the easy way, and smile upon her lawful wedded husband for the sake of peace and quietness. It was a crazy proceeding, placed as she was, and dealing with such a man as he was, but then craziness apparently ran in the family.

The launch collided with a large tree that was drifting in mid-stream, and became entangled in the half-submerged boughs; the negro engineer ran hastily forward with a boat-hook to disentangle it, while Cassalis slammed the engine recklessly into reverse and the launch lurched as if it were going under. Ngumba rolled his eyes at Nina, registering consternation and reproach better than any film-star; then shook his head and flapped his hands in a melancholy manner, and finally made a graphic gesture of someone having their throat cut, and departed. Nina shivered and tucked her feet under her, but her jaw was set.

Presently the black steward came to lay lunch, his grin drooping woefully. Evidently the whole boatload of sensitive darkies took their emotional tone from the dominating personality of Cassalis.

She heard a sound, glanced up, and saw Cassalis standing in the doorway of the cabin, looking down at her darkly.

"Well, Nina," he said, coming out and taking his place at the table, "the gilt is off the gingerbread pretty thoroughly, but I suppose we must still eat."

"I'm frightfully sorry," said Nina. "I wish things could be different."

"In what way do you want them to be different?"

"I wish you didn't do the things you do, that put you on the wrong side of the law, and cause so much suffering."

Cassalis stirred uneasily in his seat.

"It's my living, Nina. I don't see how I am to earn it in any other way. I am completely outcast, you know."

"I wouldn't mind how poor we were if you earned your living honestly."

"I would, though," said Cassalis with an ugly look, and silence fell between them again.

At the end of the meal, when the darky had gone off with the plates, Cassalis stretched out his long legs and leant back against the thwarts and said:

"Well, Nina, as we have taken each other for better or for worse, and I don't exactly see what you are going to do if you give me the chuck in the middle of the African forest, I suggest that we agree to differ, and refrain from referring to controversial subjects. I shall not do my jerry-mandering under your nose, and you must keep your conscience to yourself if you desire peace in the family."

"Yes," said Nina miserably, "I suppose that would be the best way."

"Very well, then, that's settled, and don't let's refer to it again. Now are you going to give me a kiss?"

"Yes, I suppose so."

"Oh, God!" exclaimed Cassalis savagely, and plunged through the doors into the cabin, and in a moment or two Nina felt the launch take up its erratic progress again.

The man in the conning-tower, staring out over the blinding river with eyes that saw nothing, not caring in the least what he struck, had met his Waterloo. All his successful villainy had come down on his head in one crash when the girl with whom he had fallen in love with the whole force of his headlong nature turned from him in disgust at the sound of his name.

Cassalis was hurt not only in his pride and his senses, but in the higher and better part of his nature, which had wakened from its long oblivion—to the surprise of no one more than himself—when a girl's soft hand had been placed in his on the sun-baked quay and he had looked into her eyes with quite as much pity as desire.

And when, in front of all the assorted ruffians in the bar, the lovely girl in her virginal white had come up to him and asked for his protection, he would have let himself be cut in pieces for her. If Nina had not been deliberately provocative, with her scent and her sandals and her transparent stockings, Cassalis would have made no advances to her. But as it was, he saw that his advances would evidently not be unacceptable, or so he reasoned from the way she had made herself attractive and displayed herself on the cushioned locker, and why should he not take this heaven-sent chance if the girl were willing? God knows, he would do his best to be a good husband to her. If Nina had handled him properly, she could have done anything with him. He had spoken truly when he had said that he would be a perfect fool over her.

If she had put her hand in his and said, "Lewis, give these things up for my sake," he would have dropped them like a hot coal, cost what it might. And in any case he hadn't touched the slave-dealing for years. He didn't like it any better than she did. He had not dared to refuse to lend a hand with it in his early days on the Coast because his position was very precarious with Sheik Ibrahim's sons, and it was more than his life was worth to appear squeamish; but he saw to it that precious few niggers died in his strings, and that they all arrived in fat and flourishing. His principal occupation at

75

the present moment was gun-running for the warlike Ashanti tribes to shoot each other with, and both parties were very well able to take care of themselves. He did not feel particularly conscience-stricken about that. Then he bought ivory from the illicit ivory-hunters, which caused the Government to lose its tax and was bad for the elephants, as the nigger hunters paid no attention to close seasons and suchlike, but wiped out the whole herd if they once got on its track, leaving none to reproduce their kind. He did not know whether Nina would be particularly tender over the wrongs of infant elephants, orphaned too early. None of these things weighed on his conscience, though he quite admitted Nina's point about the slave-dealing and the gin-selling; but then those were ancient history nowadays.

But equally he saw that even if gun-running and illicit ivory-trading did not weigh on the conscience unduly, it having always been accepted that the Excise, like the insurance companies, is fair game, they were not the best of occupations for a married man who had given hostages to fortune, for every police-officer on the Coast regarded Cassalis's scalp as a particularly choice one, and it not only required unceasing vigilance, but also a diabolical ruthlessness to avoid leaving evidence behind that would lead to his being "sent down" for a considerable spell of penal servitude: a particularly unpleasant prospect with Nina on his hands.

He saw quite plainly that he would have to cut out his lawlessness now that he was married, but his hackles rose at the memory of Nina's disapproving face and gesture of repulsion. The idea crossed his mind of borrowing a few slaves from one of Ibrahim's sons just to tease Nina with. But he immediately dismissed the idea as impracticable. The slaves, drawn from degenerate tribes, would be whining and imbecile nuisances. The decent blacks were the fighting blacks, and God help anyone who tried to make slaves of them!

76

Cassalis turned over in his mind what he could do if he gave up his various lawless but profitable activities. There was nothing like so much money to be made in legitimate trading, even if anyone were willing to trade with him, which he doubted. He was so utterly and completely outcast that none of the banks would handle his account nor any of the agencies do business with him. It was not going to be easy to get off the cross and run straight, even if no evidence ever cropped up about his past misdeeds, and one never knew what chance might bring to light.

There is always a thing forgotten
When the rest of the world goes well;
A thing forgotten, as long ago,
When the gods forgot the mistletoe,
And silent as an arrow of snow
The arrow of anguish fell.

In order to cover his tracks in his various illegitimate enterprises Cassalis had done a lot of killing, for he always made it a rule, if surprised, to give no quarter, but wipe out every living soul who could possibly give evidence against him. He did not even save the women for his slave-strings. The blacks understood this policy, and considered it perfectly legitimate and bore no ill-will, but the whites did not; and unfortunately white men had fallen to his gun on several occasions when he had embarked on a killing and a white man was found to be mixed up in it unexpectedly and had had to go too, in order to silence him. And the last killing of a white had taken place only a few days ago.

One of his head men had been arrested on a charge of murder on which the evidence was irrefutable; and as the murder had been committed at Cassalis's instigation, he felt it was up to him to see that his catspaw got away. So when the prisoner was being brought down to the coast, he ambushed the party and shot up the native policemen, only to find that an unexpected white officer was bringing up the rear, and Cassalis had shot him with his own hand as the only means of shutting his mouth. It was either a bullet for him or a rope for himself.

So far as he knew, he had wiped out the whole patrol, and his men had followed up the party and finished off the porters; but one never could be quite sure who was lurking in the bush, and he would be glad when the trail had grown cold and there were no signs of following it up. He very much disliked shooting white men; it preyed on his mind for long afterwards, cropping up in dreams at night; but there was nothing else for it when it was that or hang. Moreover, the killing of a white man was followed up with a tenacity and determination to leave no stone unturned that did not prevail when a few of Africa's teeming millions were gathered to their fathers prematurely. That he was suspected of the crime he knew, for the men in the bar had been openly chaffing him about it when Nina came up to him and the whole current of his life changed.

It was not in the man to yield to pressure or reproaches, but he made up his mind that the first time Nina made any response to his advances he would say to her: "Look here, Nina, I will cut out the slaving and all that, if you really want me to." In his heart he breathed something very like a prayer that this last killing would blow over safely, and that he might be permitted to turn over a new leaf. It was, perhaps, one of the most curious petitions which have ever gone up to the Throne of Grace, for it implied that the killing should have been so thorough and comprehensive that no living soul had got away alive to give evidence against him.

He knew that the authorities had been really roused by this murder of yet another white man in which suspicion pointed strongly to himself, and that bloodhounds had been fetched by sea from Cape Coast Castle, where an enterprising police-officer had introduced them. But the bloodhounds had not been feeling very well, the climate apparently disagreeing with them, and had declined to trail. Cassalis wondered what Nina would say if she knew that her bridegroom was being hunted for his life by bloodhounds. It was a nice start for their marriage. But to do him justice, in all the excitement over getting Nina away in his launch—in which his head had been completely turned till he hardly knew what he was doing, with this ravishing white beauty coming into his hands after the long years of isolation from his own kind—he had completely forgotten such a commonplace matter as a killing. In fact, if it had not been that he wanted to settle down and make a home with his bride he would never have given it another thought, regarding the risk of being hanged by the neck till he was dead as all in the day's work among the many risks that Africa imposes upon her sons and step-sons.

He promised himself that once this business had blown over safely, and the authorities had made up their minds that sufficient evidence was not forthcoming on which to issue a warrant, he would take the first opportunity to drop in on the Governor and say, "Look here, sir, let bygones be bygones. I have married a wife, and I want to settle down. I won't give you any more trouble if you will let me alone," hinting in a tactful manner that if the authorities persisted in bearing malice, rifles would be cheap and plentiful in the district for some time to come. That was an argument which had worked once before when authority had shown signs of really bestirring itself. Authority, being near the end of its period of service, had agreed to let sleeping dogs lie for another six months, at which time it was going home for good to tend its liver.

Cassalis made up his mind to concede Nina's point in

the long run, but he greatly disliked the idea of yielding to reproaches and black looks; he thought that they would have a few scenes from *The Taming of the Shrew*, which would be quite an enjoyable entertainment, and at the first sign of entreaty he would allow himself to be persuaded. He whistled to Ngumba to take the wheel, dropped down on to the half-deck and slipped with his silent cat-like movements, learnt from the forest blacks, into the cabin, whence he could observe Nina without her observing him.

He could see the curve of a round white neck and the tip of a small ear appearing under the silken cap of her hair. A bare white arm, an elbow with a dimple in it, and a trail of white organdie skirt were also visible, and that was all. Nina sat as still as a statue, her back against the forward bulkhead of the cabin, her feet up on the cushions, ankles crossed, in her habitual attitude.

Cassalis did not know exactly how to approach her. He had come out to the Coast as a very young man, before he had had the chance to gain much experience of English girls of his own class. There had been assorted synthetic charmers in the coastal ports, and any quantity of dusky belles in the forests; but what he wanted of Nina was not what he wanted of frightened negro maidens in the raided villages. It was the best that was in the man that her fair virginity had called to. And as he sat on the bunk in which she had slept, staring at the little bits of her that were all that was visible to him, he began to wonder whether even the sacrifice of his illicit interests, which he was now quite prepared to make, for his own sake as well as hers, would serve to propitiate her, or whether she would still recoil with a gesture of repulsion at the name of Cassalis and all it evidently implied to her. His hands were steeped in blood and violence, the blood of his last crime hardly dry upon them. Would all the scents of Araby avail to cleanse them in her eyes? He could feel the pressure on his groin of the revolver in its concealed holster with which he had shot the police-officer less than a week ago.

Nina, for all her talk of African gods, was a daughter of the manse, and he, from his own experience, knew the effect of that drastic upbringing. In his case it had caused him to react into lawlessness and violence; but in the case of a girl it might hold its own and strait-lace her most effectually. He saw his budding romance, the most precious thing that had ever come into his life, going west beyond recall, and an unwilling bride on his hands who would turn away her face from his kisses, feeling herself contaminated by them.

They had long since, though unobserved by Nina, left the main river, and after dodging through a network of islands had begun to work up a good-sized tributary. The mountain ranges, that had hung like a cloud on the horizon at the beginning of their journey, were now looming just ahead of them, and the oozy alluvial forest lands were giving place to steep bluffs. Cliff-like banks were beginning to close in on the river, and a peculiar chill struck up from the water, telling Cassalis that they were approaching their journey's end. He dared not leave the negroes to negotiate this part of the journey, therefore it was inadvisable to start a discussion with Nina which might prove inconclusive and lead to still further estrangement. So he slipped out of the cabin as quietly as he had entered it, unobserved by the girl sitting brooding outside. The air got steadily colder as they advanced, and Cassalis sent Ngumba down for his shooting-jacket and bid him take the camel-hair cloak to Nina; he himself dared not leave the conning-tower as the launch fought its way against foaming rapids between towering rock walls.

Nina, sitting rigid with misery, watching with increasing nervousness the progress of the launch through the roaring white water, sprang up at a touch on her elbow, a tremulous smile dawning on her lips. But it was not Cassalis, but the big steersman, who beckoned her to enter the cabin, and began to get in the cushions, and furl the awning, and generally snug down for rough weather.

The noise of the rapids was deafening, and the rocky walls seemed almost to meet overhead. She guessed that Cassalis was in the conning-tower, bringing them steadily through all this turmoil, where the slightest slip meant instant death. She was thankful he was there, for, horrified as she had been to find that the man she had married was the notorious Cassalis, she knew that she could not be in safer hands when it came to a tight corner.

Then suddenly she saw a weird witch-light dancing on the white water ahead, and realized that the big headlight had been switched on. A moment later she realized why, for as they rounded a rockbound bend she saw the dark mouth of a cave ahead of them, with the river pouring out of it. The launch toiled on against the tremendous current and passed under the rocky arch into echoing, roaring darkness, lit only by the shaft of the headlight, which revealed the dancing white waves of rapids. Then the struggle against the water relaxed, and Nina saw that they were moving over the tranquil surface of an underground lake. It was icy cold, and she shivered in her thin organdie as she drew Lewis's camel-hair cloak around her. The cloak seemed full of his personality, and she wondered what scenes of violence and crime it had witnessed.

But even if she shrank from the villainous Cassalis, she could not help longing for the man whom she had known as Lewis to come to her and keep her company in all this terrifying din and darkness.

They had drawn clear of the rapids now, and the noise was dying away behind them into a dull echoing roar as they advanced swiftly across an underground lake of considerable

82

size. Nina could see neither banks nor roof in the beam of the headlight, but only empty, glittering darkness, and there was dead silence as the voice of the rapids faded in the distance.

Then her eyes detected a flickering spot of light in the black void ahead, which grew brighter as they approached, and proved to be a small bonfire with a number of negroes huddled round it, apparently for warmth, as they waited in the chilly air of the great cavern.

They ran down to the edge of the water chattering volubly as the launch drew in, caught the mooring-ropes that were thrown to them, and secured her stem and stern to stout bollards sunk in the cave floor.

Nina heard Cassalis climbing down from the conning tower over her head, and in a moment he was beside her, the collar of his shooting-jacket turned up to his ears against the cold of the cave.

"Well," he said, "the first stage of our journey is over, and we are getting near home."

Nina shuddered, wondering whether she were going to live in a cavern in perpetual darkness, and whether the secret of Cassalis's excellent health was the chilly cave air.

"If you will put your belongings together, we will get a move on," said the man. "I want to get home before dark. Better change into something a bit warmer than that muslin. We shall be in the cave for several hours, and it will be considerably cooler when we come out, high up the mountain."

Nina took possession of the cabin, and changed into the suit in which she had come on board the steamer, and then waited in the cockpit while Cassalis also changed out of his tropical kit, to reappear in cord breeches and a flannel shirt. She saw that the Coaster's guess had been correct, and that Cassalis owed his immunity from the ill effects of the terrible

West African climate to his wisdom in making his home at a high altitude, and wondered why everyone else did not do the same, forgetting that trade must follow the means of access, which in that country were the big rivers, and that probably no one but Cassalis knew of this route up the mountains.

He put her into an awninged hammock slung from a stout pole, borne by two magnificent buck niggers, who were immensely elated by the honour, and blew out their great chests and set off at a spanking pace, the hammock swinging from side to side till Nina began to fear a recurrence of her old enemy the sea-sickness. But their pace soon slackened, for after following the shore of the lake for a little way, the track began to climb an overhanging cliff, borne on a shelf obviously cut by the hand of man. It was none too wide, and on her left hand she could look straight over the hammock-side into an ever-increasing drop, from which presently arose the sound of another stretch of rapids.

The wavering light of the lanterns that were being carried by the marching negroes revealed the white of the racing water as the dark underground river plunged over a small fall. Nina, who had a very poor head for heights, shut her eyes, and clung convulsively to the edges of the hammock with both hands, trying not to think of what would happen if one of her bearers stumbled in the darkness. She could not see Cassalis, who was away at the rear, the only proper place for the leader of an expedition to march, for then he knows what is happening to his party.

She herself was being carried head foremost, so that the steep pitch of the path should not lift her feet into the air, and all she could see from under her awning was the brawny black chest of the rear porter. She could tell from the puffing and blowing of the porters that they were climbing steeply. On her right was a sheer cliff-face against which the hammock bumped as it swung; on her left was a sheer

84

drop whose bottom she could not see, though the sound of roaring water came up to her, getting gradually fainter as they climbed, and she guessed that they were making their way up an enormous split in the mountains, like a canyon turned upside down.

Her reason told her that there was probably no real danger; that the negroes were coming and going up and down this path all the time, and that they were Cassalis's faithful servants who would no more have thought of harming her than of attacking the King on his throne. But all the same, imagination had much to work on in that cave, with its echoing darkness and roaring water, and Nina lay in the hammock rigid with terror—terror of the ugly drop under her very elbow, over which she swung at every step of the porters; terror of the wild black men who surrounded her with never a glimpse of Lewis; terror of the noise and darkness and weirdness of it all, and of what fate might await her at the end of the journey now that she knew that her Lewis was the terrible Cassalis of many murders and unspeakable atrocities.

It was an alarming home-coming for any bride.

At length the panting porters drew in to a kind of side cave that led up like a gully off the narrow man-made ledge, rounded a rocky bend, set the hammock down upon two pairs of crutched poles that were evidently carried as a support for it, and withdrew, leaving the girl alone in pitch blackness and silence, too terrified to make a sound, wondering whether this was Cassalis's punishment of her for having defied him—to carry her far into the heart of the mountain and leave her alone to a terrible death in the darkness.

But in a few moments she saw the light of a lantern shining on the bend, and round came Cassalis himself.

"Why, Nina," he exclaimed, "did those fools leave you alone in the dark without giving you a lantern? What a pair of prize idiots! But it is just like them. One has to be after them the whole time. I hope you haven't been too scared."

"I've been horribly scared," said Nina.

He bent over her. "What have you been scared about?"

"Oh, I don't know. I don't suppose there was anything really to be scared of. I expect it was safe enough. But I've got a rotten head for heights, and I simply hated that path over the river."

Cassalis heaved a sigh of relief. He had feared that she was going to say she was afraid of him. He patted her shoulder, to see how she would take it, and to his delight felt a pair of small hands clutching at him.

"Oh, Lewis, please don't go away and leave me alone in the dark again. I know I'm a fool, but I'm simply scared stiff."

Nina found herself being kissed so vigorously that all thought of darkness and precipices was driven completely out of her mind—all thought, in fact, of the slave trade and the misdeeds of the notorious Cassalis; and she put her arms round his neck, only too thankful that the estrangement was over between them, for she had liked him tremendously before she knew he was Cassalis.

Cassalis, kneeling there on the uneven rock floor in the icy darkness of the great cave, felt as if all heaven were about him, with his beloved in his arms and clinging to him. All the outcast years of violence and cruelty fell from his shoulders like Christian's burden, and he felt as if he had been freed from his sins by the soft kisses of his beloved's lips, just as men are supposed to feel freed by more orthodox means of grace.

He rose to his feet as a darky in white nightshirt and crimson fez, evidently of a different type, and considering himself vastly superior to the negro porters, came into the cave bearing a small suit-case in his hand, which, when a spring was pressed, let down four legs and became a table for an *alfresco* meal, a vacuum flask and packets of sandwiches being unpacked from its inside. Cassalis evidently believed in travelling in comfort, for another nightshirted nigger trotted up with a couple of folding camp-chairs.

"We don't live on tins when we are at home, as you can see," said Cassalis, passing Nina a plate of sandwiches. "This is Mammy Jonah's bread. Pretty creditable, don't you think, for an old black dame who has never set eyes on any white man except me?"

"Very creditable indeed," said Nina, munching hungrily at the excellent egg sandwiches, thankful for the hot coffee in the dank chill of the cave. "But how did she come by her name? Is she really a Jonah?"

"Well, you see, she lost three husbands, one after the other, and her village made up its mind that she must be a Jonah, so they were going to sacrifice the poor old dame to the local crocodile god in the hope of improving the local luck. And I came along in the nick of time and rescued the portly damsel; and knowing what a decent old party she was, I made her my housekeeper, and she has been a great success. She's a first-class cook, within the limits of the raw material I can provide her with. You'll be surprised how well we live in our eyrie."

Nina was relieved to learn that there was no jealous young nigger mistress to be disposed of upon her advent, for she had always understood that that was how outcast white men lived. She did not know enough of human nature to realize that the name of Cassalis's dusky donahs was legion, and that his half-caste bastards were the pride of innumerable villages all up and down the Coast. In fact the Coasters declared that it was impossible that one man could have done it, and he must have had help from the missionaries. Her chosen mate had merely been shrewd enough not to embarrass himself with anything half so respectable as a mistress.

The meal and rest finished, they started off again with a fresh pair of porters at the hammock-poles, and as the track had now forsaken its dizzy ledge and was winding up a kind of gulch, Cassalis came and walked beside Nina, to give her the consolation of his company, and himself the happiness of hers.

"What is this unearthly place?" demanded Nina as they settled down to their march.

"Partly natural cave, partly old mine workings. This may have been King Solomon's mines, for all we know to the contrary. It is very, very old. I believe the Phoenicians were supposed to have come trading around these parts, and mines like these were old in their day."

"Is it a gold-mine?"

"No, copper. And there's plenty more to be got out of it, too, by modern methods." He threw the light of the lantern he carried on to the rocky walls, and showed her the green streaks of verdigris. "It could be got out very cheaply, too, owing to the easy access by river. There is a path like this one all the way along the river till it joins the main stream. You didn't see it today because the river was in spate, for some reason best known to itself; you never know how or why these underground rivers rise and fall. The whole range is full of them, and honey combed with caves like a gruyere cheese. It reminds me of the Mendips, where I was brought up. This place is Wookey Hole on a large scale, if you come to think of it. Same formation, too, in the limestone. Yes, somebody is going to make easy money here, for a tug with barges could come right up to the place where we landed."

"Why don't you become that somebody?"

"I did try to, Nina. I put in for a concession, but they wouldn't give it me. Stymied it in the Governor's Council The Governor is not exactly a pal of mine. The late one, I mean. I believe the watch is changing just about now. He has had as much as he can stick of the Coast, and is retiring on a premature pension, his innards all rotted out with whisky and quinine. What a life! I prefer my pirate lair in the hills."

"Why wouldn't they give it you, Lewis?"

"Well, you see, I have not got the best of reputations in these parts, as I gather you already know. And the Governor looked at me in much the same way as you did, when I applied for the concession."

"But surely, if you wanted to run straight, they should have been only too glad to give you a chance?"

"You'd think so, wouldn't you? It would have saved them no end of trouble. But I've cocked altogether too many snooks at law and order ever to be forgiven at Government House. I was very disappointed over it at the time, but I suppose it was only human nature for him to want to get a bit of his own back.

"And do you know what I did?" continued Cassalis reminiscently, chuckling softly to himself, forgetting who was his hearer. "I ran consignment after consignment of rifles in right under his nose, and sold 'em to the niggers dirt cheap, just enough to pay my out-of-pockets, and every nigger in the district laid in supplies, and they shot each other up like one perpetual Guy Fawkes night for weeks on end. You never heard such poppings and bangings, and all under his very windows!"

He could have bitten his tongue off, the moment he had spoken, but his wife's comment made him gasp.

"Serve him jolly well right," she said viciously; and he was left marvelling still further at the vagaries of human nature, especially feminine human nature.

CHAPTER V

"**WE** are getting to the end of our troubles now, Nina," said Cassalis at last, when it seemed to Nina as if they had been travelling through the heart of the range for years, and must expect to come out in the middle of the Sahara. His words were confirmed by a greying of the darkness, and when they rounded a bend they saw daylight ahead. Nina heaved a sigh of thankfulness; she did not like caves.

They came out into the brilliant African sunshine, but with a difference. For the air here, instead of being heavy with moisture, was clear, thin, mountain air that did not hold the heat. Consequently, although the sunlight blazed and scorched, there was a cool freshness with it, and in the shade it was almost chilly, for the sun was near setting. They were moving up a small glade among scrub-oaks and fir, and Nina exclaimed with delight at the freshness and beauty of it all.

"Oh, how perfectly delightful! Am I going to live up here?"

Cassalis was enraptured. It seemed as if life had nothing left to offer him. All memory of the recent crime, of which the trail was not yet cold, was effaced from his memory as if it had never happened. He was in a state of ecstatic happiness, up here with his bride.

"I hope you'll like the shack," he said. "At any rate, it can soon be altered if you don't. We stick on bits here and there as the fancy takes us in these parts."

They came out of the wood into a little Alpine meadow of smooth mountain turf, with a stream running across it and a waterfall coming down a miniature cliff in a series of rocky leaps at the far end. Far above their heads great peaks hung in the sky, with streaks of snow here and there in the gullies. Away to the right the low cliffs opened in a gap, and Nina saw in the far distance what looked like a grey sea curtained with mist, and guessed that it was the great tropical forest rolling fold upon fold to the coast. She thought of what life must be like on those steaming levels, and breathed a sigh of thankfulness for the eyrie to which her lover had brought her.

In the centre of the glade stood a one-storey structure, built of rough stone by amateur masons, but well and truly thatched with a deep thatch of reeds after the manner of the native huts in that locality. As Cassalis had said, it had evidently had many additions stuck on at the rear without any attempt at architectural design, as domestic exigencies required it; but in front, in the part that faced the gap in the cliffs, it consisted of two wings forming a right angle, with the space between them roofed over to form a deep verandah. It had, in fact, the butterfly design of one of the modern, popular, jerry-built villas of the garden suburbs, from a picture of which in an illustrated magazine Cassalis had taken the idea.

The steps leading up to this verandah were decorated by a magnificent figure. Nearly six feet high, fat as a haystack, arrayed in nothing but a very full grass petticoat and innumerable strings of beads, was Mammy Jonah, almost overcome with excitement and hospitality and general rejoicing at the sight of her white master's bride. Here was no jealous and lamenting mistress whose vindictiveness might prove a source of potential trouble, but a faithful and adoring servitor, who thought that the most wonderful thing that had ever happened in Africa was now taking place. Nina felt a sigh of relief go all through her at the sight of that beaming black face with its ecstatic grin, the very cream of the milk of human kindness. Childless old Mammy Jonah, three times widowed and long since without hope of piccaninnies of her own, had visions of little white children for her to play with, and cuddle, and sing plaintive melodies to the children of her adored master.

Mammy Jonah executed a sort of war-dance as Nina came up the steps, and patted her with her big black hands, grinning till it looked as if she would dislocate her jaw. Nina smiled at her and patted back. Mammy threw up her hands, and threw back her head, and only just stopped short of a back somersault. Her cup of happiness was full. Cassalis, supremely happy and deeply thankful, for he saw that Nina was going to take the niggers the right way, put his arm round his bride and led her over the threshold and kissed her. To the outcast man it seemed the most sacred moment of his life. Too deeply moved to speak, he led his bride into his house and sat her down beside his hearth and stood and looked at her.

And Nina, gazing at his face at that moment, had a sudden flash of understanding of how a man could be at once both good and bad. At that moment Cassalis, for all his villainous record, had the stuff in him of which martyrs are made. He would willingly have died for an ideal, provided that ideal was Nina. He had no concept of an abstract God of righteousness, or any care at all for moral law; but Nina, simply by being what she was, unspoilt, bonny, loving, with her own high but simple ideals, had very effectually "showed him the Father".

All unconsciously, despite her rejection of its restrictions, Nina had brought to this African home the atmosphere of the country vicarage in its garden in a hollow of the moors, the atmosphere of reverence for sacred things; of regard for the good and the true; of clean simplicity and virginity, soon to be exchanged for wifehood, which, in its way, is another kind of virginity. All these things Cassalis felt without being able to express them even to himself. The sense of the sacredness of a good woman came upon him and overwhelmed him: his house made a home by her presence; its hearth sanctified by her tendance; his own wild and turbulent manhood ordered, calmed, filled with peace by her chastity. Cassalis was too reserved, too controlled, too thoroughly English to do anything openly, but in his heart he knelt down and worshipped her.

The days that followed were days of wonder and marvel to the man and the girl up alone on the African mountain. Cassalis could never have enough of playing with his bride, and rejoicing in her, and making love to her. And as he played and rejoiced and made love, she gradually changed from a rather startled and bewildered but adventurous maiden into the full flowering of womanhood and love; for these things are not done in a day, and though a girl may technically lose her virginity in one night, she takes longer than that to change from maiden into wife; and sometimes she never changes, and then the marriage goes wrong. And when she comes to marriage without her virginity, having played lightly at love and been passed from hand to hand, she never knows that wonderful flowering at the touch of one man, and its sacredness. And when a man has given a woman that flowering, no other woman can ever be to him what she is.

Equally marked was the change in Cassalis. From a wild reckless adventurer, loving risk and violence for their own sakes quite as much as for the big profits and quick returns they yielded in his able and ruthless hands, he had become a householder who desired nothing so much as to settle down quietly and build up the happiness and beauty of his home. He and Nina spent hours together going through the advertisement pages of the illustrated magazines and cutting out the particulars of the things which he would have sent up to him next time he went down to the coast.

Harold had been forgotten as completely as if he had never existed. The only thing that troubled Nina was the difficulty of communicating with her people. When she had spoken to her husband of writing to tell them about her new-found happiness, he looked worried and said:

"My God, Nina, this is going to be awkward. You will have to be dashed careful what you say."

"In what way?" asked Nina, surprised.

"Well, darling, it wouldn't do for a hint of the whereabouts of my lair to leak out. Not even that it is at a high altitude, because that would give them a pointer towards the mountains. The whole of my affairs really hang on the fact that no one knows where I lie up. I'd like you to let me see the letter, Nina, before you send it, if you don't mind. Not that I want to spy on your affairs, but in order to see that you haven't given away any clues accidentally, without realizing you've done it."

"But why all this elaborate precaution? Are you wanted by the police?"

Nina spoke jokingly, and it startled her to find that Cassalis took the question perfectly seriously.

"Not at the moment, so far as I know. But one never can tell what may crop up, and it may mean everything to me to have this place to lie up in till the hunt goes by."

"But, Lewis, I thought you had promised me you would drop all that?"

"So I will, darling, but it takes a bit of disentangling, and I'm not clear of it yet. But I give you my word that there's nothing I want so much as to get clear of it. Once I'm clear, it

94

will be all right, and we shall be able to put in an appearance in such polite society as the Coast affords. Pedro's damsel, for instance—I don't fancy she's his wife. But until then I am still something of a fly-by-night. I am frightfully sorry, darling; I hate letting you in for this sort of thing. It didn't matter when I was a giddy bachelor, but by God, it does now, and no mistake. I am realizing it more every day I am with you."

He spoke the literal truth. His nerve for lawlessness had completely gone now that he had got Nina on his hands; and with its going he began to worry, a thing he had never done in his life before, and to add up the possibilities of treachery, and of that bit of pure bad luck which is always to be expected in the best-laid schemes.

Finally the day came when his honeymoon had to end, and he set off for the plains in response to an urgent call to go down and settle the differences between two slave-hunting caravans which were encroaching on each other's territory, and had begun to shoot one another up instead of attending strictly to business. He gave Nina a revolver and left her in the care of Mammy Jonah and his own special headman, who had been with various hunting expeditions and spoke and understood a few words of English. Nina by this time had picked up a few words of the native language, and he thought that between the three of them—for Mammy Jonah was an eloquent sign-talker—they ought to be able to manage until he got back. He did not expect to be absent very long. Two days going, two days returning, and whatever the matter required at the other end.

He parted from his bride at the entrance to the great cavern amid the slag-heaps thrown out by the prehistoric miners, and went down into the darkness feeling as if something had been torn out of him, leaving an aching void, and wishing to God that he did not care for Nina quite so much.

Nina, for her part, having watched the last gleam of the

95

lanterns die away in the darkness, wandered slowly back through the little wood of scrub-oak and across the small open Alpine meadow, and stood looking out through the gap in the cliffs over the forest floor that stretched below her, mile upon mile, to end in the mists of the coast. Here and there among the dark velvet of the trees she could see the gleam of the river up which she had travelled a few short weeks before. There were no foot hills to take off the height of the steep escarpment of the range, and from where she stood, well back from the terrible edge, a cliff dropped sheer to the sea-level, at its foot lying a malarious marsh. Of an evening the mists rose from that marsh till it looked as if the clouds were beneath them. It was also the kitchen midden, and Mammy Jonah would march out from her kitchen with the sink-basket in her hand (for Cassalis believed in labour saving domestic equipment) and empty it into two thousand feet of space, leaning out nonchalantly over the giddy verge so that the tea-leaves should fall clear, for she was not blessed with civilized nerves like Nina, who had a horror of the great drop, and could never be induced to go near it even to admire the marvellous view unrolled at the feet of those bold enough to approach the edge.

Nina wandered desolately about the little domain between the last of the trees and the first of the rocks, and then went in to the house and tried to occupy her mind with Cassalis's books. She had never known it was possible to miss anyone so desperately, and wondered if it was going to be like this every time he went off on one of his expeditions, and if so how was she going to bear it.

Then she wandered forth again, unable to settle to anything, and began to walk slowly through the shaggy wood of scrub-oak and stone-pine down the path to the cave. It was nearly a mile in length, and afforded quite a pleasant stroll. Walks were limited for anyone who was not a rock-climber.

She had got, perhaps, half-way to the cave, when there was a slight sound behind her that caused her to turn her head, and there in the path she had just come by, evidently having stepped out of a near-by thicket, stood a white man. She peered, startled, under the shade of the sun-helmet at the baffling glare-glasses that he wore, not really frightened, for she was unused to the exigencies of a savage land, but perplexed, and a little puzzled as to what line she should take with the newcomer in view of Lewis's very strong ideas on the subject of privacy. She was about to greet him politely and demand his name and business, for one surely did not have to wait to be introduced before speaking when one met a stranger in the heart of Africa, when he solved her problem by addressing her by her Christian name, and with something of a shock she realized that the newcomer was no other than her late fiancé.

"Well, Nina," he said, "haven't you got anything to say to me?"

"Not very much," Nina replied. "You see, I am married now, Harold. I have made my choice, and I must abide by it."

She thought it best to speak him fair, not knowing in what state of sobriety he might be.

"Married to Cassalis?"

"Yes."

"Good God!"

Nina did not answer. She was casting about in her mind as to the best way of getting rid of him, for she was exceedingly anxious not to have to ask him to lunch. It was not a pleasant position for a bride of a few weeks to find herself in; she knew her husband to be a man of violent temperament, and, on his own showing, prone to jealousy. There was a party of some fifty black bucks, under the command of a gentleman who looked like the demon king in the pantomime, encamped in a nearby gully, and she had a notion that, with the restraining influence of Cassalis removed, any uninvited visitors would receive extremely short shrift at their hands. She also knew that if Harold were not sober, and according to Lewis he very seldom was, there was no knowing what rash act he might not be capable of, that would bring the whole fifty down on his head, armed with their own stabbing-spears and Cassalis's modern shotguns. She decided to work tactfully towards a dismissal and a warning.

" However did you manage to get in here?" she asked.

"That's an easy one," replied the man. "I was brought in."

"But how? By whom?"

"By certain friends of the gentleman whom I suppose I must refer to as your husband, who do not approve of the marriage."

"But who are they?"

"His partners in crime, I fancy, who would have preferred him to remain a bachelor."

"But what was their motive in bringing you in here?"

"It was hinted to me that I might be able to get you away while Cassalis was kept occupied elsewhere."

"But supposing I won't come?"

"But, Nina, surely you will come? You can't possibly live with this scoundrel. He's the biggest blackguard in Africa, and that's saying a good deal. He's got nigger mistresses and half-caste kids in every village on the Coast."

"I've made my choice, Harold, and I intend to stick to it."

"But, Nina, you know what we mean to each other, and how I have waited for you, and got a home together for you—"

Nina thought of the dreadful bedroom at the hotel furnished mainly with empty whisky-bottles and soiled undergarments, and turned away in disgust.

"I think you had better go back the way you came," she said. "I don't want to have anything further to do with you. I am very happy with Lewis; he is very kind to me."

"Nina! And after all we've been to each other!"

"Well, that won't help us much, for I'm married now."

" Married! To a scoundrel like that—wanted for twenty murders and sure to be hanged sooner or later. You can't do it, Nina. Come away with me while you can."

"I'd be glad if you would let me pass. I want to go back to the bungalow."

He stepped close to her, and his whisky-laden breath told her that the persons who had enabled him to gain access to Cassalis's eyrie had also been at pains to bring up supplies of alcohol with him. She wondered for what purpose they had gone to all this trouble.

"I am not going to give you up," he muttered sullenly, looking as if trying to screw himself up for some desperate deed.

"If you lay a finger on me, I shall scream," said Nina, "and then you're for it."

"Oh yes, I'm very much for it. I am under no delusions on that score. It is death for me if I am discovered."

With a sudden sinking of the heart Nina realized that in spite of his heroics he spoke the truth. If she called for assistance from Cassalis's black guard, they would certainly kill him. She saw plainly that he was counting on her not calling. She had not got Cassalis's ruthlessness, and he knew it. She saw, too, how inevitable was Cassalis's ruthlessness in his position. Once he had stepped aside out of the straight and narrow way he could not afford to stick at anything. The most fundamental instinct of self-preservation required that she should call the blacks and let them dispose of Harold in their own way, lest he carry the secret of the eyrie back with him to the outer world and Lewis should no longer have anywhere to lie up in safety when he was in danger. For her own sake, too, it was very inadvisable for her to be found by a man of Cassalis's temperament concealing and protecting her late lover. She would be in for a considerable upset with him, if for nothing worse. And yet how was she to hand a living man over to certain death? She simply couldn't do it.

"Oh, do go back!" she cried miserably. "I don't want you to come to any harm, but I can't let you stop here."

At that moment the sound of chattering negro voices came to their ears; Harold dropped back silently into the scrub, and a party of nigger porters came up the path from the cave bearing supplies of fresh vegetables on their heads. Nina followed in their rear, reached the bungalow in safety, and sank into a long chair on the verandah with a sigh of relief.

But her relief was short-lived. The clouds that had been rolling all morning out of the west suddenly assembled and met together and a tropical thunder-storm broke over the peaks with a crash. Nina had never heard such a din in her life and was terrified. She rushed into the kitchen to Mammy Jonah, ideas of taking refuge in the great cave filling her head, but Mammy was nonchalantly frying sweet potatoes for lunch, quite unconcerned, and Nina took heart of hope from her demeanour. She sat down in the kitchen for the sake of the company of the kindly old black, all thought of her unpleasant visitor driven from her mind by what sounded like the end of the world.

But the storm ran its course, as tropical storms will, and at sunset Nina ventured forth to look at the great clouds rolling back over Africa in a terrific sunset, broken branches and torn leaves strewing the ground all round the house. Out over the forest levels in the distance she could see the gleam of water in every direction, showing that the floods were out. For the first time she wondered how Harold had fared in the downpour and pandemonium when the heavens seemed to open, like the bottom dropping out of a cistern. She imagined that he would have taken refuge in the cave, and probably be dry enough, and sincerely hoped that by now he would have accepted her refusal and be safely on his way back to civilization.

But this hope was not to be fulfilled. The following day it was still too wet to set foot to ground, but by the day after, the keen mountain air had dried out the shallow soil, and, save for the volume of water that was coming over the waterfall, no signs remained of the hell let loose forty-eight hours before. So Nina set off for a walk through the scrub-oak wood, which was the only practicable walk about the place.

She was hardly within the shelter of the trees, when there, to her horror, was Harold.

"Good heavens!" she exclaimed in no very cordial tone. "What are you doing here? I hoped you'd gone."

"Gone?" said the man sulkily. "I'd be glad enough to be gone if I could, but the river's in spate and there's no getting out till it subsides. I say, Nina, you couldn't let me have a drop of whisky, could you? I think I've got a touch of fever, and I'm feeling rotten."

"No, I couldn't," said Nina. "We haven't got any. Or, at any rate, I don't know where it is if we have."

Harold moistened his dry lips and looked at her hungrily.

"You had better go," said Nina.

"I can't go till the river goes down," said the man sullenly.

Nina turned on her heel and walked away and he made no attempt to stop her. He was not the Young Lochinvar type.

She went back to the bungalow, determined not to set

foot outside it again until Lewis got back, and turning over in her mind whether or not she should tell him about Harold's visit. She knew that the black guard did not suspect his presence, for they would have made short work of him if they had. She also knew that there was no kick left in Harold, and that he desired nothing so much as to return to a spot where whisky was available and bullets were not. Someone for some reason best known to themselves had carted him up there in the hope of luring her away from her husband so that he might return whole-heartedly to his villainy, and it was to be presumed that they would now cart him back again. At any rate she hoped they would; Harold was not the sort of person who could get about Africa on his own.

CHAPTER VI

SHE had not as long to wait for the return of Cassalis as she had expected. He had told her that he would be gone at least five days, allowing two days each way for the journey and a day at the other end sorting things out. If they proved to be complicated, it might take longer. He might be away anything up to a week or ten days. But on the late afternoon of the third day after his departure she glanced up from the book she was reading on the verandah to find him standing before her, and in another moment she was in his arms.

But, alas, the joy of their first reunion was damped by her anxiety as to whether her former lover had got safely away, and, if not, what would happen; and even if he had, what consequences his visit might give rise to, and how Lewis would take it if he learnt that she had allowed Harold to get away instead of putting the demon king on to him forthwith. Cassalis, who was keenly observant, saw at once that Nina was uneasy, and although her welcome left nothing to be desired on the score of warmth, he got a sense of something at the back of her mind that was worrying her, and which she had no intention of confiding to him.

He was too shrewd to cross-question her in this moment of reunion, for he felt pretty certain that such a transparently honest little person as Nina would not be very good at covering her tracks.

He, for his part, was decidedly worried; when he had ar-

rived at his journey's end, making good time on the trip so
that he might the sooner return to his bride, he found that
the dispute between the two caravans did not amount to anything. There was no need to have sent for him; everybody
was very surprised to see him, and no one knew, or at least no
one would admit that they knew, the origin of the message
that had summoned him. Cassalis, who was a very experienced handler of negroes, thought that they were telling the
truth.

It followed, therefore, that someone with a considerable
knowledge of his affairs had sent that message, since they
knew how to communicate with him in his eyrie. It also followed that that someone wanted him to be away from home
for a few days. What was afoot? Was something intended
against his bride? It looked like it. One of the headmen with
the caravans had told him that Sheik Ibrahim was furious
over his marriage, giving expression to the Arab equivalent
of "another good man ruined". Cassalis turned his porters
round almost before they had set down their loads, and, despite the floods, was breaking all cross-country records for
Africa.

But that was not all. When he got back to the village at the
forks of the river, where the launch was always left on these
inland journeys and messages for the eyrie were received and
forwarded, he was met by word from Ibrahim to the effect
that a warrant had been issued for him in connection with
the murder of the white police officer and his underlings.

That would not have meant much to him in the ordinary way; warrants had been issued for him for everything
under the sun except bigamy at one time or another, but he
had always been discharged for the simple reason that in this
land of few white men and many black, the man who held
the blacks held all the trumps. There was not a negro who
could be got to give evidence against Cassalis because of his

104

influence with the Leopards and other agreeable institutions of a murder-and-magic nature. There was also always an abundance of negroes, Arabs, Portuguese, poor whites, and in fact all and sundry, who could be got to give evidence for him, and swear to anything and everything until their imaginations gave out. He could have had cast-iron alibis at all four points of the compass simultaneously for any crime he chose to commit. The only difficulty was to prevent the cloud of witnesses willing and anxious to bear false evidence from contradicting one another.

Consequently he did not give a hoot in hell for anything that official justice, with its hands tied by the rules of evidence, could do against him. The only thing he feared was private vengeance, and it looked as if something of that nature was at work at the moment. And when he got back to his eyrie, and found Nina uneasy, he guessed that whatever it was had got busy.

But although he felt quite certain that Nina would not be very long before she "came clean", as the exponents of the third degree put it, it hurt him keenly that she had not poured out her story the moment she was in his arms. He suspected that in some way her late fiancé was connected with it and that she was shielding him, and a smouldering jealousy began to burn within him that promised future trouble.

But nothing of all this showed in the inscrutable poker face of the professional adventurer that he turned to his bride, and although she was greatly relieved to find that he apparently suspected nothing, she was also exceedingly worried as to what would be the ultimate result of her silence, for it was obvious that, with the safe return of Harold to civilization, Lewis's secret would become known. It was a terrible position for her, and it did not require a particularly acute student of human nature to observe that Nina was very worried. Her manner was distrait, her face was white, and her eyes were forever looking out of the window towards the wood as if she expected to see something. Cassalis, shrewd soldier of fortune that he was, watched her and said nothing. They had an almost happy evening together. In the joy of their reunion and renewed love-making they both forgot their troubles for a while. But after the lights were out and thought was free to wander, both of them did more thinking than sleeping.

Cassalis was turning over in his mind what he would do about the warrant that was out against him. His usual policy was to have all the witnesses thoroughly intimidated, and then, looking the picture of injured innocence, stalk into the police headquarters at the place where the trial would be held, just as the assizes were coming off, and give himself up to justice, demanding the opportunity to have his character cleared forthwith. And cleared it was. For every witness and every juryman knew that they had their choice between an ample supply of either bullets or *baksheesh*.

He had learnt as much as was generally known of the nature of the evidence against him in the present case. It was, as he suspected, the thing forgotten when the rest of the world goes well: the nigger overlooked in the bush. At the time when the party had walked into the ambush, the nigger interpreter attached to the young white man, newly out from home and blissfully ignorant of the tongue of the men he had to deal with, had been sent on to the next village to arrange about canoes, and had been on his way back to report results when he heard the sound of firing. Dropping on his belly, he had seen the whole ambush, including the shooting of the white man by Cassalis at point-blank range. His was the only evidence, but it was, of course, absolutely conclusive if he stuck to it.

The bloodhounds, however, had proved themselves witnesses for the defence, for although laid on the trail with an

106

old tie of Cassalis's they had resolutely declined to do anything about it. One of them, the best of the two, was sickening for the canine equivalent of jaundice, of which he subsequently died, and would have nothing to do with the matter, having troubles enough of his own; and the other had been uncertain and capricious, some times giving tongue on the trail, sometimes hesitating and declining—the fact of the matter being that Cassalis, who always took off his boots when there was prospect of trouble so as not to leave identifiable foot-prints, was wearing a pair of sandals borrowed from old Ibrahim, so sometimes the poor bloodhound got a whiff of Cassalis, and sometimes it got another and much stronger whiff of Ibrahim.

In view of the artistic temperament displayed by the bloodhounds, of which counsel for the defence could make much, and that there was only one witness for the prosecution, and him a nigger, Cassalis would have considered the verdict a foregone conclusion and had no hesitation whatever in facing his trial (he always preferred to face a trial and be done with it rather than be "wanted", but an expert had been brought out from England, and Cassalis did not quite know what that expert was for, or what his potentialities might prove to be. The expert from England would not be frightened by beating a witch drum while he was giving his evidence. Time and again the court, with wrath in its heart, had heard that steady thrum-thrum begin, and seen native witnesses turn the colour of ashes and withdraw everything they had said. But this was not to be expected with a white man. Cassalis was up against an unknown factor this time, and had it not been for Nina he would have thought twice about going down to face his trial, accepting instead the final outlawry of being definitely, "wanted by the police".

But he saw only too clearly that life for Nina would be impossible in such circumstances. Supposing she were to have

107

a child? Negro midwives could hardly see her through that. Lying awake in the moonlit room, not caring to smoke for fear of disturbing Nina, who seemed to be asleep at his side, he made up his mind to the last bold cast of his career-he would go down to the coast, face the only outstanding charge against him, and, if acquitted, run straight for the rest of his days. If not acquitted, there would be no long sentence to be faced, but a short walk one early morning, and then oblivion. He did not fear death. The thing he dreaded was the parting from his beloved; but he had a vision of Nina struggling in the pangs of a birth that wouldn't come off, as he had seen many a negro woman struggle, when he had given them such clumsy first aid as was in his power, and he steeled his heart. He felt he would much prefer the scaffold for himself than to have to stand by helplessly and watch that. Having come to his decision, he turned over and slept, having a Napoleonic power of closing the drawers of his mind.

But Nina did not sleep for a long while, and the grey was in the sky when finally her anxious imaginings began to drift into dreams; but the first beams of the sun had hardly shone golden over the rocky wall bounding their meadow when a call from the verandah recalled her to her troubles and brought Lewis swiftly and silently out of bed.

She pretended sleep, and heard him go out in his pyjamas and talk in low tones with the demon king on the verandah, then she heard him return and get hastily dressed and go out again. She knew that something was afoot, and wondered in tense anxiety whether Harold had been captured. She slipped out of bed and got dressed in her turn. She felt that she could no longer bear the situation and that she would tell Lewis everything that had happened as soon as ever he got back, and that Harold must take his chance. Her dressing completed, she stood looking out of the bedroom window, which faced in the direction of the wood towards which Lewis had gone, awaiting his return. She had not long to wait. She saw two big negroes coming along, carrying between them the limp form of a white man whose face was bandaged, and recognized Harold by his boots and belt. Lewis walked at his side.

He must have met with an accident, she thought, or been injured when captured, and they were bringing him up to the bungalow to be nursed. The prospect was an embarrassing one, full of all sorts of complications, but anything was better than feeling that his death lay at her door, or, alternatively, that the betrayal of Lewis's eyrie also lay there; for that was what she now realized her shielding of her lover had amounted to.

But the little procession did not turn in at the verandah steps, but continued its way across the meadow, and Nina saw that a piece of cloth that was tied across the lower part of Harold's face looked much more like a gag than a bandage. They passed out of sight of the window, and she slipped out on to the verandah to keep them in view.

They were making their way slowly, hampered by their awkward burden, towards the gap in the cliffs where the great precipice fell sheer to the marsh below. At the verge they paused. Cassalis bent over the man lying helpless in the hands of the two huge negroes and untied the knot of the gag, retaining it in position with his hand. Then the two blacks gave a mighty swing and a heave, Cassalis whipped the gag clear, and Harold went flying out into space with no scrap of evidence on him that could inculpate anybody. He gave one yell as he turned over in mid-air, his arms and legs flailing wildly, and then vanished. The two negroes hung over the edge, watching with interest his progress through two thousand feet of space, but Cassalis turned away hastily and walked slowly back towards the house with his head bent. He was walking slowly because he was wondering whether he was going to be sick. He had done some pretty cold-blooded jobs in his time, but never anything quite as cold-blooded as that.

But he could not see what else he could do. Morley obviously had to be put out of the way, as he knew the secret of the eyrie. Moreover, he had to be put out of the way in such a manner that he did not merely disappear, but that his death should appear to be an accident. A search-party would, of course, go after him when he failed to return to civilization after a reasonable time. The guides attached to the search-party would know what was to be found and where to find it, and after a decent interval would lead their masters to the place where the broken body of a white man lay at the foot of a cliff and let it be found. It would be obvious that the man had died owing to a fall from a height, and not by violence, his revolver being fully loaded and in its holster. Cassalis had seen to that.

Everything was O.K. so far as he could see, apart, of course, from just plain bad luck. It was what the writers of detective tales call "the perfect murder".

But as he set foot on the verandah steps he glanced up and saw standing above him a woman with a face he hardly knew. It was a hard white mask, with the blue eyes so dilated that they looked black. Cassalis was already looking pretty white himself after the happenings at the cliff-edge, but he went several shades whiter when he saw that face. Nina looked down at him with a fixed intensity of gaze, neither moving nor speaking, and Cassalis, his harsh features ash-grey under their tan, looked up at her with the eyes of a whipped collie. He reckoned that this was the end of their love.

He came slowly up the steps and stood close to her, but did not touch her. She never turned her head. "It was him or me, Nina," he said at length, but she did not reply. He sat down on a deck-chair and lit a cigarette, and sat smoking and watching her. She did not move. Finally, his cigarette finished, he got up and went into the house.

He went into the bedroom and sat down on the tumbled bed and looked round his once bachelor apartment, now strewn with Nina's belongings—all the pretty things that she had originally prepared for the home that Harold Morley was supposed to be making for her. He lit another cigarette. He was quite clear on one point. If Nina had done with him, he certainly was not going down to the coast to take his chance of being hanged. He was going to end things now, with his own hand, and take her with him.

He had given up carrying his revolver in its secret holster on his groin, whence it could be reached a split second quicker than the other fellow could reach his, carried in the more usual place on the hip. Nina, sitting on his knee, sat on the gun and complained of the discomfort. He went over to the dressing-table, unlocked one of the drawers, took out a small black American shooting-iron, spun the magazine, released the safety catch, and sat down on the bed again to wait. His first thought had been to shoot Nina as she came through the door, but he decided to hear what she had to say for herself first. There was just a chance she might show signs that would give him hope.

He waited a considerable time; so long, in fact, that he had almost forgotten he was going to shoot Nina, and he felt as if he were waiting for lion. But at length she came. He heard the click of her high heels on the polished boards, and braced himself.

She came in at the bedroom door, as he had expected she would, and stopped with a start when she saw him sitting there on the bed, with a revolver in his hand. She did not take in the significance of that revolver—she thought he had been cleaning it. It was only the curious expression on his face that made her realize that something was afoot. He looked very worn and weary, and his eyes were more than half mad. It was the contrast between the fatigued face and the wild eyes that so startled her.

"Well, Nina," he said, "what about it? Are you going to stand by me?"

"No," she said, "I am not. I will not give you away, because that won't help the dead, but I won't live with you any longer."

"What do you want to do?"

"I would be glad if you would send me down to the mission station in the launch, as was originally planned. After that I will fend for myself."

"Thought it all out, have you?"

"Yes, I have thought it out, and I've made up my mind."

"So have I."

Nina looked at him questioningly.

"If you want to go, you shall go, but we'll go together."

"I have told you that I won't live with you any longer."

"I'm not asking you to."

"Then what do you mean?"

"If you won't live with me, you'll die with me, Nina."

It was only then that she grasped the significance of the revolver. Her first instinct was to run to Mammy Jonah for protection, but luckily for her she stood paralysed, unable to stir hand or foot, for had she run Cassalis would certainly have shot her in the back and then turned his revolver on himself. As it was, he found it impossible to shoot her in cold blood, as she stood there looking more bewildered than frightened.

Still more luckily for her, the door was open behind her, and Mammy Jonah—ignorant old black though she was, and understanding not a word of what they were saying, but skilled in every inflection of their voices, for she adored them

112

both—suddenly shot into the room looking like nothing so much as a gigantic and infuriated hen with all its feathers out, and, seeing her chance of white piccaninnies slipping from her, went for Cassalis like a Dutch aunt. She stood between him and Nina, regardless of the revolver; what she said to him Nina could not understand, but it sounded exceedingly homely. Then catching sight of the demon king passing the window, she gave a yell and called him in, and he added a few remarks to hers that sounded rather pointed. Cassalis sat with his head down and the revolver hanging in his limp hand while the two of them rated him. Nina knew that, whatever difficulties might be before them, he would not shoot her now.

The two blacks between them had made him see sense, though not, perhaps, quite in the way they had intended. Mammy had pointed out, with more vigour than elegance, that although it might be the time honoured custom to dispose of your wife like this if she did not please you, no one but a fool did it when women were scarce. In such circumstances the sensible man beat but did not kill. The demon king added his logic to hers. He, for his part, was in favour of killing every time, whether women were scarce or not, as a matter of principle, but he was not prepared to stand by while such a loss to society occurred as would happen if the great chief elected to follow his bride into the kingdom of the shades. In other words, Cassalis was at liberty to kill his wife if he wanted to, as was only right and reasonable, but he was not at liberty to turn his gun on himself, and would be thrown down and sat on if he made the attempt.

Cassalis, now that the first heat had passed, saw the point in Mammy Jonah's argument—that if Nina were given something that was the equivalent of a beating instead of being killed outright, she might eventually become amenable again; at any rate, it was worth trying. He also saw the point

113

in the demon king's argument, and that his last state would be worse than his first if he had killed Nina and were then prevented from killing himself.

He rose wearily to his feet and tossed the revolver into the drawer without troubling to secure the safety catch, whereupon it promptly went off with a bang, scaring them all, and putting the last touch to the sobering of Cassalis, were any such needed. He gave a few curt instructions to the demon king, dispatched Mammy to the kitchen with a wave of his hand, and turning to Nina, said:

"I will take you down to the coast with me now. I have to go there on business. When we get there, I will put you into the hands of my lawyer, to make what arrangements you like. Will that suit you?"

"Yes," said Nina. "Thank you. It will. When do we start?"

"Right away. Put what you want for a week or two into your suit-case, and I will have your other stuff packed and sent on after you. Mammy knows what is yours and what is mine."

"O-oh!" cried Nina, raising her hand to her face in startled distress. It had never somehow occurred to her that Lewis would take her at her word like this. She saw her home being broken up, and herself flung on the world defenceless, and she was not prepared for it. Deep in her heart she had cleaved to her husband for more than she realized. Once the shock of the terrible sight she had seen had passed, she would put it out of her mind even as she had put out of her mind the fact that he was the villainous Cassalis. The human mind, especially the female human mind, has a remarkable gift for not seeing what it does not wish to see.

But Cassalis knew that this was the only thing to do, for if the trial went against him and he were executed, Nina would never get out alive, for the blacks would send her to join him as a matter of course, this being the proper thing for the wife of a great chief, as they considered him to be. He did not choose to tell her this, however, at present, for he proposed to take Mammy Jonah's advice and give her the psychological equivalent of a good beating. Let her think she had been taken at her word, and was going to be sent back to her family in England, and she would soon come to her senses. He could see that by her face, and thanked God for the old black woman and her sage advice, that had saved him from an act of madness and misery.

For the first time in his life his subconscious certainty of security and ultimate triumph, that had brought him through so many tight corners, was shaken. It seemed as if his love for Nina had let fear into his life, and with the coming of fear the old charmed circle in which he had lived was broken, and his luck had turned. It was his usual experience to have an almost phenomenal run of good luck. He counted on it, just as other men always allow a little over for bad luck. But all that had changed. Bits of purely gratuitous bad luck seemed to be cropping up at every turn. The nigger in the bush; Nina waking up early; treachery and cross-purposes with the men with whom he worked. Cassalis's nerve was shaken; he could feel the rope round his neck, and broke out in a cold sweat at the thought. He determined to keep the knowledge of the coming trial from Nina as long as possible so as to spare her anxiety and retain some rags of reputation in her eyes, if it were in any way possible. He planned to leave her on board the launch, moored well out in the estuary, while the trial was going on, and there was just a chance that she would never learn its nature but believe it to be some kind of lawsuit. The African equivalent of the assizes were on at the next town down the coast from Okiki at the time, and it was for this reason that he wanted to get off quickly, so that his case might come on there instead of at Georgetown, the administrative headquarters of the colony, where he would have had more difficulty with the jury. There is not as much formality on the Coast in criminal matters as there is in England; the judges have to cover big distances, and if he applied for summary trial he thought he would get it. Ibrahim, together with the message that warned him of his peril, had sent the assurance that he was getting busy with the secret societies, and everything would be in order by the time the trial came off. In other words, all arrangements would be made for intimidating witnesses and jury, and for rushing the gaol should these arrangements prove insufficient. It was indeed African Tammany. But for his shaken nerve, Cassalis would have felt perfectly secure.

Nina, hardly able to see for tears, packed her suit-case most inadequately, gave Mammy Jonah all manner of presents, and hugged the weeping old black as if she had been her own mother. Then she wrapped herself in Cassalis's camel-hair cloak against the chill of the great cave, let him help her into the travelling-hammock without speaking, and was borne quietly weeping away from the home to which she had come as a bride a few short weeks before.

Cassalis did not march beside her litter during the first part of the journey because he was little better off than she was as far as emotional upset went; during the second part the narrowness of the track overhanging the river made it impossible to do so, and once on board the launch he had to take the wheel as he would not trust the negro steersman in the rapids.

He went in to speak to Nina in the cabin once, but she had gone to bed with a blinding headache, and had turned her face to the wall and would not answer. How was she to know that he was going down to give himself up to justice to be tried for his life? He went back to the conning-tower, and

116

brought the launch down the rock-staked river in a manner that made the negro steersman, standing at his side, pray to all the gods of Africa.

Coming down with the current was a very different matter to going up against the current, and the launch was fast. Sitting up in her bunk next morning, Nina was amazed to see that they were passing Okiki and heading for the open sea. A few minutes later they were in tumble on the bar and she was hanging on to the bunk for dear life. Then they found themselves rising and falling to a heavy swell as the launch turned down the coast, and Nina's old enemy fell upon her till it seemed as if body and soul would be torn asunder. Cassalis, hearing the sounds of her distress, came down and ministered to her, but she was in no state to be talked to, and all she could do was to cling to his hand and retch; and he could not be sure, in the state she was in, that she knew it was his hand she was clinging to. She would probably have clung to anything she had touched in that wildly pitching launch. He was at his wits' end to know what to do with her. He thought she was going to die on his hands. Finally he had the bright idea of giving her a heavy dose of chlorodyne, that faithful frontier stand-by, and the laudanum in it put her off to sleep.

It was only a few hours' run down the coast for Cassalis's fast launch, and Nina was still asleep when they passed over the bar into the calm water of another river mouth, with just such another town as Okiki, but considerably larger, surrounding it. Cassalis dropped the small anchor well out in the estuary, so that Nina should have as pleasant quarters as possible while she was living on the launch, as he intended she should during his trial. He himself would go ashore in the collapsible canvas dinghy the launch carried. His nerve had come back to him now that the time had come to face arrest. He disliked very much indeed the thought of the days, or even weeks, he would have to spend in an African gaol, but subconsciously he was certain of the outcome of the trial. It would go as all the others had gone—complete collapse of the prosecution when the intimidated witnesses let it down.

He sat down on the other bunk in the cabin to watch beside Nina until she woke. He wanted to have a talk with her before he went, and he knew it was no use to wake her from the laudanum-induced sleep for that purpose.

She lay there under a light rug, her dishevelled hair spread over the pillow, her face white with exhaustion from the sea-sickness, looking like a tired child. Cassalis, watching her as she slept, realized for the hundredth time how terribly vulnerable he was now that he had got Nina. Before, nothing had mattered; he would have gone down to death shouting and swearing and thoroughly enjoying himself. But with Nina everything was different. He dreaded death because it meant separation from her, and because it meant casting her defenceless on the world. She would be well provided for, if only his lawyer were honest in his dealings with her; but as he had expressly picked him for qualities among which honesty was not numbered, he was by no means free from anxiety on that score.

And if he were acquitted, what was her attitude going to be towards him? He felt pretty certain she would believe him guilty after what she had seen, and she would, of course, be right. Would she still insist on leaving him? He was particularly anxious to have a talk with her, and put things to her from his point of view, and appeal to her, and make love to her, until she came back to him again, and he should hold her in his arms once more before he parted from her, it might be for ever.

But even in this his luck had turned. Someone on the shore had recognized his launch, and he heard a boat come alongside. He went out to see who it was, expecting a message from Willis, his lawyer; but before he could inquire the new-comer's business, a man had come aboard without waiting to be asked, and then another.

"Are you Lewis Cassalis?" inquired the first-comer.

"I am."

"I have a warrant for your arrest to answer for the murder of Robert Saunders, assistant superintendent of police, Nkimbe Gumba, sergeant of police . . ." and then followed a string of native names that startled even Cassalis, and at the end he was warned that anything he said might be used in evidence against him.

"Right," he said. "I came here for the express purpose of answering these charges and clearing myself. Can I bring my dunnage?" He picked up a haversack that lay ready packed with such small amenities as experience had taught him that a man awaiting trial would require. It was taken out of his hands almost before they had touched it, and he felt cold steel on his wrists.

His first instinct was to go berserk and fight the lot. He had never been handcuffed before when he had been arrested. But he saw by their eyes that they were ready for this, and with a supreme effort he controlled himself. They helped him into the police launch, and he dropped down on the thwart awkwardly, thanking God in his heart for the inspiration that had made him drug Nina into oblivion and spare him the sight of her witness of his shame. To a man of his nature, being handcuffed was a great deal worse than being hanged.

CHAPTER VII

NINA did not awake till next morning. She felt better, and she felt saner. The unaccustomed sedative had brought her nerves back to normal, and she told herself that the best thing to do with her erring and blood-thirsty husband was not to leave him in a fit of temper, but to use his love for her, and her love for him, to bring him to better things. She knew that he had spoken the truth when he had said that it was he or Harold who would have to be sacrificed, and in her heart she felt that it was the better man who was the survivor. It was curious that, wicked as Cassalis was, she could never think of him as a bad man. She was much more inclined to think of him as a naughty boy and minimize his peccadilloes. She had, in fact, completely forgotten that he had ever proposed shooting her.

Having dressed herself in one of her crisp organdies, she went and sat outside in the cockpit, expecting that Lewis would join her as soon as he heard her moving about. But he did not appear, and her heart sank. Was there going to be a feud between them? She got up and went through the cabin to the crew's quarters aft. The three niggers, engineer, steersman, and steward, were squatting on their hunkers chattering thirteen to the dozen with anxious faces. She addressed them in a phrase of their own language, "Where is the master?" but could not understand a word of the verbose answer. She shook her head.

The nigger engineer, who was an exceptionally intelligent darky, took in the situation. He saw from her unconcerned face that she had no glimmer of the state of affairs, and he began a vigorous pantomime, intended to be explanatory. First of all he held out his hands with the wrists together in the attitude of a handcuffed man. Then he clasped his two hands round his neck, and ran his fingers up an imaginary rope under his ear. The youthful steward completed the pantomime by bursting into tears.

Nina did not know what to make of it. She interpreted the imaginary handcuffs as an attitude of prayer, and concluded that Cassalis had gone ashore to attend the funeral of a friend who had hanged himself. She smiled, nodded, and withdrew to the cockpit contented, and the three darkies looked after her in perplexity. They knew that their master's lawyer, Mr. Willis, would give them instructions as the need arose, and that Sheik Ibrahim was also in the offing and could be referred to, and they decided to sit tight and await events. They were all three men picked for their intelligence, and though ignorant and emotional, as are all darkies, they were by no means fools. Nina therefore ate her lunch in peace, and was sitting reading a book from Cassalis's little travelling library, when she saw a small launch coming alongside, and sprang up, expecting the white man under the awning to be Lewis, and eagerly anticipating a reconciliation.

But he proved to be a stranger, and not a very prepossessing stranger. Though his manner was that of an educated man, she did not at all like the looks of him. He had a cadaverous countenance, lemon-yellow and jaundice-eyed; his nose looked as if he drank, and his eyes were shifty.

But although his eyes did not meet hers, they zig zagged all over her from head to heel, especially heel, or rather ankles. He evidently found her good to look at, for there was a decidedly friendly expression, in fact a too friendly expression, in them when they finally met hers for the brief second necessary to make an introduction.

"Mrs. Cassalis?" he inquired.

Nina acquiesced, feeling very self-conscious, for it was the first time she had answered to that name.

"My name is Willis," he continued. "I am your husband's man of law," and he smiled as pleasantly as he knew how.

Nina greeted him politely. "I would offer you a cocktail," she said, "only my husband has gone off with the keys."

"That is all right," said the man of law genially, "I have them here. He gave them me to bring to you," and he proffered her Lewis's bunch of private keys that never left his person. Nina, rather startled by this, took them and stared at him questioningly. Why had the keys been sent her in this way? What mischief was Lewis up to now?

"Well, Mrs. Cassalis," said her new acquaintance, seeing that she showed no signs of producing a cocktail even though she had the key of the cupboard, "I am afraid this must be a very anxious time for you."

Nina stared at him, not knowing quite what to answer. Was he trying to "draw" her as to her knowledge of the manner in which Harold had met his death? However violently she might quarrel with Lewis over that ghastly incident, however long their estrangement might last, nothing would induce her to give him away. Her whole nature stood upon the defence instinctively.

"In what way should it be anxious?" she demanded, determined that he should show his hand before she showed hers.

Willis expressed no surprise. Cassalis had told him that he had intended to keep the knowledge of the impending trial from her till the last possible moment, and then had been prevented by his unexpected arrest from telling her, and had asked him to come and see her and break the unpleasant

news and arrange to look after her while they were awaiting the result of the trial—and possibly longer. Willis, having seen the girl whom he already thought of as a widow,
for he knew the nature of the evidence against Cassalis, had
formed the opinion that he would find the task by no means
distasteful, provided, of course, she did not prove inconsolable.

"Your husband told me that he had kept the knowledge
of his forthcoming trial from you as long as possible in order
to spare you anxiety, and then you were asleep when he—
had to leave."

The girl went deadly white at his words, and sat rigid,
her hands gripping the cushions. Willis had the grace to feel
uncomfortable. He would have dealt with a girl who wept
and threw herself about by putting a fatherly arm round her,
and enjoyed doing it; but this white stillness was not so easy
to handle.

"What is my husband being tried for?" She had never
spoken of Cassalis as that before, and again she felt self
conscious—the young wife, not yet accustomed to her new
status. She twisted her wedding-ring nervously on her finger.

Willis cleared his throat, and his eyes shot about like bee-
tles, looking anywhere but into hers.

"He fell foul of a police patrol, and there was some shooting."

He could not bring himself to discharge the task en-
trusted to him, and tell her that her husband was being tried
for murder.

"Where is he now?" she demanded.

"They have got him up at the courthouse. I have managed to get them to agree to a summary trial. Their case is all
ready, and there is nothing much for me to do. I have briefed
the best man on the circuit for the defence."

123

"Then—then what will happen?" asked Nina.

"When they have finished all the cases that are down for hearing, they will take his and get it over. Much the best thing to do. These local gaols are very trying for a white man."

"How long will that take?"

"Difficult to say. They have got four more cases to deal with, one part heard. Give them not more than two days for that. Might be less. Once his comes on, it won't take long. There are only four witnesses for the Crown. I am proving an alibi. I shall put up two witnesses, and they won't be in the box more than two minutes each."

"If he has got an alibi, will he get off?"

"If they believe it."

"Do you doubt their believing it?"

Willis shrugged his shoulders.

"What do you think his chances are of getting off?" Willis noted that Cassalis's wife seemed to take it for granted that he was guilty and had got to wriggle clear as best he might. She did not inquire the nature of the crime, and she did not express any belief in his innocence.

"It is impossible to forecast what his chances are," he said. He himself had no doubt whatever in his mind. He believed his client to be a "goner", but there was no point in telling this white-faced girl so. Let her hope as long as she could. "We shall pick over the jury very carefully, and we may succeed in getting a disagreement."

That, he knew, was the only hope. But, on the other hand, the prosecution would probably pick over the jury equally carefully, and try to arrange that it should consist of white men of substance, unlikely to be intimidated by the beating of witch-drums during their deliberations.

"Can I visit my husband while he—is in prison?"

Willis hesitated. " I shouldn't, if I were you," he said. "He won't be there long. The trial will be coming on in a couple of days." He knew he would have to be her escort, and he did not relish the job.

But Nina was not to be put off so easily.

"I must see him if I can," she said. "You see, I was asleep when he left, and we did not have a chance to say good-bye, and—and I had been rather cross with him just before. I really must see him."

Willis acquiesced with an ill grace.

"Well, in those circumstances, I suppose you must," he said. "I had better take you now and get it over." There would be less chance of drawing a crowd if they went before the news of Cassalis's arrest had had time to spread. He rose; there was no point in prolonging the interview since cocktails were evidently not going to be forthcoming. He helped her into his launch a good deal more carefully than was necessary, and they set out for the jetty.

They made their way up the small pier with no more staring than Nina's girlish freshness always called forth in that womanless land, but as they approached the official looking building that was evidently the courthouse a rather raffish individual came up to them.

"Mrs. Cassalis, I am the representative of the *West African Times*—" he began, beginning to unship his camera.

"No, you don't, Leary," said Willis, getting in front of Nina before the camera could be brought into play.

"Yes, I do, Willis," said the reporter, starting to walk round him.

Nina looked from one to the other in perplexity. "What is the matter?" she inquired.

"You don't want to be interviewed, do you, Mrs. Cassalis?" said Willis fretfully, all his legal instincts being against saying anything, to anybody, on any subject, while a case was *sub judice*.

But Nina took a more human view of the situation. It

125

struck her that there could be no harm in making friends with the Press and putting in a bid for sympathy.

"I—I don't know, I'm sure," she said tentatively. It would not do to appear to be too eager, but all the same she gave the reporter a glimmer of a smile.

He took his cue.

"Right you are, Mrs. Cassalis. You are going in to see your husband now, I take it? I will have a word with you when you come out."

There would be more to be got out of her then.

Nina and her escort went up the wide, shallow steps and passed through the fly-screens into a large entrance hall, handsomely panelled in native woods. Small groups of men in tropical white were standing about talking in low voices, and from an inner chamber could be heard the cold, measured tones of the judge, evidently getting ready to pronounce sentence.

"And after taking into account everything that your counsel has said in mitigation of your conduct, I consider that I should be failing in my duty if I sentenced you to less than five years penal servitude."

There was a slight stir at one end of the entrance-hall as several native policemen came out of a small door in the corner and pushed back the whispering groups. The door opened again, and out came three men, two black and one white, the one white, young, fair-haired, good-looking, and smartly dressed, between the two black. They walked quickly across the hall and disappeared through the fly screens, none of the whispering groups, intent on their own affairs, even turning a head to observe them. The court house was badly designed. It had not got a separate entrance for prisoners, being used as a cinema and dance hall between sessions. Nina, watching the young fellow going off to spend the best years of his life in prison, suddenly wondered whether she would see Cassalis marched out like that, and a pang shot through her, a sudden pang of realization; for hitherto, what with the unexpectedness of the shock and the aftermath of the chlorodyne, everything had seemed unreal and dream-like.

Willis deposited her in a secluded corner and went into court to speak to some official, and Nina found eyes beginning to be turned on her from all directions. She was the only woman in the place. Willis was well known to everybody. The news of Cassalis's arrest had already got about, and they guessed the rest. Everybody stared with great interest at the bandit's bride.

Willis returned in a few minutes accompanied by a tall, emaciated man, whose red face clashed violently with his even redder hair. He wore the uniform of a senior police-officer.

He greeted Nina courteously but distantly. The dead policeman had been his immediate subordinate.

"Will you come this way?" he said, and Nina, with Willis at her heels, followed him along a stone passage and down a flight of stone stairs that looked like cellar steps. She realized that they were following in the wake of the fair-haired young man and his two dusky guards.

They entered a small room, furnished like a station waiting-room, save that across one side ran an elbow-high iron rail, exactly like that in the lion-house at the Zoo, and six feet behind that, also like the lion-house, was a grill of heavy iron bars reaching from floor to ceiling. The red-headed policeman disappeared, and Nina and Willis sat down to wait, Willis shuffling his feet and humming under his breath, for his nerves were in a bad state and he hated such an interview as this. Nina hoped he would have the grace to take himself off when Lewis appeared and let them have a chance to talk together quietly. In fact, she made up her mind that she would tell him to do so in no uncertain terms if he had not the manners to do it of his own accord.

Then she heard footsteps on the flagged passages, the footsteps of several persons, but she was waiting for one man only, so it could not be he. The door of the waiting room opened, and the red-headed policeman returned, nodded to Willis, and dropped into a chair beside him. Then into the narrow space behind the heavy iron grill walked three men, two black and one white, and the one white man was Lewis Cassalis. The two black men dropped back a pace, grounded their rifles with a crash, and stood to attention. Lewis walked forward to the bars, lent his elbow on them, and smiled at her. The two black men were the same ones who had marched off to his penal servitude the prisoner she had heard sentenced, and again realization forced its way in to Nina's reluctant mind.

"Well, Nina, getting on all right?" said Cassalis. She nodded. She could not speak.

"I'm here for the next few days," Cassalis went on, talking to cover his emotion and hers, " and then we'll know where we are."

Still Nina could not speak. She had not realized she would have to conduct the interview in public, like this. She had imagined that they might be locked in a cell together, but not that they would have to talk to each other under a battery of watching eyes. As a matter of fact, there were no watching eyes. The negro policemen stared blankly into space, and Willis and the officer were gazing at their respective boots, hating the ordeal just as much as she was. The only person who appeared to be cheerful and unembarrassed was Cassalis, and God knows what vultures were tearing at his vitals in private.

It was impossible to ask questions or discuss the case with him in front of all these listeners. The very things Nina wanted to learn—his chances, his danger—were the last things that could be mentioned.

Nina rose from her chair and walked to the iron bar that prevented her from coming within arm's reach of the grill, and leant across it towards Cassalis. She was closer to him now, and she could see a little muscle at the corner of his mouth twitching continuously. Willis hissed nervously between his teeth, and the police-officer stirred uneasily in his seat; the two negro constables, under the eye of their superior, stared into space like graven images, as discipline bade them. Nina had a curious sense of being alone, as if she and Lewis were under a bell-jar; the others could see them, but could not touch them. She leant across the bar towards her husband.

"I want you to know," she said in a low voice, " that I will stand by you."

"Thanks, Nina," said Cassalis, and for a second the mask that was over his face slipped aside, and she saw that he was a man without hope. She had no need to ask what chance he had of acquittal. She knew all there was to know. Everything went dark for a moment, and it was only because she had the bar to lean on that she kept on her feet. Then the mists cleared, and she saw Cassalis smiling at her, his mask in place again. Then, to everyone's surprise, he took a pace backwards, and came to a halt between his two guards, who gaped at him in amazement, not knowing quite what to do. Fifteen minutes were allowed for an interview, and only five of them had passed.

But the shrewd though unsavoury Willis knew what to do. He took Nina by the arm and marched her out of the interview-room as quickly as might be.

CHAPTER VIII

NINA had no means of knowing that her interview had not gone according to plan, and accepted its briefness without demur. Willis bustled her up the stairs and along the passage till she was breathless, so anxious was he to get to the end of his painful task and go and have a drink.

Now, a law-court is not a "place within the meaning of the Act", and stowed away in the back premises is usually a spot where refreshments can be obtained by the elect, that is to say by those who have business about the court, a fact not generally known but easily verifiable. Willis's one idea was to park Nina in a suitable place and make for that spot. He found a wide, hard seat between two pillars in the entrance-hall, and lost no time in depositing her on it. But someone else lost no time either, and in two seconds the Irish reporter was also sitting on it, smiling ingratiatingly.

"The old boy's gone to get a drink. Several, if I know him. Come and have some tea with me? He'll never come back. He'll forget all about you."

Nina considered her new acquaintance. Raffish as he looked, he was vastly to be preferred to the unsavoury and irritable Willis. She smiled back and accepted. She might learn much from him that the cautious lawyer would never tell her. She might also be able to put in a good word for her husband. She must, however, be very careful that no damaging information was extracted from her by the wily newspaper-man. But she had not had a puritanical father who kept track of all her comings and goings for nothing. Information was not easily extracted from Nina.

Her new escort led her triumphantly out of the court house, amid the smiles of the onlookers who had seen Willis chase him off earlier in the proceedings, and took her to a nearby hotel, where, in a deep verandah under a swinging fan, they seated themselves in comfortable basket-chairs. Nina thought of that other Coast hotel whose acquaintance she had made, which also sported basket-chairs that were the poor relations of these, and wondered whether, if she had known what lay before her, she would ever have had the courage to embark on her venture, or whether she would now be safely in the moorland vicarage, arranging the flowers or taking the dog for a walk. And something very deep in her rose up and answered that even this price was not too high, and that she could no more go back into that moorland vicarage again than the chick could go back into the egg.

She heard her companion speaking:

"First you shall have some tea, and then you shall talk to me. I guess you could do with some tea."

Nina agreed fervently.

"It's cruelty to animals, those interviews," said her host. "Next time you want an interview, you let me take you. I know when to start catching flies on the wall."

"There won't be another," said Nina. "The case is coming on almost at once."

"Is it, now? Has Willis applied for summary trial?"

"Yes, I fancy so."

Leary meditated a moment. "Yes, I suppose he would," he said at length. "You can have confidence in one thing, Mrs. Cassalis, there are no flies on Willis. What he doesn't know isn't worth knowing."

A white-coated negro boy brought the tea, and Leary

settled down to enjoy having his tea poured out for him by the attractive Nina, amid the envious glances of the passers-by. He had not lost his eye to the main chance, however, and proceeded to combine business with pleasure in no half-hearted fashion.

"I have heard the story of your romance, Mrs. Cassalis. Tell me, is it really true?"

Nina smiled. "I cannot say unless I know what you have heard."

"I heard that you came out to be married to a fellow at Okiki, and as he didn't come up to specification you went off with Cassalis and made the padre up the river marry you, which he hated doing more than he'd hate blessing the devil."

"Yes, I saw he was cross. But why should he be?"

"Oh, well, I'd better not tell tales out of school. Now, tell me, did Cassalis take you to his famous lair?"

"Yes, he did."

"And what's it like?"

"Very nice."

"No, I don't mean that. What sort of a place is it? High up in the mountains, or low down near the river?"

"I couldn't say. It is all surrounded by trees. It's in a clearing in a wood, and, yes, there is a stream running past it."

"Ah, then it must be down in the plain, not up in the mountains, as everybody thought it was."

"Yes, I suppose so," said the mendacious Nina.

Under the skilful questioning of the reporter, Nina's story unfolded. She told him frankly of her experience with Harold, and how Cassalis had come to the rescue, treating her honourably and courteously, and taking her to the padre at the mission station up the river for safe keeping; and how, having fallen in love with each other during the brief trip, they had made the padre marry them, in spite of his black

132

looks, and she had then gone on with the outlaw to his hidden lying-up place, where the sudden romance had grown into a deeper love and he had promised her that there should be no more lawlessness. Then, when Cassalis was looking forward to peace and security, the past had risen up and smitten him, and here he was, answering a charge of murder when there was nothing so much he desired as to settle down into a peaceful citizen.

Nina pleaded her husband's cause with the newspaper man as skilfully as any counsel, and far more subtly. He never suspected that any special pleading was going on, it all sounded so artless; yet all the time she was thinking: "If I can make him see things as I see them, perhaps the jury, who will read his paper, may be influenced by it."

Whether she really made the hard-bitten newspaper man see Cassalis as a prospective saint nipped in the bud she had no means of knowing, but she felt that she had his sympathy. There was something in the wild Kelt that responded to the wildness of Cassalis and made him subconsciously partisan; and anyway he was, by right of birth, permanently on the opposite side to law and order.

Having elicited the minutest details of her early history, her meeting with Cassalis, and his dealings with her and her feelings towards him, concerning all of which Nina resolutely bared her heart for the sake of propaganda, the spate of questions began to slacken, and Nina felt that her turn had come at last. She put her elbows on the table and leant towards Leary.

"You do know my husband, don't you?" she said.

"I've run across him a number of times, if that is what you call knowing him. I'm not intimate wit him. He isn't intimate with any white man. It's against his principles, I believe. He sticks to the natives, and the natives stick to him."

"I heard a lot of talk about him on the boat. They spoke

133

of him as if he were the devil. It was the shock of my life when I found I had married him. I thought his surname was Lewis. But, all the same, he has been very good to me.

"Now will you tell me something frankly? I have no one to ask, and I do really want to understand things. It would help me a lot if I did. Will you be frank with me and not mince matters? I mean to stick to Lewis whatever happens, but I want to understand the situation. Tell me, what is this case all about?"

"Well, Mrs. Cassalis, there was a patrol of half a dozen native police under a white officer, and any quantity of porters, engaged in bringing a prisoner down for trial. This prisoner was one of your husband's headmen, and he was being brought in for a murder he had done in the course of his work for your husband, some say at your husband's specific orders. Your husband shot up the police party and got him away, and they are trying him for the job."

"But surely my husband didn't shoot up the party single-handed? How do they know he actually killed anybody?"

"Ah, you have the makings of a lawyer in you, Mrs. Cassalis. That is the thing they have got to prove. There have been lots of shootings of the same kind, and they have never actually been able to bring it home to him. But in this case there is an eye-witness, the interpreter, who was not with the party when the attack started. If he sticks to his evidence, there may be a conviction, provided the jury doesn't disagree."

"Is the jury likely to disagree?"

Leary pointed a finger towards the crowded street. "Do you see all those up-country niggers with a sprinkling of Arabs? Well, they've come in for the trial, and they keep on coming in. There'll be the hell of a row if the jury doesn't disagree. I shouldn't care to be on that jury if it didn't disagree or acquit. It would certainly disagree if I were on it.

I wouldn't face the racket. I've seen your husband tried five times, and the jury disagreed every time."

"You think he'll get off, then?"

"I honestly do, Mrs. Cassalis. I shouldn't worry if I were you. They think they've got him taped, but I'm dead certain they haven't. And even if they convicted, these niggers would rush the gaol. They've got a stiffening of Arabs behind them, and old Sheik Ibrahim's in town. They're packing into the town in thousands. I've never seen anything like it."

Nina wondered to herself why it was that Cassalis had seemed to her to be a man without hope if these assurances were true; and yet she felt that the journalist was sincere. At that moment a darky messenger-boy appeared with a note for Leary.

"Hang it all, Mrs. Cassalis," he exclaimed as he read it, "I have got to go back to court at once. If you don't mind waiting a little, I'll either come for you myself or send someone to take you back to the boat."

"Don't trouble. I can find my way back to the boat myself."

"My dear girl, you can't wander about in the midst of all these niggers."

"Yes, I can. I'm not scared of niggers. I've lived with them all these months. And, after all, these are my husband's friends. They won't meddle with me."

"No, I don't suppose they will; you're sacrosanct. But you've got a pretty good nerve to go through all those savages by yourself. Wouldn't you sooner wait for me?"

"I'll see how long you are. If I get tired of waiting, I shall go on."

Left alone, Nina turned her chair so that she could watch the kaleidoscopic crowd outside the verandah rails. She soon realized that the crowd was also watching her. As she watched, she saw them make way respectfully for someone,

135

and a tall, lean, elderly Arab in a camel-hair cloak like Cassalis's stalked slowly past the length of the verandah rail, eyeing her fixedly. With his venerable grey beard and dignified bearing, he looked just like a patriarch out of the pages of the illustrated Bible in the vicarage drawing-room. But she guessed he was no saint, in spite of his air of intense respectability, but was the redoubtable Sheik Ibrahim, slave-dealer and gun-runner, who disapproved of her marriage to Cassalis.

The burning heat of the afternoon was passing off, and it was pleasant in the shade of the verandah under the big electric fan. Nina stayed on contentedly, watching the ever-changing crowd. Then suddenly the peaceful scene was shattered as if a stone had been flung into a pool as a party of mounted troopers came through, thrusting the crowding negroes aside right and left and making way for a couple of cars. In a moment the drifting, amiable crowd became tense and hostile, though no sound was made and no sign given.

The men in the cars got out and passed into the hotel through the verandah, glancing curiously at her as they went by. She saw that they were men of an entirely different type to the down-at-heel Coasters she had hitherto met, and guessed that these must be the law-officers and Governor coming from the court.

She turned back to watch the crowds and wait for Leary. She could see that it would be an unpleasant if not an impossible business, forcing way through this densely packed mass of savage humanity, and that she had better wait for an escort. Sheik Ibrahim passed slowly back again eyeing her. She had a momentary impulse to ask for his escort back to the jetty, but hesitated, not knowing what the attitude of a Mohammedan would be towards women. As she hesitated, she heard a voice at her elbow—a woman's voice, and that of an educated woman. She turned in surprise, and saw a

136

tall, slender, pretty, grey-haired woman standing over her.

"Mrs. Cassalis?" she said. "I am Lady Piercy. My husband is the new Governor; I dare say you know. Tell me, are you alone here? Have you no friends?"

" I happen to be alone at the moment because the man I was with has just been called away by a message, but I am expecting him back again any minute, thank you very much," replied Nina. Lady Piercy charmed and attracted her, but she felt instinctively that all the dark eyes beyond the verandah rail were on her to see if she were loyal or not, or whether she would go over to the enemy.

"But have you no women friends here?" urged Lady Piercy, who had already gathered that the girl's escort was the raffish Leary, vice the considerably less agreeable Willis, who was at the moment being seen home by his clerk.

"No, I do not know any women on the Coast," said Nina evenly. "And I do not know that I particularly want to, either, from what I have seen of them."

Lady Piercy was a little nonplussed. She knew Nina's story and her exceedingly forlorn position, with the conviction of Cassalis as certain as anything in the law-courts can be certain and no one to turn to but the rascally Willis. It was, in fact, at her husband's suggestion that she had approached the friendless girl to see what could be done for her; for Nina's position, quite apart from her girlish prettiness and the fact that she was obviously a gentlewoman, had roused the sympathies of even the not very susceptible Government officials. She was meditating her next move when the girl took the wind out of her sails by rising to her feet.

"I do not think I will wait any longer for my friend," she said, smiled, bowed slightly, and walked straight out into the thick of the native crowd, which opened to let her through and closed after her like water in the wake of a ship. Lady Piercy was horrified at the sight of an English girl engulfed

137

in the midst of all these odoriferous savages, but there was nothing she could do; Nina had vanished as completely as if she had been sunk in the sea.

Lady Piercy returned to her husband and told him of the rebuff she had received. He shrugged his shoulders.

"The girl probably has no realization of the situation," he said. "She will sing a different tune after the verdict, poor child. You can look her up again then, and see what can be done for her."

"But what will happen to her in all that crowd of natives?" asked Lady Piercy anxiously.

"She will be safe enough if she has a grain of sense," said her husband. "Those are all Cassalis's supporters. They won't lay a finger on her. It is we who are in a tight corner. I shall not be sorry to see the troops arrive."

CHAPTER IX

THE crowd, to whom Nina was an object of awe, made way
respectfully, pushing one another aside as the more curious
pressed forward, and she had no difficulty in making her way
down to the jetty. It was something like the progress of the
queen bee through the hive. Finally arrived there, the entire
crowd hailed the launch for her simultaneously, making a din
that brought heads out of every window round the harbour,
for the white men in the little town, outnumbered by fifty to
one, were decidedly jumpy.

The launch lay far out, and Nina could see the collapsible canvas dinghy, looking no bigger than a toy, being put
together on the after-deck by the darky crew, and wondered
how long she would have to stand in the midst of the staring,
pushing, strongly scented crowd before they took her off, and
began to feel a vague sense of alarm and uneasiness, which
deepened as the minutes passed and the tiny craft slowly
crept towards her over the broad expanse of the harbour.
The crowding negroes were obviously not hostile, but were
highly inquisitive, and very alien.

Then, as she waited, she heard a curious thrumming, no
louder than the throbbing of an artery in the throat. Forget-
ful of the watching eyes all round her, she lifted her head
like a startled deer and listened. All the eyes watched her
eagerly to see her reactions. They were exceedingly anxious
to know whether the new white wife could be counted upon

to be loyal to her lord, or whether all their secrets were going to be betrayed, above all the secret of the way through the mountain, so all-important to the slavers and others engaged in nefarious traffics.

The girl stood poised, listening to the mysterious heart beat of the bush, and then suddenly it dawned on her what it was and why it had thrilled her so. It was a distant signalling-drum, beating the same rhythm that Cassalis had thrummed out with knuckle and palm that night on the river, when the oldest stream in the world had risen in flood and come over its banks. And it seemed to her that that thrumming was the voice of a friend, promising help in her dark hour. The thrumming of an African war drum, which to most white people is a thing of horror and frayed nerves, to her was a message of hope and lifting-up of heart. She drew a long sigh of relief. Help was at hand. Her tension relaxed. The sound of the bagpipes to the beleaguered Scotsmen in Lucknow was not more heartening than the throb of those African drums to the girl who had given herself in marriage to the outcast man.

And the black men all round her, watching her, interpreted every breath she drew and every move she made; and as they saw the look of relief that passed over her face at the sound of the war-drum, they smiled one to another and were satisfied. Nina was accepted by the Dark Continent. Sheik Ibrahim would be reassured by a cloud of witnesses that the one great difficulty in the way of their schemes did not exist.

Then another drum from the other side of the harbour began to answer the first one, and Nina smiled in response, caught the eyes of the nearer darkies, who were grinning from ear to ear in sympathy, and smiled at them also. It seemed to her that she too was in the secret of those war drums, and she felt that they felt as she did.

140

Then someone, greatly daring, began to beat a war drum in the very town itself, making a most fearful shindy for a few seconds and then stopping abruptly. Then another drum in another quarter of the town took up the deafening tale. Then it stopped, and a third spoke, to be answered by a fourth. Then the first spoke again. The beating of war-drums was not permitted inside the city limits; but hidden in all sorts of courts and wynds in the native quarters were these big drums, and as first one and then another kept on starting and stopping, and as never less than two or three were going at the same time, it was impossible to locate them. The effect was not only deafening and nerve-racking, but seriously alarming to the handful of white men, who knew that it meant open and organized defiance and would play the very deuce with the morale of the native witnesses, who had had to be promised free transport to out-of-the-way districts in order to get them to testify at all. If the white men could not stop the beating of war-drums in the very town itself, what chance had the unfortunate black men to do a get-away?

The dinghy arrived. Nina was helped in, waved her hand to her new friends, who waved back delightedly, and was rowed over the glassy surface of the harbour to her floating home. She nodded and smiled in response to the anxious black faces that gazed at her dumbly and inquiringly, indicating that all was not lost, and they grinned their relief, quickly up and down, like children.

The war-drums in the nearer bush kept it up all night, but one by one the drums in the town were routed out and silenced. Next morning, however, when Nina came on deck, she saw that a good-sized steamer, which she had heard come in during the night, was busily engaged in discharging white troops and machine-guns on to the quay. Justice was going to have a fair trial. Before the court opened at ten, every nigger in the town, except the permanent ones, had been pushed

141

back into the bush. The bush, however, was alive with drumming. And as it is not an offence, much less a crime, to bang a drum in the bush, the white man, with his legal mind, could do nothing, but had to put up as best he could with the devastating syncopation of the rhythms, knowing perfectly well, as he was intended to do, what all that drumming meant; knowing also that, if it came to trouble, the negroes would be stiffened and directed by the superior intelligence of the Arabs; that among all those dusky crowds, though indistinguishable from them by the eyes of the white man, were Cassalis's famous fighting blacks, accustomed to operate together under their own leaders and armed with modern rifles, and not a few machine-guns too, if rumour spoke the truth. The court might convict its prisoner, but whether it would ever carry out the sentence was another matter.

Cassalis, sitting in his cell after a final interview with Willis, was also listening to the drums, and feeling pretty certain that whatever the sentence might be, he would not hear much more about it, once it was passed. But all the same, what sort of a life was he going to have as a fugitive from justice with Nina on his hands? He thought again of the horrors of unhelped childbirth in the forests, and groaned inwardly. Willis had made no secret of his opinion concerning the certainty of a conviction if the case ever got a fair trial, and when Cassalis learnt the nature of the evidence against him, he too threw up the sponge. He knew that the only chance was to pack the jury and intimidate the witnesses.

But there are limits to which these two processes can be carried, even in an uncivilized land. The prosecution would try to get a substantial jury of well-to-do, well educated white men, and under the property qualification it could probably manage it. Willis and his counsel, on the other hand, would strive with might and main to get a few Dagoes and poor whitcs included, who could be relied on to rat at the sound of a war-drum, and decline to offer themselves as sacrifices on the altar of abstract justice.

The native witnesses were easy game; to intimidate them was like shooting sitting hens. But there was a white witness whom Willis believed not only to be formidable, but well-nigh invincible: an expensive expert fetched out from England, so anxious were the authorities to rid the Coast of its plague-spot; and it was an open secret that he was prepared to swear that the marks on the bullets found in the white police-officer were caused by the rifling of the revolver found on Cassalis after his arrest, and he had a number of enlarged photographs, very convincing to the enlightened eye, which showed the kind of marks that guns make on the bullets they fire, and that no two are alike, and that they are as individual as finger-prints. The lawyer did not see how Cassalis was going to get away from that; and neither did he, after he had had it explained to him. So he sat in his cell and considered his future as a fugitive from justice.

When the jury had disagreed on previous occasions, the authorities had always given it up as a bad job and dropped the case; but then he had never been put on trial for the murder of a white man before; that was not a case that would be dropped at all readily, and they had already shown by fetching the expert out from England and the bloodhounds from Cape Coast Castle that they meant to make a thorough job of it. If the jury disagreed, the case would probably be removed to Georgetown, and another jury empanelled that could be relied on to return a verdict in accordance with the evidence. They were also bringing up a detachment of white troops and machine guns, so the chance of a rescue was slender.

And supposing he got away, what about Nina ? It was only a matter of time till he was hunted down if they really meant business. The new Governor was a very different man to his predecessor, as the conduct of the trial had already shown. Could Lewis ask Nina to share his fate as a hunted fugitive, and if he could, would she? What line would Nina take in the matter? How was the visit to the prison to be assessed? Loyalty? Pity? Love? He did not know. That could only be told by her subsequent behaviour. How deep had that business over Morley gone? There had been an ugly reaction. He knew Arab psychology—an Arab who had turned on him would never forgive him; any apparent forgiveness was only a prelude to treachery, and deceived no one but a fool.

He also knew negro psychology. They never stayed put for five minutes; however great their fury today, they would come up smiling tomorrow. A nigger never let the sun go down upon his wrath, in fact he hardly let the next meal go down up on it; but then his good resolutions were equally fleeting, and no one but a fool relied on them either. Nigger psychology was child psychology, lovable and unreliable.

But what about woman psychology? He knew nothing about woman psychology. True, he had known innumerable women, from *café au lait* to black as the Pit, but he had never known any of them well enough to know anything about their psychology. He had never stopped long enough with them even to know if they were changeable. That was part of his policy, just as his avoidance of whites was also a carefully thought-out policy, many complications being avoided in these ways.

Cassalis gave it up, turned over on the narrow prison bunk, closed the drawers of his mind, and went to sleep —which was more than his captors did.

There was an anxious meeting in a private room at the hotel, consisting of the Governor, the public prosecutor, the ginger-haired police-officer, and the technical expert out from England .

144

Nobody was very happy. The police-officer was like a cat on hot bricks pending the arrival of the troops, expecting every minute to be shot in the back as his subordinate had been, and that is a thing which wears down even the toughest. The public prosecutor was sore because the Governor, not knowing the ropes, had granted Willis's application for a summary trial without consulting him, and he knew that a jury anywhere except at Georgetown would disagree, to a certainty, and his work would have to be done twice over, with the principal witness vanishing into thin air or thick earth in the meantime. The expert out from England was gradually grasping the fact that he stood an excellent chance of martyrdom. Only the Governor was cool and collected, which, in the opinion of the local men, was due to his ignorance of local conditions.

"There will be no violence until there is a conviction," he said, "and then we must act quickly. The fellow will get off legally if he can, because of his wife; he won't want to be on the run now he is a married man."

"A horrible thing for the girl," said the expert, who was beginning to hate his job and wish that love of adventure had not led him into accepting it. "I saw her in the verandah. An uncommonly pretty girl, and a lady."

"Yes, my wife had a word with her. But she seems able to take care of herself. Declined any help and walked straight into the crowd, and they made way for her without a murmur. Evidently quite at home with them."

"Hm," said the police-officer, "that is an additional complication. How to safeguard the girl? They say Sheik Ibraham is furious at the marriage; he would murder the girl, given half a chance. And that creature Willis, who seems to be the only person looking after her, is the most unsavoury swine on the Coast. If he looked at my wife as he looks at her, I'd knock his head off."

145

"Have the girl watched, for her own sake, and see how things shape," said the Governor. "It is very difficult to help people who don't want to be helped. I suppose Cassalis is one of these fascinating scoundrels that women will do anything for."

CHAPTER X

NEXT morning Willis's dinghy drew alongside the launch, to the great surprise of Nina, and Willis dropped clumsily into the cockpit, looking exceedingly liverish. He had a strong sense of grievance against her, but could not remember what it was about. He had left her sitting on a bench in the ante-room of the courthouse, but he remembered nothing after that till he woke up to find himself lying on his bed with his clothes on; and though he could not remember whether he had abandoned her or she had abandoned him, he felt sore on general principles.

However, she greeted him pleasantly, not wishing to quarrel with him, and having no means of knowing that he had no recollection of having been given the slip. Her welcome immediately restored his good humour, and he set himself to the task of cheering her up by telling her all about himself and his grievances. As, however, she denied having the key of the cocktail cupboard, he did not stop very long. He stopped long enough, however, for a scheme to ferment in his brain, and he proceeded to pave the way for it.

"I think it would be a very good plan," he said, "if you had a room at a little hotel just behind the courthouse. A decent, quiet little place that I know of." He did not mention that it was the place where he himself hung out, and that they always put him to bed without troubling to remove his boots.

"I shouldn't care for that," said Nina; "I would much sooner sleep on the launch, where it is cool."

"You would find it a great convenience, while the trial is on, to have somewhere handy, so that you will not have to keep on going backwards and forwards to the launch. You can still sleep out here at night, and use the room to have a rest and a wash in by day. You'll be very glad of it, believe me."

Nina saw his point, which was a sensible one, and accepted his offer to make the necessary arrangements. He suggested that he should take the room for her as from the following morning, as the trial might start any time after that. He knew it couldn't, but he wanted to make the most of his opportunities; for if by any unforeseen chance his client got off, these were likely to be limited. He was already calculating how much of Cassalis's funds that were in his hands would have to be handed over to his widow, and how much he could stick to. It was a moot question whether Cassalis was worth more to him dead than alive. If his wife reformed him, he would be worth little or nothing. Marriage to his wealthy widow was far and away the best bargain. Cassalis's chances of acquittal sank lower than ever.

Next morning Willis came out to her again in a dinghy, and accompanied her to the room he had selected for her. She was annoyed to find that it was in a broken-down Dago hash-house instead of a decent hotel such as the one under whose verandah she had sat with Leary, but Willis assured her that that one was full. The room to which he took her was a large double room, unnecessarily large, she thought, for the purpose for which she required it. She told him that a small single room would have been quite sufficient, but he said that this was all there was, the town being very full, as she could see for herself. He seemed disposed to hang about and make himself at home, ringing the bell and ordering refreshments, and she was at a loss to know how to get rid of him. She did not know what was the etiquette on the West Coast of Africa; was it usual for gentlemen to join ladies in hotel bedrooms in this manner? He seemed to take it for granted that it was, and so did the people of the hotel, apparently, for refreshments for two came up without demur, and Willis started getting outside a double whisky. Nina endured him as best she might. If wishes could kill, he would have been stretched a corpse. A knock at the door disturbed this idyll, and the house boy announced that there was a gentleman downstairs who wished to speak to the lady. Willis glared with rage.

"Tell him the lady is engaged," he said.

"Tell him nothing of the sort," said Nina, with relief, hoping it was the raffish but decent Leary, and slipped out of the room and down to the lounge before Willis had time to protest. There she found not Leary, but the ginger haired police-officer.

"Mrs. Cassalis," he said, "I think it would be best if you stopped on board the launch till the trial starts. Then I will arrange for you to come and go under escort. It is not safe for a woman to go about like this."

"I thought the trial might be starting any time now."

"Oh no. It certainly won't start till the day after tomorrow, if then."

"My husband's solicitor tells me otherwise."

"If your husband's solicitor thinks that, he is mistaken."

" Yes, if he thinks that ..." said Nina thoughtfully.

The police-officer looked at her sharply.

"Is it the usual thing in this part of the world for ladies to entertain men in hotel bedrooms?" said Nina.

"No, it is not."

"I thought as much. Yes, I should be glad to go back on

149

board the launch, provided I can get my suit-case out of here."

"Where is it?"

"In my room, with Mr. Willis sitting on it."

The policeman made no comment, but beckoned a black-and-tan sort of creature that appeared to act as hall porter.

"Fetch the lady's suit-case down," he said.

The creature padded upstairs obediently. A moment later they heard the sound of a bellow of rage, and the creature came padding down again, minus the suit-case.

"De gentleman no willing," he said.

The police-officer went upstairs, beckoning the porter to follow him. The sounds of a short, sharp altercation were heard, and down they came again, but this time with the suit-case.

"Lady no pay?" wailed the porter.

"Ask the gentleman for that," said the police-officer. A smart official car was outside, and in two minutes Nina was at the quay and embarked in a Government craft and being ferried swiftly out to the launch.

Back in the familiar surroundings, that felt like home to her after the sordid hotel, she sank thankfully down on a locker and asked herself what manner of peril she had escaped from. She felt perfectly certain that the opportune visit of the police-officer was of a piece with the approach of Lady Piercy: Government House was alive to her position and was doing what it could to help her. She also suspected that she had now made a dangerous enemy of the vain and bad-tempered Willis. Nina felt utterly and miserably helpless, not knowing where to turn for the help she so badly needed. Lady Piercy she had instinctively liked, but to turn to her was to estrange the Cassalis faction still further. She wanted desperately to see Lewis again and ask his advice, but did not know how to get through to him apart from Willis.

150

Finally she wrote a desperate little note and gave it to the nigger engineer, bidding him, in a few words she knew of the native language, to take it to the master. He understood her perfectly, and she had the satisfaction of seeing him immediately put off in the skiff; but she had no means of knowing that he had taken the note to Willis's office, and that Willis, as soon as his back was turned, had opened it and, smiling sourly, had placed it in his pocket-book and returned it to his pocket. Consequently Nina waited in vain for a reply, and miserably concluded that she and Lewis were estranged beyond redemption.

But short as Nina's sojourn in that miserable hotel had been, it was not without results. In the morning she woke up with a headache, by the evening she had a temperature, and by next morning she was light-headed in her first bout of malaria. Thenceforth she knew neither time nor space while the nigger engineer, who considered himself acting skipper vice his boss, placidly dosed her with the same doses of quinine that he was in the habit of giving to the fourteen-stone Cassalis in similar circumstances; and, as she had not told him to tell anyone, he did not tell anyone, having been well trained by his boss. Consequently, when the trial came on, Nina did not show up in court.

When Cassalis came into the dock from his dimly lit cell he blinked at the brightly lit court and looked round for Nina, but she was not there. He told himself that he could hardly blame her for not caring to face this ordeal; all the same, he was deeply disappointed. He had wanted very much to see her sitting there.

The trial commenced its leisurely course, as trials will; all the same, there was a sense of tension in the air, and it was not the prisoner only who felt the strain. The town was full of troops, but the woods were also full of natives, and there was no knowing when there might be a clash between the two; and the result was by no means a foregone conclusion, for there was a stiffening of Arab slavers among them, armed with modern weapons, and the Governor would not allow the military to entrench because of the unfortunate political impression it might make.

Both parties, of course, picked over the jury till there was nothing left of it. Cassalis's counsel was certainly a better type than his solicitor, but it is a tradition of the Bar that the hand shall be subdued to what it works in, and he toiled diligently at the packing of the jury. Finally both sides reached the limit of what the law allows them to challenge, and settled down to make the best of it.

When Cassalis heard the opening speech, he thanked his stars that Nina was not there, for the prosecuting counsel was out for blood if anyone ever was. Then came the witnesses. First the ginger-haired police-officer who had sent out the detachment that never came back; and then the Crown's *piece de resistance*, the interpreter who had been promised everything from the moon downwards provided he stuck to his story. And stick he did, manfully. Cassalis smiled bitterly and his counsel toiled in vain. Then came the bloodhound expert; but he had to admit that his beasts had been temperamental, and was more help to the defence than the prosecution. He did not know, and Cassalis did not inform him, that Sheik Ibrahim's highly flavoured footgear were enough to put any bloodhound off its stroke.

Lastly came a small, precise little man in pince-nez, who came into the witness-box armed with a packet of photographs. These were passed to the jury, and he explained clearly and uncompromisingly what they meant—how the barrel of a gun or pistol left marks on any bullet fired from it, and that these were as individual as finger-prints. He showed photographs of the bullets found in the unlucky young policeman, one of which had been fired at such close range that the flash of the shot had scorched the skin of his forehead; had been fired, in fact, obviously to finish him off as he lay dying, shot through the lungs; he also showed photographs of the bullets found in the prisoner's revolver and subsequently fired therefrom experimentally. The markings were identical. There could be no getting away from the fact that the unfortunate lad had not only been shot down, but deliberately finished off by the same hand. It was an ugly story; even Cassalis himself felt sick as he heard it. It all sounded so different in the calm, frigid atmosphere of the court to what it had been in the wild flurry in the pitch darkness of the tropical forest with everyone fighting mad. He was horrified to learn that the dead lad was only twenty. Sick at heart, sick with himself, thanking his God that Nina was not there to hear the damning story, but wondering all the time why in the world she wasn't, and where in the world she was, Cassalis sat in the dock between his two black guards, paying up the first instalment of his debt to God and man.

In the luncheon interval he had a word with Willis and asked him where Nina was. Willis shrugged his shoulders and told him that she had been seen at the hotel where all the bigwigs put up, interviewing the Governor's wife, and that the chief of the local police had fetched her away from another hotel where she had taken a room, and she had gone off with him without saying where she was going. Cassalis asked why in the world she had left the launch, where she was both safe and comfortable. Willis shrugged his shoulders, and said he had no idea. He suggested that if his client cared to write a note, he would give it to the police chief, who probably knew where she was. Cassalis, all unsuspecting, hastily scribbled the first love letter of his life, anxiously watched Willis put the unsealed slip away in his pocket-book, hoping against hope that he would have the decency to seal it unread, little

153

knowing that in that pocket-book it was destined to remain.

Then they went back to court again, and the case for the defence was opened. There were only two witnesses for the defence—an up-country store-keeper who neither looked nor was at all respectable, and whom only the vast experience and positively motherly care of Willis were at the present moment preserving from the D.T.s.; and a fly-by-night individual who when asked who and what he was, didn't even seem to know himself. These were not very good, but they were the best that could be done, and they kissed the Book, and said their bit, and stuck to their story like glue under cross-examination. With any other jury than a colonial jury, where everybody knew everybody, their evidence might have gone down. But as everybody knew both Cassalis and them, it didn't. Grins went round the court in which even Cassalis, with a perverted sense of humour, found himself joining.

Then came the closing speeches, counsel for the Crown representing Cassalis as a fiend from the Pit and counsel for the defence representing him as a mass of clotted virtue, no one, not even the prisoner, taking either party seriously. What really mattered would happen when the jury got to itself, and a couple of up-river traders and a dithering quadroon had to make up their minds whether it was worth the risk to do their duty. The judge's summing up left them in very little doubt what their duty was.

The prisoner disappeared below, the judge disappeared into the back premises, and the slow tropical hours began to go by one after the other. Everyone knew that the town mice were trying to get the country mice to bell the cat, and that the country mice were not relishing the job, and small blame to them.

Meanwhile, out on the launch things were reaching a pitch when even the darky engineer was beginning to wonder whether the malaria germs would not prove more resistant to quinine than Nina, and finally paddled ashore and took counsel with Sheik Ibrahim, who said it was undoubtedly the will of Allah. When Ngumba not unreasonably inquired what was the will of Allah, the Sheik replied that that was a thing which no man knew. Ngumba, with a primitive's intuition, knew that Sheik Ibrahim wished that his master's wife should die, so took his leave politely and went in search of more helpful counsellors. He had been bidden in an emergency to refer to Willis, but to Willis he did not refer, for the same instinct had warned him that the man of law desired the master's wife for himself, and would not be a trustworthy counsellor either, and he believed according to his primitive code that a dead Penelope was better than a living Helen. So he padded up and down the dusty street seeking the heathen equivalent of light from above, and Providence threw Leary in his path. Leary, recognizing him as Cassalis's number one, made shift to pump him in a patchwork of Coast dialects, and Ngumba poured out his story.

There was only one reputable doctor in the town, the one who had come there in the Governor's suite, so Leary went to him. He, knowing the story of Nina and her lover, went to Lady Piercy, and so it came about that Nina, unconscious on a stretcher, was brought into the hotel that served as Government House and taken to the Governor's private apartments, none of which was lost on Ibrahim's spies. Consequently, when Willis had a word with his client that evening, the jury still being just as much locked up as the prisoner and having sent out for eleven suppers and a bunch of thistles, he was able to tell him that Nina was at the Government headquarters with Lady Piercy and that there was no answer to his note—as there naturally would not be, firstly because it had not been delivered, and secondly because, even if it had, Nina had a temperature of a hundred and four and was babbling of green fields—but of neither of these facts, needless

155

to say, did he inform his client.

He was relieved to find that Cassalis received unmoved the information vouchsafed him. But as he left the prisoners' quarters in the company of the ginger-haired police-officer, who combined the office of gaoler with his other jobs, a noise broke out behind them that caused them to pause and look at each other, and then shrug their shoulders and pass on as men well accustomed to that sort of thing, for the sounds they heard were Cassalis wrecking his cell.

There was one thing they did not know, however, or they would not have passed by on the other side after the manner of the Pharisee and the Sadducee—that cell had been the scene of a determined attempt at escape, a prisoner having succeeded in picking out a good deal of the mortar that held the bars before he took his last short walk in the early morning; and when Cassalis seized and shook those bars in his madness, they came away in his hands, leaving him staring dazedly at the heavy weapons with which the Providence he had been cursing had supplied him.

Cassalis was clad in his usual inconspicuous khaki kit, such as all men in the tropics wear, and he was sinewy rather than heavily built. Without giving himself time to think, he was through the gap and chancing his luck on the drop.

Consequently when the jury at last came back into court and the nigger turnkeys went to fetch the prisoner to hear his fate, they found no prisoner, but only the yawning gap through which he had gone. In his absence, therefore, the outraged judge demanded of the jury their verdict. The jury, however, informed him that they had not arrived at one, nor were they likely to; so he reluctantly discharged them after a few scathing remarks on the subject of public duty and moral courage, to which the up-river store-keepers listened with sickly smiles. But the quadroon, unable to keep his bilingual tongue quiet, cried out:

"We got to live here!"

CHAPTER XI

IN consequence of all this, Lady Piercy found herself with a very sick girl on her hands, and no immediate prospect of getting her off them. It was proposed first of all to send Nina round to Cape Coast Castle by sea in the troop-ship that would now be taking back the troops, the *casus belli* having vanished into the bush; but when they learnt what a deplorably bad sailor she was, they decided not to risk it, and when the Governor and his party moved inland to the next town where the assizes were held, they took Nina with them on a stretcher in Lady Piercy's car.

Once away from the dreadful humidity of the Coast, she began to pick up, and when they went yet further inland to the next trading centre where the tribes came in for their disputes to be settled, Nina was able to dispense with the stretcher and sit up beside Lady Piercy, and had, in fact, become quite one of the family, for the childless couple had grown much attached to her.

It was here, in camp in the heart of the primeval forest with the tribes all around them, that Lady Piercy undertook the task of breaking to Nina a piece of painful news that had been very wisely kept from her during her illness—a few days after Cassalis's escape a crocodile had been killed in a village just above the town, and in its belly were found Cassalis's belt-buckle, and the assorted metal buttons and clasps on a man's gear that even a crocodile cannot digest.

Nina heard her apathetically, the aftermath of malaria still upon her. There was nowhere in the camp where she could go to be alone with her grief, and it was strictly forbidden to go out into the dense tropical forest that pressed close on every hand, for the Governor was more than uneasy at the demeanour of the natives. They should have turned up in their thousands to trade, get their disputes settled, and generally take part in the fun of the fair, but the big justice tent was pitched in vain; no dusky suitors came to have their cases heard, and even the usual train of camp followers had mysteriously melted away, leaving only the regular servants of the suite, and even they huddled together apprehensively and would not go out to gather firewood without an armed escort. And meanwhile the drums that meant all Africa to Nina throbbed and throbbed unceasingly away in the impenetrable woods.

A very curious story was afloat among the tribes—the rumour of a monkey Messiah. Blacks as well as whites had accepted Cassalis's death as a proven fact, but whereas the whites thanked the God of justice that He had taken their problem off their hands, the blacks believed that the soul of Cassalis had immediately re-incarnated in a huge ape which had been captured and lodged in a ju-ju house in the heart of the bush. This ape, by the manner in which it ate yams, acted as an oracle, apparently, and at the present moment it was eating them in a manner that pointed to war.

The ginger-haired police-officer, who had pieced together the story bit by bit, urged the Governor to send his womenfolk down to the coast in case the reincarnated Cassalis began to eat yams in a manner that indicated that he wanted his wife returned to him. Some of this had to be explained to Nina when walks even under escort had to be put a stop to, but she showed no more outward emotion than she had shown when the news of her husband's death was broken to her. She had asked for and obtained Cassalis's belt-buckle, a twisted gilt serpent, that had been taken from the belly of the crocodile, and from a native goldsmith she had obtained a Brummagem rolled gold chain, and the buckle now hung round her neck, under her frock, never leaving her night or day. It was the only memorial she had of Cassalis: save for that one bit of twisted metal, he might have been no more than a figment of her fancy, and there were times when her fever-daze brain sometimes thought he was. She asked whether Cassalis's cigarette case and wrist-watch and lighter had also been found in the belly of the crocodile, but was told that the finding of them had not been reported, the finders having probably melted them down for the sake of the not inconsiderable amount of gold they contained.

It was reported that the lodges of all the secret societies that rule Darkest Africa had called up their members, and that only women, children, and a few ancients were left in the villages; this beyond all question meant war, but war organized in a way never before achieved by the childish mentality of the primitive folk dwelling behind that ill-omened coast. Native opinion declared the brains behind the organization to be those of the great ape, chained to a stout post in his ju-ju house and fed on yams; white opinion naturally discounted this, but knew that a brain there must be somewhere, to gather up the tribes and yet hold them in check till all was ready, and prevent the sporadic raiding in which native warfare usually petered out, all discipline disappearing with the first loot.

The Governor dared not send his womenfolk back because he could not provide them with an adequate escort. His one hope was to push on as fast as possible to the next big river, where it was arranged that a launch should meet the party and take off the women.

By fatiguing journeys through the steaming forests they

pressed on, drenching themselves in quinine till their heads buzzed like bells and all food tasted of it; at last they came to the bank of a great sluggish river studded with a maze of islands, and saw moored near the bank Cassalis's launch.

To Nina the sight of those graceful lines, the pride of Lewis's heart, was a bitter reminder of her tragedy; and when she learnt that she, Lady Piercy, Lady Piercy's maid, and the ginger-haired policeman's wife were to make the trip to the coast in her, Nina wondered how she was to bear it. It was not quite so bad when they got on board, however, for all personal touches of Cassalis had been removed, and she was just a Government launch, like any other, her crew wearing the snowy ducks of His Majesty's service instead of the inconspicuous khaki affected by Cassalis. Nina had one shock, however—the nigger engineer was so like Ngumba that she addressed him by name when she first saw him; but he shook his head, and, when she spoke to him in the dialect Cassalis had taught her, answered in another which she did not understand. The four women packed into the little cabin, camp-beds being placed in the centre of the scanty floor-space between the bunks, and settled down to make the best of the sweltering night. Nina, however, soon had enough of it, and followed Cassalis's plan of sleeping in the cockpit on cushions taken from the lockers, the swift movement of the launch preventing the attentions of mosquitoes.

Unable to sleep, she lay watching the launch thread its way through the maze of islands, the river at this point having degenerated into a network of channels through a swamp without any main stream. All sense of direction was lost as they twisted in and out, and for all Nina knew to the contrary they might have been heading straight for the heart of Africa instead of down to the coast and safety.

They passed so close to a party of crocodiles lying like stranded logs on a sandbank that she caught the vile musky

161

stench of the great brutes, and shudderingly wondered what the last struggles of Cassalis had been like; and, memory re-awakening, she wept for a while, and then fell asleep, only to be disturbed by the blazing tropical moonlight falling full on her face. They had drawn clear of the maze of islands now, and were moving steadily over the broad expanse of the river again. Nina was puzzled by this, for she knew that the estuaries of most African rivers are a tangle of choked-up channels, only to be kept clear for the passage of boats by constant dredging. Why had this river suddenly developed a broad, clear channel as it got towards its mouth, and why was the rising moon shining in under the awning over the cockpit? And why was there a chuckling bow-wave under the fore-foot of the launch, as if she were breasting the cur-rent instead of being carried down by it? Nina did not know much about African rivers, but her common sense told her that this one was acting oddly.

They rounded a bend and saw ahead of them a gap in the dense forest that showed where a tributary stream came in; the launch crossed the broad expanse of water diagonally and, abandoning the main channel, entered the tributary. There was not the slightest doubt about it now—they were progressing up-stream and away from the coast and safety with every throb of the engine.

Nina's mind flashed back to the guarded information that had been given her about the great ape in the ju-ju house and the reason for the curtailment of even the scanty and guarded exercise that was permitted to her. Cassalis was dead—was dead! Eaten by crocodiles while escaping. Both blacks and whites were agreed that he was dead; but was his hand reaching out to her from the grave through the hairy paw of the great monkey? The idea was a thing of horror that her mind recoiled from, refusing to take in its implica-tions.

Ahead of them the channel forked again, the long trail of drift wood on the spit showing that it was more likely to be divided by an island than receiving a tributary. Into the bank of the island the launch drew softly and came to rest, its engine still running. One dark figure and then another dropped from the bank on to the bows, and before she could gather her wits together sufficiently to cry out, Nina felt a sweating black hand clapped over her mouth, and found herself lifted out of the launch and passed to other hands reaching out from the bank. The engine of the launch took up its beat again, its sound dying slowly away across the water. Nina made a vain effort to struggle and scream, but dozens of hands held her and she could do no more than jerk and quiver, half smothered by the pressure of the padded leathery palm on her mouth.

She could see that she was being carried in the midst of a party of blacks down a comparatively broad path on the wooded island on which she had been landed. It was not as densely wooded as the mainland, and through the interlaced boughs overhead the moonlight shone in glittering patches. After a few minutes of this uncomfortable progress they came out into a clearing of some dimensions, perfectly circular, the firm beaten earth underfoot showing that it was a place that was either diligently weeded or had hard wear. In the centre of what Nina guessed to be one of the magical dancing places of which she had heard, stood a stout stockade, inside which rose the pointed, reed-thatched roof of a circular hut of considerable size. Beside the gate that gave entrance to the stockade were two weird carved figures decorated with bunches of dried grass and elephants' tails, showing that the structure inside the stockade was a ju-ju house. On the far side of the clearing, lights could be seen among the trees, indicating the presence of a village.

Nina's captors carried her rapidly up to the gate of the

stockade, and in response to a knock thereon, an old man, toothless, shrivelled, and evidently of immense age and so feeble that he could hardly fulfil his function of gate-man, opened the doors to them; Nina's captors hastily deposited her just inside the gates and then ran for their lives. The ancient dodderer closed the doors behind them, and Nina, thus unexpectedly released from constraint, sat up and looked around her.

Within the ring of the stockade was bare beaten earth, the same as outside, wide as a road. From the big, round, mushroom-shaped hut in the centre dim lamplight shone out here and there from under the over-hanging eaves of deep thatch, indicating the narrow slits between roof and wall that supplied air to the windowless structure. The entrance was sealed by a heavy hanging mat. In response to a faint piping call from the old gate-man, two figures in the huge head dresses and fantastic frills of witch-doctors pushed out from under this curtain, letting it fall to behind them so that no glimpse of the interior was visible to those outside. Without a word spoken they lifted Nina to her feet, and she, not wishing to repeat the very unpleasant experience of being carried, and knowing resistance to be useless, walked with them. Someone from within lifted the mat curtain, and Nina found herself inside the ju-ju house.

It was dimly lit by a semicircle of lamps upon the floor, each lamp consisting of a wick floating in oil in a coconut-shell. The circular floor-space was divided in half by a partition running right up to the roof, and in the centre of this partition was a low dark hole, like an outsize hen-hole in a poultry-shed. Outside the circle of lights sat a ring of witch-doctors and warriors in full war-paint, their black skins hideously striped with white, and frills and plumes sticking out in every direction. In front of each little lamp lay a small pile of yams. In a sudden horrible flash of realization Nina knew

164

what was expected to come out from the pitch-dark inner chamber through that exaggerated hen-hole. Why she had been brought, and what her part in the proceedings was to be, she could not imagine.

The rattle of a chain from the darkness behind the partition told her that whatever was within was on the move; and then the massive head and shoulders of a huge gorilla appeared in the low mouth of the entrance, and the creature hirpled clumsily through, walking on knees and knuckles like a man on all fours. As it advanced towards the circle of light, Nina saw that underneath the huge ridged brows the eye sockets were empty pits of darkness—the creature was blind!

It seated itself clumsily in the centre of the circle, lifted its hideous head, and seemed to gaze round at the silent assembly out of its sightless eyes, the squatting crowd bowing, heads between knees, as the creature turned from side to side, as if surveying them. Finally the dreadful eyeless face turned full towards Nina where she stood between her escort, at the back of the ring of sitting men, and to her intense surprise she saw the creature give a distinct start. A witch-doctor, so bedizened as to be more like a wind-blown hayrick than a human being, who appeared to be in charge of the proceedings, gave a brief order, the circle of squatting men parted, Nina was brought forward by her guards right up to the clumsy huddled heap in the centre, forced to her knees, and her head bent forward till it touched the ground in front of the great beast.

Evidently the animal was tame, since her escort had come fearlessly within its reach, but even so, it was a thing of horror, a monstrous parody of the human, with God only knows what thoughts going on inside its dim animal mind.

A harsh, dry palm was laid on Nina's head, and the sweating hands gripping her shoulders were removed. She over-

165

balanced and fell forward right on to the hairy knees of the great ape, and the hand on her head pinned her there. Then the roaring darkness of fainting descended on her, and the last thing she remembered as she slipped into unconsciousness was the ticking of a wrist-watch close to her ear.

When Nina recovered consciousness she found herself lying on a camp-bed in what she guessed from its shape must be the partitioned-off part of the ju-ju house. Daylight coming in through the ventilation slits under the eaves lit it dimly, and in the half-light she saw Cassalis's familiar camp equipment standing about, right down to the portable table and chairs that they had used at the meal in the cave. This was no lair of a beast, but the room of a man, and a civilized man at that. Before she had time to take in all she saw, a mat curtain hanging over the hen-hole entrance was pushed aside and a figure in voluminous Arab draperies came crawling through, which, when it rose to its height and resumed its dignity, turned out to be Sheik Ibrahim.

"Much danger," said Sheik Ibrahim in English. "Big monkey in medicine sleep. Lady run away." And he held out to her a camel-hair cloak such as Lewis had been in the habit of wearing as a protection against the sun.

Nina rose shakily from the camp-bed, took the cloak from his hand, and wrapped it about her, pulling the hood over her head; as she did so, she knew by the smell of tobacco-smoke clinging to it that this was none other than the identical cloak that Lewis had been in the habit of wearing. For a moment memories rose up so overwhelmingly that she forgot the danger and horror of her position and stood motionless till recalled by the hand of Sheik Ibrahim on her arm and his voice saying:

"Lady come quick. Big monkey wake."

He held aside the mat curtain, and Nina crawled through the hen-hole to find herself in the other half of the ju-ju

166

house. The little lamps had burnt themselves out, the piles of yams had been removed, the audience had departed; and alone at the end of its chain the great ape lay in a dead sleep, the drugged "medicine sleep" described by Sheik Ibrahim.

Nina gave that dark hairy bulk a wide berth, oblivious though it was, and, guided by the Sheik, passed out through the mat-closed entrance into the stockaded enclosure and the grey light of dawn. At the gate, secured by a huge beam pushed through sockets, the old gateman toddled out and gave a squawk of surprise at the sight of them. Then, to the amazement and horror of Nina, who had never seen a blow struck in anger before, Sheik Ibrahim suddenly produced a great curved knife from his voluminous draperies, clapped his hand over the gate-man's mouth, and slashed him with the curved blade where neck joins shoulder; a jet of blood spurted high in the air, and the old man collapsed in a heap, dead without a sound.

The Arab wiped his knife on the poor old creature's ragged garments and returned it to his draperies without a word, unshipped the great beam that secured the gate, opened it just wide enough for Nina to pass and then pulled it shut behind her, wedging it in position with a bit of stick, being, of course, unable to replace the beam from outside now that he had thus summarily disposed of the gate-man.

Then he hustled Nina as fast as she could put foot to the ground down the path to the water-side up which she had been carried a few short hours ago. Held in to the water's edge was a large canoe with a mat awning amidships; without word spoken, Nina was helped down the steep bank and pushed under the awning, the rowers dipped their paddles, and without any form of explanation or farewell Nina left the mysterious island after a sojourn as brief as it was inexplicable.

Moving swiftly with the current, the canoe was soon back

again in the main stream; and a few hours' paddling took them to the maze of islands, through which they threaded their way by a definite channel and Nina saw how misleading had been their route of the previous day, dodging and out and round about till all sense of direction was lost.

In the late afternoon they tied up at the bank, putting blankets over their heads against the mosquitoes. As soon as the swift tropical darkness fell at dusk they pushed on again, paddling a short while till lights appeared round a bend, the bright lights of white men, and they drew in to a timbered jetty, put Nina ashore—indicating by gestures that she should make her way up a path leading to the lights—and disappeared into the darkness of the broad river, returning whence they had come. No choice being hers, Nina did as she was bid. On her left loomed a small barn-like building, all in darkness, so she kept on her way towards the lights, to find herself in a few minutes in front of a good-sized European house, deeply verandahed, with a raffle of huts for native servants in the background.

The door stood open, shielded only by a fly-screen. One cannot knock with one's knuckles on wire gauze, so Nina pushed it open and called huskily:

"Is anyone there?"

She heard an exclamation of surprise and the sound of a chair being pushed back, and there came out, marvel of marvels, the padre who had performed the marriage ceremony, a table-napkin in his hand and crumbs in the creases of his waistcoat, evidently having been disturbed at his supper.

"Mrs. Cassalis!" he exclaimed. "But where are the others?"

"What others?" said Nina, not grasping the import of his question.

"Lady Piercy, and Mrs. Grigson, and the maid. What has

168

become of them?"

"I don't know," said Nina. "May I sit down?"

And she walked unsteadily towards a chair and collapsed into it.

This recalled the padre to the duties of hospitality, and he dosed her with brandy and set to work to extract her story from her. Briefly and barely, for she did not like him, she told of the kidnapping in the launch and the visit to the ju-ju house and its unholy occupant; but some instinct she could not define prevented her from giving any indication of the whereabouts of the island, or in fact even that it was an island, and for all the padre learned to the contrary that ju-ju house might be any where within a day's journey on either forest-clad bank of the river or any of its tributaries.

Then, having learnt as much as he saw he was likely to learn, he handed Nina over to his negro housekeeper, a bowdlerized and dispirited edition of Mammy Jonah, and routed out a native boy to take a message down to Okiki by canoe.

Nina kept her bed the following day, as much in order to avoid being cross-examined as to recover from her ordeal. Early next morning she heard the sound of booted feet on the path outside, and, hastily dressing, came down to find the padre in counsel with Sir Robert Piercy and the ginger-haired policeman, while a big white launch, with a machine-gun in the bows and a bargeful of native police in tow behind, lay off the jetty.

Now if Mr. Grigson had started his inquisition by an inquiry into the location of the ju-ju house, he might have learnt something that was of use to him, but, as luck would have it, he began on the more spectacular subject of the monkey Messiah, and when he learnt that the celestial beast owned a washstand he and the Governor looked at each other.

"That explains a good deal," said Mr. Grigson.

"It does not explain the buckle and buttons inside the crocodile," said Sir Robert.

"It explains the finding of them—why that crocodile of all the crocodiles in the river should have got killed at that particular moment. And why the wrist-watch and cigarette-case were not found with the other things."

Nina, still suffering from the after-effects of malaria and the repeated shocks she had been through, was paying little attention to these speculations, having heard them *ad nauseam* during her sojourn with the Governor's party; but the sudden raising of Sir Robert's eyebrows and the abrupt cessation of the flow of Mr. Grigson's speech riveted her attention. She too had been puzzled by the presence of camp furniture in the lair of a great ape, who ought to have required no more than a heap of straw; but it had never occurred to her to speculate upon any link between their presence in that lair and the presence of identifiable relics of Cassalis in the belly of the crocodile. They were both mysteries, and if any link existed between them it eluded her.

The rasping voice of Mr. Grigson recalled her wandering mind.

"Now, tell me, Mrs. Cassalis: you say that the ape had no eyes. Do you mean by that that the eyeballs appeared to be missing, and the lids closed and sunken, or were there empty holes where the eyes ought to have been? Try and remember. It is an important point."

Concentrating her malaria-poisoned brain with difficulty, Nina cast her mind back to the scene in the dim lit ju-ju house as the great ape came crawling through the low hole in the partition. She could see its hideous face sunk between its great shoulders as clearly as if it were before her; she could see it slowly turn its head, surveying its audience; and then she could see, perfectly clearly, that the little bright eyes of its kind were lacking and in their place were large black

170

holes. For the first time it struck her that there was something unnatural about those black holes, for the lids should have closed over the eyeless sockets. Whatever injuries the beast had received, some sort of healing should have taken place, and one would not see right inside its head. And then there flashed into her mind hardly even the thought, but a kind of dreamlike echo of the ticking of a wrist-watch close to her ear as she sank into unconsciousness beside the great ape. How often had she heard that exact ticking as she dropped off to sleep at night, her head on Cassalis's shoulder and his arm around her!

The sudden return of the blood to numbed limbs is a painful process, and so is the sudden reawakening of hope when all hope has been abandoned. Nina did not dare to ask any questions lest she should rouse suspicions, but Mr. Grigson might just as well have saved his breath for all the information he could henceforth extract from her. Nina knew nothing, had noticed nothing, could remember nothing, and it was only the intervention of Sir Robert that saved her from a very thorough third degree at the hands of the irritated police-officer. Concerning Lady Piercy's fate, of which she would gladly have told them if she could, she genuinely knew nothing .

Finally, realizing that no more was to be extracted from her, they departed, leaving her in the care of the not-too -hospitabl padre and his dispirited nigger housekeeper, whose soul appeared to have been saved at the expense of her wits. Nina was to be sent down to Okiki by the mission launch, which was expected any day, and advised to get in touch with her husband's lawyer. They did not know what to do with her, for she was obviously no longer on the side of the angels.

CHAPTER XII

THERE was one factor in the affair upon which Nina, like a good many other folk, had been kept completely in the dark, and which, at the present moment, was darkening Darkest Africa considerably; and that factor concerned the doings of Cassalis after he broke prison.

He knew the geography of that prison well enough, having twice assisted at the gaol-breakings of other folk, and was alive to the fact that everything depended upon catching hold of the first thing he touched as he reached earth, for upon this side of the building ran the river, and the footings of the wall were protected from the water by no more than a row of piles. If he could catch hold of and hang on to the brushwood growing among the piles, well and good; if not, he would roll off into the water, and the water was full of crocodiles. It was only a ten-foot drop, but the landing was so precarious that it had never been thought necessary to wall or patrol this side of the gaol; the crocodiles did all the sentry go that was necessary. Even Cassalis would not have risked it unaided if he had been in his sober senses.

But there is a special providence, they say, whose job is to look after fools, drunkards, and little children, all folk, in fact, who are without fear; and to its list of duties might be added the care of those who are without hope. Cassalis, in his crazy mood, came under its jurisdiction. Landing on the narrow ledge, he stayed there, and, recovering his balance, crawled along it till he came to the high, spike-topped wall that guarded its landward end. Then he did the only thing there was to do—dived into the water, nipped round the corner, and scrambled ashore before the crocodiles winded his presence.

There was not a soul about, everybody being gathered in the square in front of the Government building to await the verdict. Cassalis slipped along the tangled bank, an inconspicuous figure in his drenched khaki, and made his way over some waste ground till he came to the high mud wall of the compound of an Arab house standing on the outskirts of the town, ledged his toe in a well-known cranny, and was up over the top and down on the other side observed by no man. The only person to give tongue was an ancient dame, one of Ibrahim's earlier wives, who was engaged in grinding mealies with a pestle and mortar in the shade on the far side, and on top of whom Cassalis very nearly landed. Her yell stopped half-way as she saw who it was, and she was on the point of summoning her innumerable descendants to perform the duties of hospitality, for Cassalis was a very honoured guest, when he hastily checked her, for the fewer folk who knew of his whereabouts the better, the crocodiles having given him an idea which he thought he could see his way to carry out.

The old dame smuggled him into a shed and padlocked the door on him, and sent an urchin in search of Ibrahim, for it was essential that Cassalis should be out of the way before his escape was discovered, for this would be one of the first places to be searched.

Lying very comfortably on top of some mealy-sacks, an old burnouse of Ibrahim's replacing his sodden clothes, Cassalis's fertile mind was soon weaving a scheme for the future. There was not the slightest hope of an acquittal, he knew that; the only choice lay between a conviction and a disagreeing jury, in which latter case the warrant out for him would still hold good, and he would be hunted down and brought to trial again as soon as caught, and this time he would be tried at Georgetown, with an all-white jury, and the result was a foregone conclusion. He had to accept the fact that he was finally and irrevocably outlawed.

This would not have bothered him unduly had it not been for Nina; but to take her with him into outlawry was impossible. The rough but efficient Arab doctoring that served his needs was no use for her. To take her with him into outlawry was to lose her with her first child.

But the crocodiles had given him an idea. It was a thousand-to-one chance against the success of a getaway. If his clothes were rolled into a bundle round a piece of meat and thrown to a crocodile, the crocodile would certainly swallow them; and if that crocodile were subsequently killed quite enough in the way of metal tabs and buttons would be found in its inside to lead to identification, and no further hue and cry would be made. He could slip out by the old slave routes to Timbuctoo, reappear in French Colonial Africa, where few questions are asked, and with his energy and experience make a decent living on the right side of the law.No one could want a pleasanter place to live in than one of the oases around Tunis, the past could be decently buried, and even if the British authorities succeeded in tracing him, the French ones would be exceedingly unhelpful if he had ingratiated himself with the local bigwigs. His money had all been carefully stowed away with a view to just such an eventuality as this; in fact a lot of it was already in French banks. The only person he would have to take into his confidence would be Willis; Ibrahim he thought it better not to confide in, as it was not to be expected that he would encourage the withdrawal of his right-hand man.

Cassalis was the brains behind the whole organization of

174

graft and slaving and gun-running; the Arab mind, though both shrewd and brave, is not far-sighted, and any sort of extended co-ordination or organization is unknown to it. Cassalis, and Cassalis alone, held African Tammany together, and without him it would disintegrate into petty criminality that the police could easily cope with. Cassalis, and Cassalis alone, would the negroes follow, because he protected them from the rapacity of their Arab allies and saw that they got a square deal, which it would never have entered the head of any Arab to give them. It was an odd fact that the whole of the organized lawlessness of the Coast turned about the one man whose integrity could be relied on. It was because Cassalis was trustworthy that African Tammany had been possible.

Cassalis saw his way clearly. Working through Willis, he could arrange for Nina ostensibly to be sent home widowed, but actually to go to Tunis to await his coming by the overland route. His and Ibrahim's connections were well established in North Africa, and some of his friends were highly placed and influential, French finance not being faddy as to the sources of its profits from overseas trade. Willis had wangled passports for him before, and could do it again with the minimum of trouble. Cassalis did not think there would be any difficulty in the execution of his scheme provided Ibrahim did not get wind of it prematurely and spoke his wheel.

A key grated in the clumsy lock on the door, and Cassalis sat up hastily, eager to receive Ibrahim and arrange a getaway. But the person who entered was not Ibrahim, but Ibrahim's eldest son, Yussuf, between whom and Cassalis no love was lost; the Arab resenting his father's partiality for the infidel, and the Englishman distrusting the narrow fanaticism of the Arab's not very intelligent mind.

Today, however, Yussuf was positively cordial, and ready to give his father's favourite any assistance he could. Two tins of Nugget boot-polish were produced, a brown and a black, mixed together, and diluted with melted mutton-fat; and then, with a poor relation at work on every limb and the old grandmother herself doing his back, Cassalis was turned into a Mohammedan negro, cheekbones and nose cunningly built up with plasticine and sticking-plaster till no semblance of European features remained, and Cassalis issued forth in the company of Yussuf ben Ibrahim in the likeness of a darky who had had the worst of a fight, one eye closed and a piece of sticking-plaster going from cheek to forehead diagonally as if holding a gash. Clad in Arab robes, he passed as one of the negro converts of the Prophet; negroes letting him alone because of his religion, and Arabs letting him alone because of his race. In this guise he stood with the crowd in the square awaiting the verdict, saw the jury shuffle out looking very self-conscious and disconsolate, and heard the rumour of his escape leap from mouth to mouth in a dozen different dialects. Then, sitting in an Arab coffee-house, he watched the patrols go out to search the town. Presently another of Ibrahim's innumerable descendants appeared with the news that the headquarters of the clan had been duly searched, the searchers had departed, and he could come home now; so he and Yussuf, swinging their robes insolently among the negro crowds, strolled back to supper at their leisure, well knowing that the darkest place is under the lamp.

Not wishing to tempt Providence, either Mohammedan or Christian, unduly, Cassalis did not linger under the hospitable roof of Sheik Ibrahim's premier spouse, but set off at moonrise as one of the paddle-men of a canoe going up-river with trade-goods. But although Nugget boot-polish might deceive his fellow men, it did not deceive the mosquitoes, and the trip was a penitential one in consequence, and he was thankful to drop off towards dawn at one of Ibrahim's depots up a back water, where he proposed to lie up while his plans matured, for it was within easy reach of the persons with whom he intended to work.

Following the disappearance of his client, Willis had felt justified in letting himself go and getting properly drunk to make up for the self-denial he had practised during the trial. Luckily for him, he had remained in court from the moment he left Cassalis's cell in the company of the police-chief until that functionary returned to announce to the court that his prisoner had given him the slip; consequently there could be no question of his complicity in the escape, for with his reputation he was suspected of anything and everything.

His celebration was such that it occasioned no surprise when he did not put in an appearance at his office next day; and when his black-and-tan clerk announced that he was suffering from a bout of fever, everybody grinned and translated fever as delirium tremens and gave him leave of absence from all inquiries. But as a matter of fact, though a heavy drinker, Willis was not nearly as heavy a drinker as he allowed it to be believed, his supposed debauches frequently serving as a cover for business trips into quarters where no reputable attorney should be seen.

In due course, therefore, he joined Cassalis at his lay-up, where he found his client in that state of de-Nuggetation when he looked like a leprous Arab. He himself, clad in filthy white drill, with his drink-reddened nose and unshaven jaw, looked the complete beach-comber. Nevertheless, he listened with as professional an air of legal wisdom as if he occupied historic chambers in the Inner Temple.

Cassalis explained what he wanted done. He never asked Willis for his advice on anything save legal technicalities, which was a sore point with that vain and touchy egoist, and bullied him outrageously when his truculent adventurer's

177

temper got the upper hand.

Three things Cassalis wanted done. Firstly, certain securities were to be sold and the proceeds placed to the credit of a mysterious trading company of which Cassalis was the board of directors and all the shareholders. Secondly, means of communication were to be established with Ibrahim *via* Willis's office, for although Cassalis quite agreed that it was as well for the Sheik to have disported himself in public all the time the hunt was on, caution could be carried too far if it meant constantly having to communicate through a third party, especially when that third party was one that he neither liked nor trusted. Thirdly, Willis was to see Nina, ostensibly with a view to settling up her affairs as a widow, but actually to persuade her to carry out her share of the scheme for getting clear of crime and making a fresh start.

To all these several points Willis nodded his agreement, made no notes, and stowed his instructions away in his head. Waiting for the turn of the tide that should carry his canoe back to the coast, he sat chatting with his client. He was probably more intimate with Cassalis than anyone, with the exception of Sheik Ibrahim, for he had been a man of both brains and culture before that happened which led to his coming to the Coast—a talent as an amateur lightning artist turned to account in signing and witnessing what had been only a draft agreement. A jury had declined to accept the evidence of experts, but other folk had not, and, although Willis was whitewashed by the law, there was no place left for him in legal England.

Cassalis was glad to have someone of his own class and calibre to talk to among the riff-raff with which his outlawry condemned him to associate, and, although he often found Willis distasteful, made a friend of him for lack of anything better. Consequently Willis had no difficulty in getting him to open his heart on the subject of his hopes for the future, when he should be able to establish himself as a law-abiding citizen in North Africa and make a home for Nina. It never occurred to Cassalis that Willis would have any objection to this scheme, for he would still handle all his affairs, a shady lawyer being as great a need as ever if he were not to lose the fruits of his West Coast enterprises. It never entered his head that Willis, as far as he was capable of such a thing, had fallen in love with Nina, and had not the slightest intention of helping her to settle down with her lawful husband. It may be that hell knows no fury like a woman spurned, but a tipsy solicitor runs her a close second.

As soon as the voice of the river announced that the tide had turned, Willis crawled under the mat awning of a canoe and disappeared into a hollow pile of native produce. But although he returned to town as arranged, it was not Nina he sought out, but Sheik Ibrahim, the very person he had been pledged not to enlighten, and told that grim patriarch Cassalis's story.

Then he proceeded to do a little bargaining on his own account. He pointed out to the wily Arab what he already knew, that the real cause of all the trouble was Nina. Ibrahim replied that that need not worry anybody unduly; there were many ways of quitting life in West Africa, all of which could be made to look perfectly natural. Willis replied that a broken-hearted widower might not be of much use to them, but a deserted husband, properly disillusioned, might return from the paths of virtue with renewed energy. Ibrahim, a connoisseur in the human heart, as are all oriental epicureans, saw the point and approved it.

Willis knew that once the fact of Cassalis's death was held to be established, as it would be as soon as the crocodile had finished digesting what had been given to him and could be opened and his contents revealed, the obvious thing for Nina to do would be to return to her family, and he could interview her with that end in view. He could also probably extract from her a letter on the subject that, with suitable additions, if his hand had not lost its cunning, could be shown to Cassalis, who should be led to believe that Nina had been pleaded with in vain and was determined to have no more to do with outlawry. To Sheik Ibrahim, to whom women were a matter of barter, there was nothing particularly outrageous in all this; he firmly believed that he was acting in Cassalis's best interests. Nina was easily replaced; in fact he himself could lay his hands on a very competent mulatto who was capable of supplying the consolations of Paradise. He was in a position to know, for he spoke from experience. Willis's price for co-operation was Nina; and as Sheik Ibrahim, like most people, was quite willing to give away what he didn't want, the arrangement suited everybody.

Nina was to be told that Cassalis had survived and awaited her in his eyrie; she was to withdraw herself from the protection of Lady Piercy and go to Okiki, ostensibly to await the boat that would take her out; actually, she would be picked up there by Sheik Ibrahim and handed over to Willis. What would happen then neither of them discussed—Ibrahim because to him it was all in the day's work; Willis because even he had his limits.

Then Willis turned him about and made the unpleasant journey back again up-stream and presented himself before the eager Cassalis with a mournful countenance.

"Nothing doing," he said, shaking his head sadly. "She won't rise to it."

"What d'you mean?" demanded Cassalis, angry and anxious.

"The Piercys have been talking to her, and she has seen the account of your career in the local papers, and what with one thing and another she's got cold feet and has packed up for home. I'm awfully sorry, old chap, I did what I could, but

180

it was no use."

Cassalis sat silent so long that Willis began to look round for a drink. Finally he broke the silence so abruptly and so inappropriately that Willis thought he had gone off his head with grief.

"What date is it?" he demanded.

His next words disillusioned Willis, however.

"Then she's missed the boat, and has got a fortnight to wait for the next. A lot can be done in a fortnight. If she thinks I am going to take this lying down, she is mistaken."

Willis turned green about the gills. This was an eventuality he had not bargained for.

"You had better talk to Ibrahim about that," he muttered hastily.

"No fear," said Cassalis; "no good asking Ibrahim to help in this," and he told Willis the story of the shipping of Harold Morley up to the eyrie and his suspicion of the complicity of Ibrahim in the matter.

"Surely not," mumbled Willis uneasily. "I can't believe it of him."

"Whether you believe it or whether you don't," said Cassalis savagely, "you're for it if you don't keep your mouth shut."

Willis shivered. Cassalis's vengeances were notorious. "What do you propose to do?" he inquired meekly. He might as well get all the information that was going. He and Ibrahim would need to be as forewarned as possible.

"What do I propose to do?" snarled Cassalis. "I propose to do what you never do—have the courage of my convictions and go the limit, double or quits. I also propose to keep my mouth shut, my friend; and if I find you've opened yours, I shall shut it for you permanently." Willis scowled, but said nothing. He saw that Cassalis was in one of his ugly moods of truculence when it was a word and a blow with him, and the blow often preceded the word.

He rose. Cassalis paid no attention. Walking sideways, crab-fashion, in case Cassalis was minded to shoot him, he sidled towards the canoe that awaited him. Once out of Cassalis's line of vision, he turned and scuttled like a rabbit— hating himself for scuttling, and above all hating the man who, without lifting a hand, could make him scuttle.

Cassalis, thankful to be relieved of the presence of Willis, who had suddenly grown unaccountably odious to him, sat on silently, trying to get his emotions in hand as one steadies a bolting horse for the jumps. It was always Cassalis's boast that nothing could ever rattle him, and in even the most urgent crises he always insisted on taking time to think. It never entered his head to question the truth of Willis's statements. Twice already Nina had turned on him, and he supposed that now, for the third time, she had turned for good. If the Piercys had been talking to her, and if she had heard his unvarnished record, it was hardly to be wondered at. Willis's statements were, moreover, confirmed by Nina's failure to communicate with him, save for that one brief visit, which, according to his own statement, Willis had had to use all his power of persuasion to bring about. Nor had she answered the notes he himself had sent her. He entirely failed to recall that all communications with Nina had been made *via* Willis, for he had no reason whatever to suspect the man of treachery; it was all to his interest to keep in with African Tammany, on which the bulk of his practice depended. Romance was the last thing that anyone would associate with the middle-aged, whisky-soaked, bad-tempered solicitor.

Cassalis therefore accepted it as axiomatic that Nina was following the line of least resistance, and his fertile mind began to revolve around the most strategic method of employing force. His death, he knew, had been satisfactorily established. There was no hue and cry. Only Ibrahim and his household knew the secret. Both black and white believed him gone whence there is no return. His stratagem was completely successful. Whatever scheme he might devise for the possession of Nina he must not throw away this enormous advantage.

But against this advantage must be set the awkward problem of the divergence of interest between himself and his allies. He did not like Yussuf ben Ibrahim's new-found cordiality; he suspected it indicated that he was out of favour with the old man, though Ibrahim himself was as affable as ever in his grim, snarling way. The attitude of the fool of the family is often a very useful indicator of the real opinions of his betters.

The situation on the Coast was a curious one. The official power, and all the transport, were in the hands of the English; the bulk of the local, as distinguished from the overseas, trade was in the hands of the Portuguese and their half-castes; but all the real power and influence was in the hands of the trading Arabs, coming down with their caravans from the north, who play the same part in Africa that the Jews played in medieval Europe. And outnumbering all this parti-coloured handful of exploiters by ten thousand to one were the blacks—an enormous potential force, capable of anything if led, and of nothing if not led. Hitherto Cassalis had used the negroes in the interests of the Arabs. Now, he thought, for a change he would use the negroes in his own interest, and if the Arab interest offered opposition, well, so much the worse for the Arab interest; it would just be swamped and sunk by sheer weight of numbers. Cassalis knew the strategic point to strike at—where the caravans came through the mountains by passes unknown to any other white man; the passes that led down to the secret lines of wells across the desert that alone made the slave trade possible. Stop the caravans from getting down into the plains to revictual, and they were in the soup, for they could only carry just enough for the desert journey.

Cassalis's hard cogitating was not long in bearing fruit. The furrow between his brows smoothed itself out and his face settled down into its usual mask-like immobility whose likeness to a basking lizard Nina had noted with her first sight of him. At daybreak, long before Ibrahim busting up-stream with double-banked rowers could get to him, Cassalis had departed by forest paths, travelling light and moving fast, slipping along the tangled trails like a shadow with no more than a couple of porters at his heels, travelling as the negroes themselves travel, setting a pace that the elderly Ibrahim had not the slightest chance of overtaking. When it came to forest travel, the Arabs were only one degree better placed than the white men; but Cassalis had right of way over all the ju-ju haunted tracks by virtue of his high attainments in the blood-stained rites that pass with the negro for religion. He was hand in glove with every medicine-man and witch doctor from end to end of that evil coast: those of the lower grades regarded him with awe as a kind of cardinal of the powers of darkness; those in the know set great store by his support, scratching his back diligently in return for getting their backs scratched whenever the need arose. Cassalis, tracking through the mysterious twilight of the woods, was making for the lair of a great friend of his—an old gentleman who, despite the fact that he wore nothing save the equivalent of an old-school tie, and that about his middle, shared Cassalis's outlook on life and enjoyed much the same sense of humour, and there is no greater bond than that.

Thirty hours' fast travel brought Cassalis to his friend, the approach to whose abode was guarded by no more than odd little bunches of grass hanging athwart the forest paths, and in the perfect seclusion ensured by those little bunches of grass Cassalis settled down in security. The scheme that was suggested caused the old gentleman to chuckle until his few remaining teeth were endangered. From the back of his hut he produced the most startling ceremonial robes that ever a high priest wore—nothing more or less than the skin of a gigantic gorilla.

The original owner of the skin must have stood close on seven feet, and his hide had not shrunk much in the tanning. Cassalis, who was six feet two, could stand up in it comfortably. But perhaps that is hardly the right word to use, for a gorilla-skin is not the most comfortable wear on the coastal plains of Africa. Cassalis, clad in nothing but a loincloth and breathing as best he could through the gaping mouth, reckoned that, of all that goes to make a god, martyrdom at least would not be lacking. The old witch-doctor, pleased as a child with a new toy, pushed Cassalis into the back of his hut to pass the time as best he might, and send out the African equivalent of the fiery cross to all the faithful. In forty-eight hours Africa had a Messiah after its own heart, formidable, sub-human, altogether fiendish, with promises of a holy war to follow. No wonder the Governor and his party drew blank as they went on circuit in the name of justice. Who wants justice if they can see a chance of getting the upper hand?

CHAPTER XIII

THE monkey Messiah having been duly launched with full military honours, Cassalis thankfully shed its skin and slipped down to the coast again in his disguise as the negro with the bunged-up eye. There he learnt the news. Nina was indubitably with the Governor's party, there was no gainsaying that. He travelled a day and a half by the secret forest trails for the bitter pleasure of seeing her drive past in a car with Lady Piercy; then back to the coast again, and a maze of tortuous wire-pulling, exclusively among the negroes, for he no longer trusted the Arabs and the Arabs no longer trusted him. African Tammany was divided against itself, and in consequence its days were numbered. Priam's private thoughts about Helen of Troy were the only things that equalled Ibrahim's outspoken comments upon the wife of Cassalis.

Cassalis found, to his great delight, that although his precious launch had been confiscated, Ngumba had been kept on as engineer because he, and he alone, understood its French super-charged engine. The rest of the crew consisted of a couple of retired naval ratings and a Portuguese steward. The steward could be corrupted by anyone with a few pence to spare; the naval ratings, being inured to discipline, would see and do nothing they were not told. One could do a massacre under their noses with impunity. Cassalis felt that his luck was at last getting back to its old form.

He had set the war-drums beating to such purpose that the whole white population of the Coast was exceedingly jumpy and the negroes were showing that peculiar kind of truculence that is theirs when they think the dice are for once weighted in their favour. From a half-caste clerk in the telegraph department Cassalis learnt that the Governor was trying to get his womenfolk out, and he could hardly believe his luck when he received the tip that the means of getting them out was to be his own launch, sent up-river from Okiki.

Nothing could have suited Cassalis better. The launch, after its coastwise trip, would be obliged to refuel at Okiki for the up-river part of the journey, and at Okiki he had reliable emissaries, notably a gentleman who rejoiced in the name of Albert Edward Victoria George de Souza and a complexion like cheap floor-stain badly applied, and who combined in nicely balanced proportions the vices of the Scotch, Irish, Portuguese, and negro strains that had gone to the making of him—but who likewise combined their variously assorted wits. With this racial *multum in parvo* Cassalis communicated by bush telegraph, and all the Irish in A. E. V. G. de Souza came uppermost and he threw himself heart and soul into the plot that was afoot.

Arrived at Okiki, the European portion of the launch's crew naturally left the nigger to do the dirty work, and themselves repaired to Pedro's unattractive establishment for drinks and other less salubrious purposes. Okiki being Cassalis's headquarters on tide-water, they equally naturally did not find the launch where they had left it when they came straggling back after an indecent interval. All they found was the tearful Portuguese, bereft of all save his singlet, which he was wearing as a kind of petticoat in a last despairing tribute to convention. Having lost their own kits also, they relieved their feelings by kicking him.

De Souza and Ngumba, meanwhile, were taking the

187

launch up-stream with a bone in her teeth, aiming at getting to the trysting-place ahead of the news of their bunk. Taking turn about at the steering, they changed into the snowy Government ducks they found on board, and none of the riverside residents, seeing the white-uniformed brass-badged steersman, his head sunk in a sun helmet, conning the launch from the top of the deck-house doubted that it was an official outfit.

Arrived at the trysting-place, where the forest trail came down to a ford, they lay well out in mid-stream to await the Government party, ready to slip their cable and be off for the head-waters if suspicion had been aroused. Ngumba changed back into his usual dungarees and got the collapsible boat into the water, for they meant to allege that it was impossible to bring the launch into the bank owing to her draught, though, as a matter of fact, being designed for just such work as this, she could have come alongside with ease. It was unlikely that any of the menfolk would insist on making the trip in the dinghy—which could only take two passengers at a time in addition to the rower—and, if they saw the white-clad, brass-badged, helmeted figure at the wheel, would never suspect that the crew had undergone a change.

So far, all had gone as planned by Cassalis without hitch or delay, in a manner that would have done credit to a General Staff, but no sooner was the launch at her moorings than the double-crossing began. A man signalled to them from the bank, and Ngumba put off in the dinghy, to find that he was one of Ibrahim's hangers-on with a message to the effect that the rendezvous was changed; Nina was not to be taken direct to the sacred island, but landed at a certain riverside village.

Knowing the man personally, and that he was often made use of as a go-between, de Souza would have acted on the message without suspicion. Not so Ngumba, however, whose primitive's intuition was backing and sidling like an uneasy horse. Nothing would suit him but that they should first put in at the original rendezvous and verify the message. De Souza grumbled, for it meant a run of some miles off their course up a side-stream, but Ngumba was adamant and declined to start the engine until de Souza agreed.

Fortune continued to favour them, and the womenfolk were ferried aboard without hitch. The launch was steered in circles in and out among the maze of islands that cluttered the river where it received its main tributary just above Waigonda, and, with the women safely asleep, was then run up the side-stream, to be met by the watchers according to plan, and Nina taken off as arranged.

But now the first-fruits of the double-crossing began to make themselves felt. Ngumba had obviously been right concerning the landing of Nina at the original rendezvous; what then could be the meaning of the message carried by Ibrahim's hanger-on? De Souza came to the conclusion that it must refer to the other women, whom he had originally been instructed to deliver to the missionary at Waigonda, to be picked up from there by whomsoever it might concern. Ngumba, not caring twopence either way, readily agreed, as the riverside village was half a day's travel nearer than Waigonda and one of his dusky inamoratas resided there.

In consequence of all this, Willis, waiting at the river-side lair, had delivered into his hands, not Nina, whom he was eagerly expecting, but the Governor's lady, the wife of the chief of police, and an hysterical French maid, none of them young or well favoured, and all of them with menfolk in a position to raise a hue and cry to high heaven. It would have been an easy matter for him to explain that he had made arrangements for the return of his client's widow to her family if inquiries were made as to her whereabouts, but he could hardly expect two angry and official husbands to accept such an explanation in the case of their spouses. Willis had decid-

189

edly bitten off more than he could chew, and the more he tried to wash it down with whisky, the less he could swallow it.

Hastily improvising the first lie that came into his head, he told the women that the native disturbances made it unsafe for them to proceed any further for the moment, and that they were to land at the riverside village and await further instructions. A trader's bungalow, reasonably wholesome, for it served Cassalis as one of his innumerable lie-ups, was placed at their disposal, and Willis took formal charge of the party as being the best way out of the difficulty. The women had no suspicion that they were really prisoners, but accepted Willis at his face value as a local resident lending a hand to the authorities as it was the duty of every white man to do in an emergency.

Sheik Ibrahim, hastily summoned to a conference upon this *contretemps*, cursed most horribly and wanted to knock the entire party on the head forthwith as the best means of shutting their mouths. Willis, however, would not agree to this, pointing out the perfectly hellish row such conduct would give rise to, and urged that the women should be kept as hostages for the moment, as they might possibly afford valuable bargaining power later. He was privately considering in his own mind the advisability of turning King's Evidence on both Cassalis and Ibrahim, and he thought that if he produced the Governor's womenfolk as a peace offering into the bargain, a good deal might be overlooked. Naturally he did not confide this motive to Ibrahim, and neither did Ibrahim confide to him that he too was doing a little cogitating, and that his cogitations turned on the advisability of murdering Willis as a damned nuisance, what with his alcoholism and his infatuation. He would have murdered Nina too, if he had dared; but he dreaded, and not without reason, Cassalis's vengeance, having seen a few of them, and guessing that that dangerous renegade would go completely berserk if Nina were meddled with. He saw clearly, despite the urging of Yussuf, that the only thing to do was to be patient.

Cassalis estranged from his wife might return to the fold; Cassalis,bereaved, would shoot up the entire Coast and then himself. The only person who could do Iago's job was a white man in Cassalis's confidence, so Willis remained alive—for the moment, at any rate. He was to stop where he was, in charge of the women, and await developments; Ibrahim was to double back with all speed to the ju-ju island and wangle things with the ju-ju men and the chiefs. The chief witch-doctor, fortunately, was quite ready to stand in with the scheme, being distinctly an un-friend of Cassalis, who had interfered on more than one occasion in matters that the witch-doctor considered were no concern of his; for though Cassalis had no qualms whatever on the subject of killings, he could not abide torture, and how was any ju-ju worth its salt to be propitiated without torture? Anyway, the soul of an artist needs expression, and the witch-doctor did not like having his speciality decried.

Having seen this functionary and found him agreeable, Ibrahim perfected his plans. Cassalis was the brain behind African Tammany, and to allow him to withdraw and earn his living honestly was out of the question. But he would be no use as an organizer if his heart were no longer in the job, and the only way to get him to return to the paths of evil contentedly was to remove Nina out of his reach in such a way that it could only be regarded as an act of God. Nina must shake the dust of Africa off her feet, ostensibly, at any rate; then she must be unostentatiously decoyed to a bungalow, inaccessible but not too remote, where Willis could give himself the pleasure of dropping in at week-ends. That was Willis's price for co-operation. What scenes would be enacted at the bungalow neither Ibrahim nor Willis thought it necessary to discuss; Ibrahim taking them as a matter of course, and Willis telling himself that, given a fair chance and no competing influences, his powers of persuasion must prevail, and Nina would see which side her bread was buttered.

Now, either of the original plans in itself was practicable, but the attempt to combine the two was not. Sheik Ibrahim could have finished Nina off in an apparently natural manner and so kept his hold on Cassalis, or Willis could have finished off Cassalis indirectly and legally, and so got Nina into his hands; but when they tried to preserve both Cassalis and Nina for their different ends, they attempted the impossible, and things soon began to tie themselves into knots, especially as they had to work mainly through the negroes, all of whom adored Cassalis and could be induced by no bribes to double-cross him. They therefore had to be kept in the dark as to the real purpose of the manoeuvres afoot, and a well-intentioned lieutenant who has been kept in the dark can tangle plans in the most extraordinary fashion if he begins to use the wits God gave him with the laudable intention of furthering them; and the more loyal and competent the lieutenant, the worse tangle he can make.

While Nina was undergoing her cross-examination at the mission station, African Tammany was holding its committee meeting in the ju-ju house; a genuine committee meeting of those more or less in the know, not the play acting that was staged in the outer chamber for the benefit of those who were being led by the nose.

It was an uneasy meeting, however, for nobody was being quite frank with anybody, and it resembled nothing so much as a game of poker among card-sharpers, each of whom had got a few aces up his sleeve.

Cassalis's original intention in stirring up trouble among the tribes had been no more than to create a smoke screen to cover his retreat; but the war fever, once started, could not be stopped, and a native insurrection was gathering like the clouds of a thunder-storm all up and down the Coast, and spreading inland far beyond what had ever been dreamt of by its originators as the restless tribes caught the infection one from another and went fighting mad. Cassalis saw for himself what it was like to try and maintain order when the tribes were armed, supplied with alcohol, and exasperated by slave-raiding.

Sheik Ibrahim had got the wind up badly, fearing he had over-reached himself. When the chief witch-doctor, who ought to have known better, had marched Nina into the open assembly at the ju-ju house, Ibrahim, in consternation, had hastily enlightened him in a whisper as to the state of affairs, and he, with admirable promptitude, had redeemed the situation by packing the divinatory yam with a native drug; so when Cassalis, performing his part as monkey Messiah and tribal oracle, ate it, he keeled over in a dead sleep and slept for forty-eight hours, thus enabling Nina to be got away again.

But in spite of the complete success of this scheme— so far as Ibrahim knew, at any rate, the canoe crew not yet having returned to inform him of the little economies they had practised in his interest—he was scared stiff as to its re-percussions, for Cassalis was taking things hard. Willis had been diligently doing his part during the past weeks by taking up an elaborately non-committal attitude whenever Cassalis spoke of Nina, as if he could say much if he would, but, be-ing charitable, wouldn't. This is a manoeuvre that is far more effective than openly blacking anyone's character, because it allows of no rebuttal and gives the imagination free scope. Cassalis, being hot tempered and passionate by nature, had brewed for himself a hell of misery during the long hours of idleness in the ju-ju house on the river island, till at last he

193

was hardly sane on the subject of Nina; which was not the end the plotters had in view, and they were beginning to be a little scared of their handiwork.

Fortunately for all concerned, the drastic drugging Cassalis had received had left him very dazed, with blank gaps in his memory for the incidents immediately proceeding his lapse into unconsciousness, and upon this they were trading, assuring him individually and collectively that it was all a bad dream. How much he believed them and how much he was "playing possum" they did not know, and were skittering about like cats on a cucumber-frame accordingly, not knowing where the wrath was going to strike.

Cassalis, clad in nothing but a loin-cloth and wrist watch, was seated on the edge of the camp-bed, elbows on knees and head in hands, in a very bad temper; his head was aching fit to burst, and his eyes were so bloodshot he could hardly see out of them. On the wall behind him hung the gorilla-skin, turned inside out to air, for he had sweated like a horse during his forty-eight hours' compulsory sleep; spread-eagled on a coat-hanger, it looked most sinister, like a murderer hanged by the neck till dead, with its great eyeless head resting limply on its deflated chest. Cassalis, after his sojourn inside its oppressive folds, felt as if he had had a dozen Turkish baths one after the other.

Willis, seated in Cassalis's folding chair, was busy getting outside a bottle of whisky, with Sheik Ibrahim, a strict Mohammedan teetotaller, watching him sourly, knowing full well the danger of drinking in a trade like theirs, and that Willis couldn't last much longer at the pace he was now going. Sheik Ibrahim, in fact, was the only person present who looked at all self-possessed or comfortable, and even he was wondering how the murdered gate-man was going to be explained away.

It was Cassalis who broke the overcharged silence. "What

I want to know," he said, "is who doped that blasted yam."

Sheik Ibrahim told him, like one who has explained the same thing many times before to a child at the question asking age, that the witch-doctors had doped it in the hopes of increasing the psychic faculties of their monkey Messiah.

"I don't believe it," said Cassalis sullenly. Willis went on with his drinking, never opening his mouth save to pour whisky into it; he would soon be incapable of speaking even if he wanted to.

Ibrahim appealed for support and confirmation to the two local kinglets, squatting on their hunkers in a corner, looking anxious; the divided counsels and obvious animosity among their leaders worried and bewildered them, and they could not understand what was afoot. The kinglets knew that it was considered advisable to keep Nina away from Cassalis, and judged it to be such " medicine" as their own magicians used when they forswore their wives for the period of certain ceremonies. They knew that a man with a new wife is apt to neglect his other affairs, especially if his affairs take him away from home, and they certainly considered it a good thing in the present crisis that Cassalis should be kept free from temptation till things were more settled for all of them; but had they suspected that a wife-stealing was afoot, they, as worthy citizens within their limits, would certainly have respected the laws of property and refused to be a party to transgressing them, for if a wife is not property, what is?

They were quite satisfied that what was being done was for Cassalis's good, and agreed with Ibrahim that it was far better he should content himself with assortments of local beauties, for whom he paid good cowrie money, than get himself involved with this white wife who was leading him astray and causing him to neglect a business so profitable to all concerned, and to which he was indispensable.

They, like everyone else on the ju-ju island, agreed that

it was a most unfortunate *faux pas* that had delivered Nina there at just the wrong moment, and that Sheik Ibrahim had certainly got the right idea when he suggested that they should all stick like glue to the story that she had never been there at all, and that what Cassalis had seen was a figment of the imagination caused by the drugs in the yam. Cassalis, feeling deadly sick and still pretty dazed, had perforce to accept the statement that was pressed on him with one voice. His plans had miscarried, how and why he would learn in due course from Ngumba, and his desire to see Nina had caused the hallucination as the drugged yam got in its work. All he cared about now was to gather together his resources and have another shot at the kidnapping.

With this end in view, he dropped into Arabic, which neither Willis nor the negroes understood, and began to discuss the re-laying of his plans with Ibrahim. But Ibrahim had no mind to entangle himself any further in the matter, and also wanted assistance from Willis while that worthy was still capable of speech. So he led the conversation into English, which he understood perfectly and talked after a fashion. Willis picked up his cue, and the next stage of the tangled plot got going. The two kinglets, understanding not a word, but listening to the tones of the voices, were not misled by what was being said, and knew that Cassalis, whom they loved like children, was upset and sincere, and that Ibrahim, whom they hated, and Willis, whom they despised, were lying to him.

Nudging each other with their elbows, they determined to double-cross the witch-doctor, their spiritual adviser, in their turn, for they suspected him to be Ibrahim's man rather than Cassalis's, Cassalis having interfered in one or two ritual matters that involved certain unpleasantnesses; for they knew that Cassalis, though he did not mind cannibalism, which he considered harmed neither eaters nor eaten, nor yet murder

196

within reason, had an invincible objection to torture, which in their hearts they shared, being kind-hearted souls except when worked up. One of the kinglets was Ngumba's half-brother, and he determined to broadcast by bush telegraph for his relative forthwith, and learn from him the facts of the case, having a great respect for the intellectual capacity that is developed by wearing trousers; not realizing in his simple soul that Ngumba owed his trousers to his wits, and not his wits to his trousers.

Another ingredient in the devil's broth that was brewing, which none of them knew of at the moment, was that the crew of the canoe charged with the task of deporting Nina had not carried out their instructions to the letter and landed her at Okiki, where the local branch of African Tammany would immediately have picked her up and delivered her into Willis's hands as instructed, after leading all and sundry to believe that she had left for England; but had deposited her at the mission station, knowing that she would be forwarded by the mission launch in the course of the next few days, and thus saving themselves the long slog back against the current. They considered this a very bright idea, and wondered why Sheik Ibrahim had not thought of it himself when he gave them their instructions as to the manner in which the white woman was to be delivered into the hands of her own people; for he was of an economical turn of mind, and would have been glad to save himself the expense of even the scanty rations of half a dozen negro rowers.

Willis, prodded by Ibrahim, lifted his sodden head and proceeded to perform his allotted task in what he fondly believed to be a well-thought-out scheme, but which was actually a soup getting ready to boil over.

"I'm not aversh to another shot," he said. "Do anything to help old friend. That ish, if the girl'sh shtill there. Better find out before you g-g-go to mush trouble or exshpensh."

197

"Why shouldn't she be there?" asked Cassalis sharply, lifting his head for the first time during the interview.

"She'sh goin' home nexsht boat—with Grigson."

"Who the devil is Grigson?"

"Ginger-haired p'leesh-offsher. Great pals. Put up at my hotel with'm durin' trial. Saw all the fun. Lov'ly girl. Nishe feller. Why not? Nexsht door to a widder."

"What d'you mean?" demanded Cassalis, exceedingly agitated, as he was meant to be.

"You nearly hanged. Widder then," said Willis, deliberately misunderstanding him, for he was not nearly so drunk as he was pretending to be.

Ibrahim took up his cue.

"You bad man, Mr. Willis, tell that."

"Not bad, only drunk," said Willis with disarming candour. "Very shorry firsht thing t' morrer mornin'."

"Do you know anything about this?" demanded Cassalis of Ibrahim.

"I know lady at Mr. Willis' hotel. I know policeman got here. Not know what happen inside. Maybe talk not true."

"Is there talk, then?"

"Maybe not true."

"Answer my question. Is there talk?"

"Maybe some."

"Who is talking?"

"White, black, everybody."

"My God!" said Cassalis, and put his head back in his hands again.

They tried to get him to discuss future plans, but it was useless; Cassalis had metaphorically turned his face to the wall.

"It will pass," said Ibrahim sagely. If a man in Paradise requires four houris to make it Paradise, why should a man in this vale of tears be expected to manage with one? It was

198

contrary to nature. He abased his dignity and led the way through the hen-hole, the rest following him, Willis only pausing for a last drink.

Cassalis, exhausted by the sweating and still feeling dazed from the drug, sighed and stretched himself out on the camp-bed and tried to sleep. In a few hours' time the evening's ju-ju stunt would start and he would have to stifle himself in the gorilla-skin and go through the solemn farce of prophetic yam-eating, and he needed to gather together his wits and his strength; it was the night of the full moon, and the chiefs would be coming in from far and near.

And as he lay between sleeping and waking, unable to sink into the deep sleep that refreshes, and yet troubled by evil half-dreams, he seemed to see the whole of his life sliding along before him like a cinematograph film. The repressive home that had made a rebel of him; the cranky upbringing that had sent him out all unprepared to cope with the world; the harsh judgment that had reacted to its own complexes and allowed him no second chance. If the truth were known, he believed that his father had been glad of the chance to rid himself of his young rebel. Then the long outcast years; the worthlessness of the degenerate whites with whom he had to associate for lack of any other society; the final resolution to have no more to do with them and stick to the clean-living blacks; and the endeavour to keep his white man's mind in spite of all, and not go completely native and sink into the inevitable demoralization which follows on that for the European.

He thought of the ugly history of African Tammany; the cruelty of the slave trade; the destruction wrought by the gin trade; the quarrels fomented for the sake of the trade in arms. And all the time, before his half-delirious eyes, moved the endless procession of the chain-gangs; whatever he thought of, to whatever he turned his imagination, they were going

199

by all the time in the background, a shadow-show over which he had no control. The weary afternoon hours slipped by and the quick tropical dusk descended, and Cassalis was considerably less rational when he rose from his bed to don the gorilla-skin and face the evening's ordeal than when he had lain down in the hope of the rest that would not come. He tossed down what Willis had left of the whisky to fortify himself for what lay before him, breaking his strictest rule in so doing; got into the stifling hide, and, with the head hanging down his back like a monk's cowl, settled down to wait for the ceremony to get going. The weird howling and chanting struck up, and as soon as the audience had warmed to its work and was at it hammer and tongs, intoxicated with its own noise, he pulled his head piece into position and crawled out into the ju-ju house to confront his followers.

He seated himself in the middle of the little circle of lamps and counted the piles of yams; each had its significance, and the thirteenth pile meant bloody war. And as he sat there, gazing into the faces of his followers, faces in which no rational thought, as the white man understands it, would ever gleam, a sudden revulsion of feeling at his outcast existence came over him, and he stretched out his hairy paw and took a yam from the fatal thirteenth pile.

In an instant the ju-ju house was filled with a mass of yelling, whirling humanity dancing a war-dance and pouring towards the door as they danced, to continue their orgy outside in the ampler space of the dancing-place, where he heard the rest of the tribe joining in. A loud crackling noise told him that the signal fire had been lit, and that war was fairly launched among the tribes; for that light would be seen all up and down the river, and beacon after beacon would blaze, taking up the message. The use of the usual war-drums had been forbidden so that no warning should come to the white men and they could fall upon them unawares.

Cassalis, left alone in the now empty ju-ju house, crawled wearily back through the hen-hole into the interior apartment, got out of his gorilla-skin, and lay down on the bed, cursing the bookless existence of an outcast that allowed him nothing to distract his mind.

He had not been lying there long when a faint scratching sound on the concealed back entrance of the ju-ju house caught his ear; he rose to investigate, and found there the one man he felt he could trust in all the orgy of double crossing—his black engineer, Ngumba. Ngumba, to his great surprise, felt his huge black sweating hand seized and shaken, a thing Cassalis seldom did with niggers, knowing the inadvisability of familiarity even with the best of them; but so glad was Cassalis to find one man in whom intelligence and loyalty were combined that there was neither black nor white for him at that moment.

Squatting on his hunkers on the earth floor, his grin gleaming white in the semi-darkness, Ngumba gazed up adoringly at his beloved master, who was to him the finest ju-ju he had ever worshipped in all his benighted heathen existence. Ngumba told his story, and for the first time since his escape from prison Cassalis felt he was dealing with sincerity and getting the truth.

He listened with growing uneasiness to Ngumba's account of the message he had received at the trysting place, and learnt to his amazement that Nina had actually been landed on the ju-ju island as planned. He began to wonder whether his dream of her presence had been an hallucination after all, and if not who was responsible for misleading him, and what were they driving at.

It was not very difficult to see what Sheik Ibrahim was driving at. On every hand he heard stories of the Sheik's outspoken comments on his lapse into domesticity and virtue. Willis, however, was gifted with the legal virtue of a shut mouth, and there was not one whisper to inculpate him. He and Ibrahim had never been on terms of more than the barest toleration of each other, the ascetic Mohammedan despising the lawyer for his intemperance, and Willis's sensitive vanity reacting like a shying horse to his undisguised contempt. It therefore never occurred to Cassalis that things had reached such a pitch with Willis that he was willing to put his pride in his pocket and co-operate with his *bête noire*.

He did not know what to make of Ngumba's suspicions concerning the carryings-on of Nina with Willis at the Makalu hotel. It was, on the face of it, exceedingly unlikely that Nina, or any other decent woman for that matter, would willingly carry on with the exceedingly unappetizing Willis; but Cassalis had reached a state when he did not know where the truth lay, and concluded that there could not be so much smoke without some fire at least, forgetting that all the smoke originated in one quarter. Sometimes he thought one thing of Nina, and sometimes he thought another. He was fast reaching a state when he ceased to be rational where she was concerned. Iago was doing his job successfully.

Cassalis had arrived independently at his suspicions of Ibrahim's duplicity. He felt sorry at having to break with the old Arab, who had given him his chance and saved him from the beachcomber's fate when he had deserted into the African landscape ten years ago; but he saw how impossible it was to find any basis of reconciliation between their respective viewpoints, and that if Ibrahim were minded to use force he had no option but to do the same, replacing the tacit and treacherous intriguing with an open breach.

There were times when Cassalis was seized with revulsion at the character of the men he had to work with, particularly Willis. Ibrahim wasn't so bad; he was a cruel and treacherous devil, but that was only to be expected of an Arab in his line of business, and he was perfectly self-respecting with it all. But Willis was sordid, and repellent, and shifty, and his linen was never really clean nor his chin properly shaved; and though Cassalis made a sort of friend of him as being the only educated white man available, and though his brains were first class and his knowledge of the law quite out of the ordinary, and although Cassalis himself was no better than his solicitor as far as conduct went, there were times when he turned against Willis as if he were an evil flavoured food, and bullied him outrageously. Willis always cringed when bullied, and that did not improve matters, for Cassalis then hated him additionally for his cowardice.

All the same, he never suspected him of treachery, for Willis had a curious kind of professional integrity, the one thing he had never prostituted in all his debasement, and Cassalis counted on that as he had always been able to do. It never occurred to him that the cadaverous lawyer was suffering the pangs of unrequited love, and that while in that state it might be possible to bully him once too often. But, supposing Cassalis broke with the Arabs, with whom should he unite himself? The whites had outlawed him, and would hang him if they caught him. There remained to him only the blacks, and they, for all their weight of numbers, had the mentality of children. Cassalis had never felt so deadly alone in all his life, not even when he first escaped into Africa from the unendurable conditions of a tramp's stokehold.

He brooded over these things in the torrid darkness of the ju-ju hut so long that Ngumba put his head on his knees and went to sleep. But there was no sleep for Cassalis till his decision had been taken; then, as his custom was, he would close the drawers of his mind and rest.

Ngumba had no idea as to what had become of Nina after he had put her ashore, but it seemed most likely that, since she was presumably in Ibrahim's hands, she would have been put for safe keeping in the same place as the other white women, his captives. Cassalis wondered what Ibrahim's motive might be in hanging on to Lady Piercy and the policeman's wife, and, guessing correctly, concluded that they would be used as hostages. He knew, however, that Ibrahim might be reckoning without his hosts, and that the negroes, egged on by the witch doctors, who were very powerful in that district, might decide that the white women could be used more advantageously for propitiating the black gods. Cassalis went cold all down his spine at the idea. If a start were made with that game, the women would be better put out of their misery than rescued. He was well aware of the way the black gods liked their female victims served up to them.

Cassalis was sick at heart with the horror he had let loose upon his own people. He had not known, when he recklessly put out his hand to the fatal thirteenth yam, that any women would be involved in the trouble. There was in him, for all his wildness, a deep-rooted chivalry, and for Nina's sake he felt for these women, dear to their menfolk as she was to him; sheltered as he would have liked to shelter her. From his own brief experience of what his home had meant to him, he reverenced the homes of other men, whether reed-thatched hut or deep-roofed bungalow. All the evil that he had done rose before him in bitterness and humiliation, and with a sudden turn of mood he determined to do what he could for those women in the up-river bungalow.

He stirred Ngumba up with his toe and bid him bring him from the launch whatever he could find in the way of civilized kit and prepare for a start up-stream.

CHAPTER XIV

LADY PIERCY was having a very trying time of it. Mrs. Grigson was down with fever; the French maid was incapable of anything save weeping into her rosary; and Willis, having run out of whisky, was engaged in drinking himself imbecile on arrack. They were still awaiting news and instructions, and Willis, when sober enough for speech, rejoiced in making their flesh creep with tales of native risings, partly in order to keep them submissive and dependent upon him, and partly because he liked horrors for their own sake.

Lady Piercy had long since decided that he was an unmitigated blackguard, but being a white man, she had perforce to put her trust in him in the present emergency, and had no reason to doubt that he was doing other than his best for them, though what that sodden best might be like if put to the test she did not care to think. Mrs. Grigson, semidelirious, declared she knew him, but could not recall where she had met him.

They were having lunch under the big tree in the compound, she and Willis, the French maid being with Mrs. Grigson, when she suddenly saw Willis, looking over her shoulder in the direction of the river-bank which bounded the compound upon one side, go grey-green and a look of sheer maniacal terror appear in his eyes. She turned hastily to see what had so alarmed him, and found a tall man dressed in the white brass-badged ducks of the Government service standing just behind her chair. What was there in this man to have alarmed Willis? She could not understand it. She looked at Willis again, and saw that he had recovered his self-control; but that moment of self-betrayal had been unmistakable. Willis was scared to the bottom of his sodden soul by the appearance of the newcomer. Nevertheless, he pulled himself together manfully.

"Well, this is a surprise," he said.

"I don't know why it should be," said the stranger. "Did you think I had gone broody? By the way, what are you doing here?"

"I'm in the same boat as the rest of the party—stuck here and can't get out."

"Well, of course I believe you, but you had better not try that yarn on the Marines."

Willis said something in the native dialect. The stranger looked at him speculatively, but finally nodded his head, and the tension relaxed perceptibly.

"Is this all there is of the party?" asked the newcomer, running a keen grey eye over the compound.

"Mrs. Grigson's inside with the maid looking after her. She's pretty bad. Fever, y'know."

"No one else?"

"No, no one else. Not set eyes on anyone else."

"Hmm."

What the stranger was thinking was impossible to tell from his face, which was as impassive as a graven image, but Willis's twittery countenance registered relief in an unmistakable fashion. Whatever it was he had so greatly feared had evidently been successfully side-stepped. Nevertheless, he was too flustered to remember to make the necessary introductions, and he must have been badly flustered to forget that, for normally he had ceremonious manners, and the drunker he was the more elaborate they became.

The stranger turned upon the silent woman at the head of the table a prolonged and steady scrutiny that yet had nothing of discourtesy in it.

"I take it that you are Lady Piercy," he said. "My name is Lewis."

A snigger came from Willis, that stopped abruptly when the grey eyes turned in his direction. This man, thought Lady Piercy, was distinctly a force; his personality stood out from among the other men of that unwholesome coast like a great rock in a weary land. She must tell her husband of him. He was a man to watch and promote; one who could be relied on amid much that was neither very energetic nor very intelligent. The previous Governor had hung on long after his health had failed, and what with his lack of grip and the influence of African Tammany, things were not all they should be in that particular section of the Colonial service, and Sir Robert had been sent out to try and pull them together.

She made her new acquaintance welcome, wondering as she did so why Willis was grinning so broadly. The darky servants set before the newcomer food of a very different quality to that with which they had previously been supplied, and gathered round him chattering while he ate, evidently telling the news of the district to a master returned after absence. From the way in which he did his share in the babble of talk, she knew that he was intimately acquainted with the dialect, for the darkies were splitting their sides at his remarks, and only a man who knows a language very intimately can crack jokes in it.

When the babble died down, she began to make conversation, partly because she was exceedingly anxious for news, and partly because she wanted to learn some thing about this stranger whom Willis obviously knew and feared, and had equally obviously no intention of introducing.

She asked concerning the native disturbances. The stranger answered guardedly.

"I know that the trouble has started, but that is all I can tell you. Mr. Willis knows more about it than I do."

"I've told you all I know," said Willis sullenly. "Mr.—er—Lewis can confirm it if he has a mind to."

"Not knowing what you've told, but knowing the kind of tales you can tell, I'm not so sure of that," said the stranger bluntly. Willis, whose vanity was one of his many weaknesses, looked like murder.

"We were warned that travel was unsafe, and that we must wait here for further instructions," said Lady Piercy. "But so far nothing has come through."

"No, I don't suppose it has," said the stranger. Lady Piercy looked at him in perplexity. Willis looked daggers.

"Have you any news?" she asked.

"None. All the same, I am prepared to take you down to Okiki in my launch if you care to come."

"Look here—er—Lewis—" Willis interposed hastily. "You will stop behind. I'm not taking you," said the stranger grimly.

"But, look here, this is sheer murder!" cried Willis agitatedly.

"Well, and what if it is?"

Willis's hand dropped beneath the table, and in another second the two men were rolling together on the dusty ground. In a further second the stranger rose, in his hand a Colt automatic. He examined it, secured the safety-catch, and dropped it into his pocket.

"Got any fodder for her?" he inquired, and turned Willis over as if he had been a sack of potatoes. Putting a hand inside his shirt, he groped about and pulled out a heavy cartridge-belt, Willis yelping as it rasped his skin. Then, assisted by the stranger's boot, he scrambled to his feet and shambled away, looking savagely over his shoulder as he went.

"Well, that's that," said the stranger in a matter-of-fact voice. "Sorry to have disturbed your lunch, but that was a job that needed doing."

"Was he really going to shoot, do you think?" asked Lady Piercy.

"He was a fool to draw if he wasn't," was the reply. Lady Piercy began to feel that she was completely out of her depth; life in a Crown colony, as seen from Government House, had never given her a close-up of tropical human nature before. She had realised that this man was lawless and reckless, and yet she felt that he was perfectly straight and absolutely trustworthy. She was prepared, without the slightest uneasiness, to embark on his launch and accept his escort down African rivers and through African forests.

At his suggestion she went to see about the packing up of their possessions and camp gear. At the far side of the compound she found Willis reviving himself with arrack after his rough-and-tumble. She went up to him; drunk though he might be, he was her only source of information.

"Mr. Willis, who is this man Lewis?"

"Friend of your husband's. Friend of Grigson's too. Oh yes, very much friend of Grigson's. Very pleased to meet'm. No one he'd like to see better. Friend of yours, too, from what I can see. Always did make a hit with the ladies, white *or* black."

Lady Piercy turned away in disgust from his leer and went to prepare Mrs. Grigson for removal to the launch. Glancing over her shoulder as she entered the bungalow, she saw the man whom Willis had addressed as Lewis crossing the compound with a whalebone cutting-whip in his hand and stand talking to Willis, drawing the whip slowly through his hands like a butcher sharpening a knife as he did so. She saw Willis eyeing the whip apprehensively, and wondered what lawlessness was now afoot in Darkest Africa. As a matter of fact,

Cassalis was offering Willis his choice between the whip and an ant-heap unless he chose to answer certain questions that were about to be put to him. A man buried up to his neck in an ant-heap is not long in answering questions, even upon the sorest subjects.

But in so doing Cassalis made an error of judgment. When it came to a war of words, he was no match for Willis, for words were Willis's trade.

Willis was in that state between drunk and sober when he was at his best. Dead sober, he was a quivering mass of inferiority complexes; dead drunk, he wept a little and lapsed into unconsciousness; but neither drunk nor sober did his subtle tongue ever betray him. He summed up his man and set to work. Cassalis might be master in every quality of manhood, but he was no match for his subordinate in subtlety.

"Now look here, Lewis," he said in a low and confidential voice, "the situation is very much more complicated than you realize. I have been wanting to have a word alone with you, but haven't been able to get it." He appeared to have completely forgotten the hiding he had just received, which Cassalis attributed to his distinctly tanked condition. It was beyond his comprehension that any man, for any reason, would overlook a thrashing.

"Lewis," said Willis, dropping his voice yet lower till it sounded like the ghost of Hamlet's father, "do you realize what Ibrahim's game is?"

"I have my suspicions," said Cassalis, and waited for Willis to show his hand. Willis proceeded to produce that assorted selection of half-truths which is much more effectual than downright lying. Cassalis listened, and, knowing from his own observation that much of what he was being told was correct, gradually began to believe the rest.

"Ibrahim is very upset about your marriage. Very upset indeed, my dear fellow, and not without reason, either. That girl is a source of potential danger to all of us. I don't say she isn't a charming girl, and a good girl too, from what I can see of her, but she hasn't got the nerve for this game, my dear chap. She means well. I don't say she doesn't mean to be loyal to you, but she's a simple-minded girl, you know, and they've got hold of her and just turned her inside out. Naturally Ibrahim's upset. You can't blame him."

"I don't blame him," said Cassalis soberly. "I can quite understand his viewpoint; but what is to be done about it? What's his game that you are referring to?"

"His game is exceedingly simple. He wants to get rid of the girl, but he is afraid to murder her because of your reactions."

"Wise man," said Cassalis drily.

"So knowing our ginger-haired friend the police wallah was blessed with a roving eye, he bagged his old cow and planted her here, and sent your wife downstream by canoe to Okiki, where she'd land into Grigson's hands. I'm supposed to be keeping an eye on the females, but it's my private belief that I'm just as much a prisoner as they are, and if I tried to move I'd soon know it."

"Hmm," said Cassalis, and Willis, eyeing him sharply, could not tell whether he believed him or not, and so shut his mouth and left the next move to Cassalis.

"What exactly happened when Nina went to the hotel at Makalu?" Cassalis asked at length.

Willis moistened his lips. This was the very opening he wanted.

"She didn't exactly go to the hotel, my dear fellow. She just took a room there so that she could have somewhere to rest and have a wash in during your trial. There's no accommodation for ladies at the courthouse, y'know."

"Why did she go to your hotel?"

"I don't suppose she knew it was my hotel."

211

"Why did she leave?"

"Grigson marched her off. Put the wind up her properly, I fancy. She'd been reading the newspapers too, and they weren't exactly jam, as you can imagine. I did what I could with her, but she was pretty upset. I got her to come and see you in gaol because I wanted to put some heart into you so that you would put up a fight at the trial, but get her to court I couldn't. She just wouldn't face it. Then I think Grigson introduced her to Lady Piercy, and Lady Piercy took her up, and I haven't set eyes on her since. The last I heard was that she would be going home with the Grigsons when he goes on leave as soon as this tour is over, Grigson's interest in her being supposed to be fatherly. I should have thought Mrs. Grigson would have known better at her time of life, but apparently not."

Cassalis listened to all he had to say without comment, but this time Willis had a feeling that his shaft had gone home.

He loosed another, at a venture.

"I suppose you know she is going to have a kid?"

"No, I didn't. Is that why they are sending her home?"

"Yes, that's why. If I were you, I'd let her go quietly, Lewis. It's best for everybody. That's a situation you can't cope with, can you?"

"No, I certainly can't," said Cassalis, and turned and walked away.

Willis looked after him, praising the gods for that lucky shot. Why hadn't he thought of it before? It all fitted in so perfectly. He had been improvising as he went along, watching Cassalis' face for reactions and telling his story accordingly; feeling his way almost subconsciously into the other man's mind. He wondered whether Nina really were going to have a baby. It was always a possibility. If she did, he'd tell Cassalis that it had red hair and post-date its birthday a bit. Iago was getting his hand in nicely.

212

Cassalis walked to the river-bank and stood looking out over the slowly swirling water, seeing nothing. He had known some bitter moments in his life, but never anything like this. There was only one possible service he could do for Nina— stand aside and let the Piercys look after her, as they seemed disposed to. He discounted Willis's carefully thought-out story about Grigson and his roving eye, but he believed the story of Nina's child, for it was the thing he greatly feared, and had feared all along. He knew that he ought to give God thanks that she was in good hands and leave her there. But it was very bitter. Cassalis stood for a long time looking out over the water, but he could not see any other way out of it. Gradually his resolution crystallized. There was one thing at least he could do for Nina and her child—his child— stamp out the smouldering sparks of the native rising, get the women down to the coast in safety, and then leave the Piercys to look after Nina, as he saw they meant to. As for himself, he just didn't care. The only way to scotch the rising was to set the negroes and Arabs fighting among themselves; that meant the end of African Tammany. A white man on the run in the bush didn't last long, so perhaps hanging was as good an end as any.

Lady Piercy, doing everybody's packing, the French maid being a hopeless heap of tears and fears, glanced out through the fly-screens from time to time at the motionless figure of the man on the river-bank, and wondered what he was watching. When she had finished, and all was ready for the departure, she went out to him. He turned at her approach, and she stood and stared at him in amazement, so complete-ly had he changed from what he had been an hour before. For a moment she wondered whether it were the same man. The veiled truculence was gone, and he had the look of a man who has heard his death sentence. They exchanged a few words, the commonplaces of travel, and then she went back to Mrs. Grigson while he went to assemble the porters. Something had shattered the man, something Willis had told him, but what it was she had no means of knowing.

But she had no time for further speculation, for Mrs. Grigson had to be prepared for her removal to the launch. Lady Piercy wondered what accommodation would be available for the sick woman. To her surprise, when they got down to the river-bank she found that it was the launch in which they had already made their river journey, and that it was alongside the bank in knee-deep water and there was no occasion to use the dinghy. The darky engineer grinned sheepishly when he saw her, but his grin was entirely friendly. Of the other member of the crew, that amazing mongrel, there was nothing to be seen, but sounds from below indicated that he was aboard, even if he chose to keep out of sight.

The sick woman being comfortably installed in the cabin with the French maid, who felt safer under a roof, however stuffy, the man who had introduced himself as Lewis joined Lady Piercy under the awning in the bows. He had recovered his nerve by now, and was sphinx-like, but she had had a glimpse of what lay below that impassive exterior.

She tried to get him to talk about himself, but beyond admitting that he had been on the Coast for ten years without going home, she could extract nothing from him.

"How do you manage to keep so fit?" she asked.

"That is a thing I am often asked," he replied, and turned the subject on to her husband and his career.

Lady Piercy came of the ruling caste, born and bred to the taking of responsibility and the preserving of the amenities; but although she knew that the first duty of a Governor's wife is silence upon all Government affairs, she found herself being turned inside out like a glove by this stranger with his brusque yet persuasive manners. Herself the daughter of a diplomat, she put him down as the cleverest diplomatist she had ever met, and wondered how a man of his calibre came to be hiding his light under the bushel of the Colonial service. This was indeed a find to be reported to her husband with joy.

From probing, her new acquaintance turned to commenting, and Lady Piercy was kept busy making mental notes of the things she meant to tell her husband; for here was knowledge and judgment worth their weight in gold to the newly appointed Governor, who had hitherto had to depend on his predecessor's leavings, who had no desire to be speeded up or have the dust of ages disturbed in their vicinity. When, however, she tried to probe him on the subject of African Tammany, he shut up like a clam, save to vouchsafe the information that the real trouble lay with the Arab traders.

"But surely it is that man Cassalis who is at the bottom of it all?" she asked.

"Same thing," said her new acquaintance. " He's in with the Arabs. It's all one."

"But surely a white man—"

"Well, he's got to be in with somebody, hasn't he?" replied Lewis in his brusque manner. "You can't expect him to exist in a vacuum."

At that moment the French maid put her head out of the cabin and summoned Lady Piercy. She went in, and saw at once that Mrs. Grigson was in a state of collapse.

"Do you know anything about doctoring?" she called to Lewis.

"I know a fair bit about doctoring, provided I can lay my hands on the drugs, but this launch has been looted pretty thoroughly. Can I come in and have a look at the patient?"

He bowed his tall height to the low doorway. Lady Piercy thought she had never felt so relieved in her life as she did when she saw her new friend take the pulse as if he knew what he was about.

"Heart's giving out. This is nasty unless we can get some stimulants."

He called Ngumba and spoke to him in his own language. Ngumba grinned broadly and began to dismantle the opposite bunk, pulled out a panel from the back, put his arm down between the panelling and the shell of the boat, and began to draw forth and hand out a most amazing collection of oddments.

"Good Lord, so that's where the loot went!" exclaimed Lewis. "Why ever couldn't he say so before?"

Whatever was in it had apparently to come out in the reverse order to that in which it had been inserted, and the first to appear was a quantity of books. The man Lewis surveyed them with evident pleasure, and began to arrange them on the little shelf over the bunk as the negro handed them out.

"That looks a bit more furnished," he said with satisfaction as the shelf filled up.

Then came maps, binoculars, an aneroid, a prismatic compass, revolvers and ammunition, note-paper, shoe polish, sealed tins of cigarettes; all manner of things that might have tempted the light-fingered in the absence of the owner of the launch, all being produced from the secret hiding-place and laid before the stranger by the grinning negro. Lady Piercy knew that this launch had originally belonged to the notorious Cassalis. To whom, then, did all this stuff belong?

Then from out the depths began to appear gear of another nature—a woman's silk stockings, her brush and comb, a pot of face-cream—all the things that a dainty woman uses in her toilet. Lady Piercy stared at the stranger as the darky dumped them one after the other into his lap, and saw that he was holding them and looking at them as if he were holding a dead child. Then, at last, medical and surgical requisites began to appear, such needful things as travellers in wild lands must carry and on which life often depends, and they all breathed a sigh of relief as they saw the brandy and the camphor and quinine handed out. Then the man got down to his doctoring and Lady Piercy watched the sick woman's lips gradually change from mauve to pink. He evidently knew how to deal with fever.

By next morning Mrs. Grigson, though almost too weak to lift her head, was in her right mind; and in the cool of the evening Lewis lifted her and her bedding and carried her out bodily to lie on the cushioned lockers of the cockpit and enjoy the breeze.

But not for long. Hardly had he got her settled when Ngumba appeared with his happy darky grin to announce that they were down to their last drop of petrol. Unsupervised by the white man, it had never occurred to him to refuel.

Lewis rose and let fly in dialect till he saw by Mrs. Grigson's scandalized face that she understood what he was saying. Then he restrained himself, and merely bid the irrepressible Ngumba to get out the sweeps and exert himself. Then, and then only, did Ngumba appear disconcerted.

"It doesn't really matter," Lewis explained to the women. "We can drop down with the current, and these two fools can sit up all night and keep her off the sand banks with the sweeps. It merely means we shall take longer over the trip."

"But suppose there is trouble with the natives?" asked Mrs. Grigson.

"I can cope with that," said Lewis curtly.

"Can you say that for certain?" asked the policeman's wife.

"Yes," said he.

"Then you can say more than anyone else on the Coast," said she.

He did not answer.

217

They drifted tranquilly down with the slow current. In the complete stillness now that the engine was silent they heard the voice of the forest all around them like the murmur of a city.

Mrs. Grigson broke the silence. "Where is Mr. Willis?" she asked.

Lady Piercy looked at Lewis, but he did not choose to reply.

"Mr. Lewis was not willing that he should come on the launch, so he had to stop behind."

Mrs. Grigson sat up on her pillows.

"Good heavens!" she exclaimed. "Do you want to murder the man?"

"Yes," said Lewis, and there was something in his voice that told them that what he said could be taken literally.

Mrs. Grigson eyed him sternly. "I cannot say I like the man," she said, "but all the same, he is a white man."

"That does not cut any ice with me," said Lewis.

"Then it should."

"Sorry, but it doesn't."

Mrs. Grigson glared at him. "Do you mean to say that you deliberately left that man behind to perish?"

"I did."

"You deserve to be hanged."

"I shall be, when we get to Okiki."

They stared at him, knowing once again by his voice that he was not jesting.

They all sat for a time in silence, and the rapid tropic dusk came down around them till they could no longer see each other's faces.

Once again Mrs. Grigson broke the silence.

"Do you know, I believe I can place Mr. Willis. It has just occurred to me who he is. I haven't seen him before, I have only had him described to me. He is the man my husband had to rescue Nina from, at that horrible hotel, when he tried to run off with her."

From out of the darkness at the bows came a man's voice:

"Perhaps now you realize why I left Willis behind?"

"I am afraid I don't," said Mrs. Grigson. "Unless, of course, you have some connection with Mrs. Cassalis."

"She is my wife."

"Good God, are you Cassalis?"

"I am."

"Then—then what are you doing with us?"

"What I told you, neither more nor less—taking you down to Okiki."

"Why?"

"Because, although I don't care much about white men, I am not minded that white women should fall into the hands of certain of my late friends. Moreover, Lady Piercy has been very kind to my wife, and I am hoping that—after I have met your husband, Mrs. Grigson, she will continue to be kind to her, for there is nothing I shall be able to do for her."

"You know there is a warrant out for you?"

"Yes, I know that. I am coming in to meet it. African Tammany is finished."

"It is a warrant on a capital charge, Mr.—Cassalis."

"That is its one redeeming feature."

They heard him brush past them in the dark and climb up to the conning-tower on the roof of the cabin, the only place in the launch where anyone could be alone.

"What do you make of that?" whispered Mrs. Grigson to Lady Piercy.

"I knew there was something funny about him, but I never suspected this."

"Do you think he is really taking us down to Okiki?"

"Yes, I am certain he is."

"He is going down to be hanged, you know. It is rather awful, isn't it? He has been so good to us."

"And I had been thinking that he was exactly the man my husband wanted, and how awfully useful he would be."

"I know. My husband always said that if Cassalis would only run straight there would be no one to touch him."

"Can't he be given a chance, don't you think?"

"A man can't be given a chance when he is wanted for murder."

"Do you think he has really done a murder?"

"Oh, my dear Lady Piercy, he does one every day of his life. He's a most ruthless scoundrel, he is really. We mustn't get soft about him."

Suddenly a vivid beam of light cut the darkness, and round a bend came the Government launch, its headlight illuminating the river for a couple of hundred yards. Cassalis, upon the roof, banged a bell; Ngumba ran forward with a boat-hook, and as the slow current brought them alongside, laid hold of the launch's gunnel and drew the two boats together.

"What boat is that?" hailed a voice from the Government launch. There was no reply from the roof, so Lady Piercy hailed back, and in another moment her husband dropped into the cockpit and took her in his arms, to be followed by the ginger-haired policeman in quest of his own wife.

Everyone was too agitated by the reunion to ask or answer any questions. Ngumba, in reply to Grigson, who spoke his language, explained that they had run out of petrol. A couple of cans were handed over from the Government craft, and the launch set out to follow her heavier consort down-stream. For some reason best known to themselves, neither of the two women revealed their knowledge of the presence of Cassalis.

But presently Grigson, sitting beside his wife in the shadowy cockpit, heard his name being spoken.

"Is that you, Grigson?" came a voice from the darkness. "I have heard you have been asking for me."

"Have I? Who are you?"

"Don't you know?"

"Can't say I do, though your voice is familiar."

Someone came into the cockpit and sat down beside him.

"I'll go quietly as long as you don't try to handcuff me, but you'll never get the handcuffs on me alive again, Grigson."

"Good Lord, who are you?"

"It's Mr. Cassalis, Jim," said Mrs. Grigson quietly, "and we owe our lives to him."

"Cassalis, is it? Have you come in to give yourself up?"

"I have."

"Why have you done that?"

Cassalis did not answer.

"I think I know," said Lady Piercy in a low voice in her husband's ear.

"It's all very well to say you won't submit to be handcuffed, Cassalis, but I am afraid that with your record we can't give you the choice. You've broken gaol once, you know."

"I happen to be armed, Grigson."

"So am I."

"Yes, but I've got you covered, and you have still to draw, and if you make any motion towards your hip pocket, I'll plug you."

"You haven't the slightest chance of getting away."

"I know I haven't, but you haven't the slightest chance of surviving."

Lady Piercy's voice came out of the dusk. "If Mr. Cassalis has come in voluntarily to give himself up, surely we can take his parole?"

Grigson, whose temper had suffered from the African climate though his integrity remained unimpeachable, snarled something about standing orders.

"I will take the responsibility of accepting Cassalis's parole, if he will give it to me," said Sir Robert.

"Right you are, sir. I'll play no tricks with you," came the voice of the man whose face they could not see.

"Tell me, Cassalis," said Sir Robert, "why have you come in like this to give yourself up?"

"African Tammany is finished."

"How do you know?"

"Because I have been engaged in the salubrious occupation of kicking the bottom out of it."

"Why have you done that?"

"Tired of it."

Sir Robert was perplexed. He knew there was more in Cassalis's surrender than met the eye, and his first thought was to suspect a trick, knowing Cassalis's tricky reputation, yet there was a curious feel about the man, as of one who has abandoned hope, that made him wonder what lay behind it all.

Lady Piercy broke the silence.

"Is it because of your wife that you have kicked the bottom out of African Tammany?"

"Yes, it is not a practical proposition with her on my hands."

"And is it for the same reason that you have given yourself up?"

"Yes, something has got to be done about her. She is going to have a child."

There was a dead silence as the realization dawned upon them of the sacrifice Cassalis was making, and his reason for making it.

It was Cassalis who broke the painful silence. "Do you

222

know where Nina is now?"

"She is at the Waigonda mission station," said Sir Robert.

"Are you sure?"

"Well, we left her there the day before yesterday, to wait for the mission launch to take her out."

"Did you leave a guard with her?"

"No, it did not appear to be necessary, everything was quiet in that district. If the mission launch has not called by the time we return, we shall pick her up ourselves."

"We shall be dashed lucky if we find her there."

"Why shouldn't we find her there?"

"Perhaps I know my friends a bit better than you do."

"What do you fear for your wife, Cassalis?"

"Well, you can't expect Sheik Ibrahim exactly to welcome my kicking the bottom out of African Tammany, and he's spotted the reason for my doings, same as Lady Piercy. He'll either use Nina as a hostage or knock her on the head. I don't know which."

"What are you planning to do in the matter? You've got something up your sleeve, I take it."

"I am planning to put you wise to Ibrahim's run-ways and lay-ups in the hope that you will be able to snaffle her out of his hands."

"And then—what about yourself? You realize we've got a warrant out for you, don't you?"

"I'd be pretty dim in the intellect if I didn't. Yes, I know all about that, but it can't be helped. I'll have to face the music. I've had a pretty good run for my money. I'll take an early morning walk without repining. But, you see, I can't possibly drag Nina round in my wake any longer. It's a perfectly hopeless proposition, quite apart from whatever Willis and Ibrahim are playing at. You've been very kind to her, Lady Piercy, and I'm hoping that you'll go on being kind to

223

her."

There was dead silence in the darkness at the bows of the launch save for the murmur of the water under the forefoot. Even the case-hardened Grigson was taken aback at this confession. It was a grim thing to sit thus quietly in the company of the man who was giving himself up to be hanged for the sake of the girl he loved and could not protect.

It was Lady Piercy who spoke first, though her voice was not under control.

"I will do everything I can for Nina, you may rest assured of that, Mr. Cassalis."

"Well, I'm dashed sorry about it, Cassalis, but we can't do anything," said Grigson. "Things have got to take their course."

"I know you can't," said Cassalis. "There's nothing I'm expecting you to do, save not to handcuff me. I'll kill you if you try to do that."

"We've got your parole, Cassalis," said Sir Robert. "There is no question of handcuffing."

"All right, I'll accept your assurance. Perhaps I had better hand over my gun. Grigson and I have both got West African tempers."

He passed it across, but in the dark the heavy holster landed in Lady Piercy's lap, not the policeman's.

CHAPTER XV

THE launch ahead of them heaved-to, and as they drew alongside, her skipper hailed Sir Robert to say that they were reaching the maze of islands, and he did not propose to try and follow that tricky channel in the dark, but would tie up till the morning.

"No need to," said Cassalis, to the Governor. "I'll pilot him through."

Grigson pressed his foot on the toe of Sir Robert's boot.

"What's the hurry?" he asked.

"Well, Grigson, if your wife were in the hands of Ibrahim, and you knew as much about Ibrahim as I do, you might think speed was indicated. But being as it is, I can quite understand your liking for a quiet night's sleep, though at the same time I think you might see my point of view. You have my parole, and you have my gun, so what more you want I don't quite know, but if you'll indicate it I'll let you have it."

"That is all right, Cassalis," came Sir Robert's voice. "I shall be just as glad as you are to press on. Perhaps you will cox your boat and give my craft a lead through."

"Right-o, I'll get up on to the roof and take the wheel. Anyone coming to keep an eye on me?"

"Yes. I'd like to come," said Sir Robert. "Not to keep an eye on you, but because I want to talk to you."

Up on the roof in the brilliant tropical moonlight that made the headlight unnecessary, Sir Robert watched Cassalis taking his fast craft lickety-split through the winding channel in and out among the maze of islands.

Watching him as he stood at the wheel, upright, sinewy tense, he was struck, as his wife had been, by the contrast between Cassalis and the general run of Coasters, and, as she had done, asked him the secret of his health.

And Cassalis told him. For the first time a man not in the inner circle of African Tammany learnt the secret of that eyrie, and the way through the cave that led to it. And Cassalis went on to tell him the carefully guarded secret of the wells in the desert, hundreds of feet deep and lined with camel-bones; marked by no landmark save the secret bearings taken by bringing the Pole Star on to a certain notch in a certain peak. There were no bones by the wayside to mark the trail, for any camel that fell was buried and the drifting sand and the wind did the rest. Sir Robert knew that the keys of the Coast were being put into his hands, and even if they hanged this man they could still clean up African Tammany.

A hail from the Government launch requested them to modify their speed, as the bigger boat could not manoeuvre as easily as the launch in the sharp bends of the channel. Cassalis swore.

"Why are you in such a desperate hurry, Cassalis? What is it you fear?" asked Sir Robert.

"I suppose you know we are in a dashed tight corner? The tribes are up."

"How do you know?"

"Because, damn fool that I was, I raised them." And he told the Governor of the eating of the fatal thirteenth yam. Then, as they travelled down the moonlit river hour after hour, the two men talked together, Cassalis's tongue unloosed by the shadow of the gallows; and the man born to the high places of the world learnt something about the point of view

226

of an outcast that stood him in good stead for the rest of his service.

At dawn Cassalis handed over the wheel to Ngumba. "Well, I think I've done my bit," he said. "Either we're ahead of the news, or we aren't. If we are, we shall get through, and if we aren't, we shan't, and that's that. I'm for a spell of shut-eye."

He went below, but Sir Robert remained in the little conning-tower watching the river unfold in the dawn. That the need for haste was no put-up job was proved by the fact that Ngumba had repeatedly to be admonished from the Government launch to slacken his speed to the pace of his consort.

Then, while they were all at breakfast on the larger craft, that which they had feared came upon them. A yell from Ngumba and a frantic banging on the bell warned them; the skipper of the launch reversed his engines, and put his helm down hard, and succeeded in converting a head-on collision into a glancing blow as they rounded the bend and found the channel completely blocked by a big raft of tree-trunks securely moored in mid-stream.

"Now we're for it," said Cassalis. "Sit down, Grigson. If you give the order to use those machine-guns you'll never see your happy home again. Run her into the bank and put me ashore and let me talk to them. It's the only chance we've got. If it's niggers only, it will come off, but if it's Arabs it won't."

"How do we know you won't disappear into the bush?" said Grigson.

"You don't know, you'll have to chance it," said Cassalis placidly. "I'd be glad if you'd let me have my gun back."

"No, no, my lad, that's a bit too steep."

"Look here, let me have my gun with one cartridge, that's all I want. But I'm not going ashore without it, I'm not really. I'll stop here with you, and we'll all die in comfort. If you

227

think I'm going to be taken alive by my late pals, you're damn' well mistaken. I don't stick at much, but I stick at that."

"Give him his gun, Grigson," said Sir Robert, and Grigson rather sullenly handed it over. This was not playing the game according to the rules as he understood them; Cassalis, having broken gaol once, ought to have been brought in in irons.

Much against his better judgment, the skipper brought the shallow-draft river gunboat into the bank and Cassalis jumped ashore before they could run out the gang-plank, lithe and active as a cat for all his size. He gave a curious wailing cry and was answered from the forest; then he disappeared among the trees.

Time went by, and Grigson sniffed portentously, and even Sir Robert began to think that their prisoner had shown a clean pair of heels, when with a sudden thud he dropped on the deck in their midst, the carefully posted sentries with their rifles never having set eyes on him.

"Sorry to have been so long," he said, "but you know what these palavers are. I think I've got things fixed with this little lot, at any rate, but they are only the local yokels. The gathering of the clans is further down the river, at the forks. I've sent off a runner to tell them to get the fathers of families together, and make the lads of the village keep quiet till I can talk to them. He'll cut across the bend and be there some time before us."

"Isn't that a risk?" said Grigson. "Surely our best chance is to make a dash for it."

"Well, of course, it isn't my launch any longer, it's Government property; and, anyway, where I'm going I don't suppose there will be enough water to float it, so if you like making a dash into tree-trunks, why, do it by all means, but I don't advise it—not from the health point of view, anyway."

Grigson looked daggers. But a man who is due to be

hanged can commit contempt of court and assault the police with impunity, for nothing can be added to his sentence.

"Did you pick up any news?" said Sir Robert, anxious to turn the conversation and stop Cassalis and Grigson from bickering. Tempers are short in tropical countries, and both parties might forget their manners if allowed to work themselves up.

"Nothing I didn't know," said Cassalis shortly. "Save that Ibrahim has got Nina."

"Good God! How did he get her?"

"Picked her up from the mission station as soon as your back was turned. By the way, they've knocked the padre on the head. At least, I hope they have."

"Mr. Cassalis, don't talk like that, please, I beg of you," said Lady Piercy, fearing ructions.

"I beg your pardon, Lady Piercy. I wasn't being nasty, I wasn't really. Being knocked on the head is the thing you pray for in these parts if you fall into the hands of the enemy."

"What do you suppose will—will happen to Nina?"

"Goodness only knows; I don't. I don't know what Ibrahim is driving at in that matter. There is some motive at the bottom of it, that is all I can tell you; but what it is I know no more than you do."

A party of negroes, waving an isabella-coloured shirt-tail on a bit of stick, came down to the bank and began to shift the boom under the protection of this nominal white flag, and the two launches slipped through the gap. Cassalis's craft had the heels of the Government launch and, despite Grigson's protests, left it behind. Lady Piercy watched with secret amusement the way their prisoner was running the show. The only person who ever seemed to remember that he was a prisoner was Grigson, and even he only remembered spasmodically. But as Cassalis merely waxed sarcastic when the police officer tried to assert his authority, his captivity was a convention that was honoured more in the breach than the observance. There was nothing to be done but await the issue of the palaver at the forks. Cassalis was driving the launch in a way that made speech impossible. Her bows were out of the water and she was roaring and shuddering like a pneumatic drill.

"Good Lord, this is a speed-boat!" said Grigson as the wash spread out in a wave that swamped the banks. "No wonder we could never catch the fellow."

Sir Robert, realizing more and more the resources at the disposal of Cassalis, wondered yet further at his surrender. When they arrived at the forks they found they were expected, and the banks were crowded with negroes.

"Let us lay out our plan of campaign," said Cassalis. "Grigson, you had better stop at home and mind the baby; you aren't *persona grata* with my late pals. You've run us in too often. Now, Sir Robert, are you game to come ashore with me and face the pow-wow? I admit there's a risk, but it's our only chance."

"I don't speak the local dialect, Cassalis; I only speak Arabic. But I'll gladly come with you if I can be of any use. What policy shall we pursue? General amnesty, if they go home quietly and refrain from looting? Except, of course, for the folk who were concerned in the attack on the padre, if that proves to be true."

"No, general amnesty won't do it now their blood is up. The young warriors won't go home without blooding their spears. What I propose to do is to set the blacks and the Arabs at each other's throats, then they'll clean up African Tammany for you automatically. It won't take much doing; the blacks have had a lot to put up with."

"I can't countenance that officially, you know, Cassalis."

"It's our only chance. And, by gum, I'm going to do it! Just you look the other way. African Tammany's going to get

230

cleaned up good and proper. It's long overdue for it. It's a dirty game, and I don't mind admitting it."

"Then why do you go in for it?"

"What else can I go in for? I've lost my place in the queue. I tried to turn honest and run a copper-mine under your predecessor, but he wasn't having any."

"We are tied hand and foot by red tape, Cassalis. We would like to be a lot more human than we are, but it would cost us our careers. But in any case I forbid you to carry out your suggestion, which is a most improper one, and I place you under close arrest."

Cassalis turned a bewildered face towards him.

Sir Robert unstrapped from his waist his cartridge belt and holster. "I suggest you go and have a wash. Here's a cake of soap for you." And he handed Cassalis the belt.

"Oh, ta!" said Cassalis. "Lavender's my favourite scent." And he took the belt and vanished into the cabin. The darky steward came in to ask if he should serve tea, or would they wait till the master returned? Sir Robert looked at the police-officer, and the police-officer looked at Sir Robert.

"No, I don't think we'll wait tea for Mr. Cassalis," said His Excellency the Governor.

He had hardly spoken when baying pandemonium broke out among the crowd on the bank. They surged backwards and forwards and then disappeared with a rush among the trees, and rifles began to speak.

"That's my revolver," said Sir Robert as a sharp, high crack rang out among the deeper notes of the trade guns. "He wasn't far out when he said it wouldn't take much to start trouble between the blacks and the Arabs. It's not taken him much more than ten minutes."

"It would not take Cassalis much more than ten minutes to start a war in heaven," said Grigson. "What do you pro-pose to do, sir? Wait a bit, and see if he honours his parole?"

"No, I propose to abandon him to his fate. In spite of being under strict arrest, he has once more broken prison. I have not the slightest doubt that he is already dead."

"Oh, Robert, do you really think so?" exclaimed Lady Piercy.

He patted her hand. "My dear, what I tell Grigson officially is one thing, and what I tell you privately might be another, since you are a woman of discretion; but I am not telling you now, as Grigson mightn't want to hear."

Grigson rubbed his nose. "I've hunted Cassalis up and down the Coast for years, and if there was one thing I wanted more than another to round off my service, it was his scalp. But when you see the scalp *in situ*, with hair growing on it, it is a different matter. Can't say I'm sorry to be cheated of my prey. The fellow has guts, and the fellow has brains, which is more than can be said for most of the local residents. What a first-class chap he'd have made if we'd recruited him for the police before he got mixed up with Ibrahim!"

"I doubt it," said Sir Robert. "There would always have been trouble over discipline. You would never have got the fellow broken in. It took Nina to do that."

The sound of shooting was moving further off through the forest; whoever was being shot at had evidently bolted.

"No good hanging about any longer," said Sir Robert. "We will go on down to the mission station and try and find out what has happened there. We have seen the last of Cassalis, for good or bad."

The sound of firing was dying away in the distance as they rounded the next bend and bore down upon the mission station. As they drew into the jetty they saw that the rumour was true, the mission station had been sacked and burnt; the tin church and the ramshackle bungalow stood roofless with blackened walls. Not a living thing was in sight. Sir Robert and Grigson went ashore and walked about among the ruins. Turning over the ash here and there, they found bits of white bone that crumbled at the touch.

"Poor devil," said Grigson. "He was a damn' nuisance, but he died for his faith all right." They removed their helmets and stood silently for a moment.

"Nothing left to bury," said the police-officer, replacing his helmet hastily as the heat struck at his skull.

"No, nothing. No use risking our necks for the sake of the dead. Cassalis has given us breathing-space. We had better get the women out and then come back and tackle this."

Grigson nodded, and they turned away; but as they turned they heard a faint moaning, wailing noise that seemed to come from underground. Grigson thrust aside a fallen beam, revealing the dark mouth of what had been cellar-steps. Cautiously they ventured down, striking matches for light. At the foot of the steps lay what looked like a bundle of dirty bedding. They raised it, and the ash-coloured face and rolling eyes of the black housekeeper appeared among the rags. Between them they carried her to the top of the steps, and sent the native orderly for a stretcher.

But by the time the stretcher arrived the old dame was on her feet. She had taken refuge in the cellar, which was also the padre's store-room, at the first alarm, and had been living on tinned milk, neat lime-juice, and all manner of luxuries ever since. She was exhausted and frightened, but uninjured.

From her they learnt the history of the raid. Ibrahim had apparently turned up in person when he learnt that his plans had miscarried, and had had a long and acrimonious wrangle with the padre, bluffing and threatening, and generally trying to drive a bargain with him, but all to no purpose. Then, failing to come to an understanding, Ibrahim had shot the padre through the head at point-blank range, hunted down and shot all the niggers about the place, mas-

233

sacred the native hamlet that had grown up around the mission, leaving no single soul alive, and finally had set fire to the mission buildings and thrown the bodies into the flames. The old dame in the cellar had made up her mind that her end had come, but fire burns upwards, and, though her exit was blocked by fallen beams, she was unscathed.

"What became of Mrs. Cassalis? Did they kill her or take her away with them?" asked Sir Robert.

"She no killed. She gone away day before with mission boat."

"Now what do you make of that?" said Sir Robert to the policeman.

"Funny. The blacks up the river thought Ibrahim had got her. What made them think that?"

"Do you suppose Ibrahim wants Cassalis to think he's got her, and started the rumour himself, and tried to get the padre to keep his mouth shut, and the padre wouldn't, so he shot him out of hand, killed everybody who could possibly know Nina had got away, and is now trying to bluff Cassalis, using Nina as a hostage?"

"Looks like it, doesn't it?" said Grigson. "And there's Cassalis chasing all over Africa after her, and she's safely at the district headquarters of the mission."

"Where is that?"

"Makalu, just behind the court house. We can ring through and see if she is all right as soon as we get to Okiki. Then we can tell Cassalis's nigger engineer to get word through to his boss. He'll know how to do that, all right."

They travelled through the night to Okiki, and at dawn tied up beside the stone quay where Nina had first set foot in Africa, and from which she had started out with Cassalis upon the journey that had led by strange paths of love and danger.

Grigson went to the Custom House, where Harold Mor-

234

ley had worked, and phoned Willis's office in Makalu for news of Nina, to learn that she had indeed arrived there safely, but had boarded the *Biafra* and was now on her way to England.

He reported to Sir Robert. Sir Robert whistled. "Lord," he said, "this will be a blow to Cassalis! Wonder how he'll take it! If he swings round and goes right back to African Tammany, we'll have our hands full." Then, the launches being refuelled, they took advantage of the fair weather to run up the coast to their headquarters.

CHAPTER XVI

CASSALIS had no very clear-cut plan in his mind as he jumped ashore among the negroes crowding the river bank, for he had no certain knowledge where the truth lay.

He was quite used to being lied to, however, for there is no honour among thieves, and was expert at assessing the amount of truth in the varying versions of his alleged friends. He reckoned Ngumba generally told the truth as far as he knew it, but how much did he know? Ngumba's intelligence had its limits. Willis, on the other hand, invariably lied all round the map—he just couldn't help it, it was his nature. It was only in matters of law that, by a curious kink in his character, he was unimpeachable; in matters of fact he was hopeless, being imbued with the idea that everything he said would be used as evidence against him. Ibrahim's word was his bond, but he was constitutionally suspicious and secretive, and Cassalis had had several very narrow squeaks from being kept in the dark by his partner. Forgetting his own share in developing African Tammany, Cassalis cursed his luck at having to do business with rascals; he thought bitterly of what it would be like to have men like Sir Robert Piercy to deal with, and what could be made of life under such conditions.

He looked hastily around among the crowd in front of him, not daring to advance from the river-bank till he had found a guard for his back. That was another drawback to having to do business with rascals—one always had to be on one's guard, a knife in the back or a shot in the dark being normal social intercourse. To his relief he saw first one and then another of the men who had hunted with him or fought beside him. He hailed them by name with jovial greetings, and the negroes, easily distracted as children, forgot all the poison that had been poured into their ears and only remembered that he was the great white chief and their hero. Grins grew wider and wider as they were reminded of various exploits in which they had distinguished themselves. Cassalis shook hands with a chief—a high honour, for he was chary of giving his hand, knowing the vital importance of prestige. Seeing him in this expansive mood, all his admirers pushed forward for the privilege of taking that rarely given hand, and in a moment Cassalis was surrounded by a pushing, shoving crowd of fans, and the chance of a knife in the back was over. Had Ibrahim come down to the bank in person and tackled his seceding lieutenant the moment he appeared, it might have been a different story, but Ibrahim's constitutional caution over-reached itself this time, and the white man's nerve carried the day. When Cassalis arrived at the stockaded village that was Ibrahim's temporary headquarters, it was at the head of a procession of hero-worshippers.

Cassalis, seeing that stockade, and knowing who was inside, sat down on a tree-trunk and sent a youth in to invite Ibrahim to the parley. The youth returned with a message from Ibrahim inviting Cassalis to the parley.

Cassalis turned to two or three young bucks standing beside him, upon whom he had already bestowed most flattering attention, and said in a loud voice:

"Since when did the Arabs own Africa? Who is he that he sends for me thus? Are we his dogs to be ordered about? There has been enough of this foolishness. He is not master here. We meet as equals or enemies."

A delighted murmur greeted these sentiments, for the ne-groes were heartily tired of being bullied and bossed by the slave-driving Arabs, and only needed leadership to turn on them.

"Shall we fetch him out for you, O great one?" cried a buck, eagerly fomenting the discord.

"Yes, fetch him out, why not?" cried Cassalis. "Shall he and his handful lord it over us? I am weary of him. Fetch him out and we will beat him."

A howl of delight and a concerted rush answered him. Taken completely by surprise, for an open breach at this mo-ment was the last thing they had expected, Ibrahim's body-guard could not get the gates of the stockade shut in time, and the yelling mob poured into the enclosure and began to shoot up the huts. Cassalis, knowing that Ibrahim always had a bolt-hole, left his friends to get on with the riot and made his way round to that side of the village that gave upon the forest. He had a pretty shrewd notion who would be the first through the bolt-hole.

He had not long to wait, and it was even as he expected. A baulk of timber that looked no different from the others slipped from its place, and Yussuf ben Ibrahim popped through the gap like a rabbit and bolted for the bush. Cas-salis yelled to him to stand, and put a shot through his fez. Yussuf threw up his arms and slid to a standstill. He knew Cassalis's shooting of old.

Cassalis walked up to him and poked the barrel of Sir Robert's revolver into his ear.

"Hostage for hostage," said he. "There is war between us, Yussuf ben Ibrahim. The blood-bond has been broken. Thy father shall account to me for my wife's blood, or I will spill thine."

As he spoke, Ibrahim and two of his headmen came through the gap in the stockade. There was no need for

238

explanation; the revolver in Yussuf's ear told them all they needed.

"Thou hast my son," said Ibrahim, with unruffled dignity. The tables had been turned on him with a vengeance, but he was a good loser.

"Yea, as thou sayest, I have thy son," said Cassalis. "But there are between us many years of comradeship, and I would not bereave thee lightly. When I have my wife, thou shalt have thy son."

Ibrahim considered him astutely. He knew his man. That Cassalis, if cornered, would shoot all and sundry and then himself there was no question. What was left after a head-on collision would hardly be worth burying. But white men invariably lacked subtlety, and a man with a new wife was very vulnerable. Perchance guile could do what force could not. Ibrahim folded his hands in his wide sleeves and prepared to revise his plans and parley.

"It is not in my power to give thee thy wife," he said, "for she has passed out of my hands."

"Then where is she?"

"She has gone to her own people."

"How do you know?"

"Because I sent her. She was willing to go, and it was well that she should go. She has made trouble between us, that were friends. She said to me: 'Spare my life, and I will trouble you no more. I go back to my own people, for there is a child to come.' Like all women, she puts the child before the man. I spared her, for the child was thine. She goes home in the care of the wife of the policeman. It is finished with her, my son. I, who have been a father to thee, tell thee that it is finished. She is afraid, and she goes home to her people."

Cassalis lowered the revolver from Yussuf's ear and stood looking at him. What he had said confirmed Willis's statement, and if Nina were indeed going to have a child, the only possible thing she could do was to go home to her people. It was not in his power to do anything for her.

Ibrahim spoke again. "My son, let us clasp hands and be friends again. There is more profit to be made at this moment than at any time since I have been upon the Coast. Let that which has been be forgotten."

Cassalis slowly slid the revolver back into its holster. "I will gladly clasp hands with thee, Father Ibrahim, for the sake of all that has been between us these many years, and I thank thee for sparing my wife and—my child; but remain with thee I cannot, for I have given my word to the white men that I will return, and it was in faith of my word that they let me come."

Ibrahim raised his eyebrows. "They will hang thee, my son. Such is their fixed intention."

"Yea, I know that. I return to be hanged."

"This is madness."

"Yea, I am mad. It is well that I be hanged." Cassalis turned on his heel and walked away, careless of a shot from behind, leaving them standing with their mouths open staring after him.

"Praise be to Allah!" said Yussuf under his breath. But his father heard him.

"Thou fool," he said savagely, "I would he had shot thee!" For he knew what was lost on the dull-witted Yussuf.

Cassalis, arrived at the river-bank, was amazed to find that the launches had gone. He addled his brains as to the reason for their departure, but failed to discover it. It never entered his head that he had been given the chance to jump his parole and do a get-away.

The feud that had been started between the blacks and the Arabs could be trusted to take care of itself. Authority could carry out the classic precept: divide and rule. Since Nina had got safely down to the coast, there was no point

240

in his hanging about in the bush. It was only prolonging the agony. He would surrender to his parole and get it over. The one thing he was anxious about was the disposal of his affairs so that Nina should be provided for. There would be no difficulty about this. Once he had surrendered to justice every facility would be given him; whereas, if he got knocked on the head in the bush, Willis would have a free hand, and if Nina got her fare home she would be lucky. No, his number was up. He could not maintain himself in the bush now that he had disorganized African Tammany, so he might just as well meet his fate in such a way that Nina would get the benefit. Knowing it was useless to try and find rowers while such a glorious fight was going on, he commandeered a canoe and dropped down the sluggish stream with the current, anxious to put as much distance as possible between himself and the scene of the trouble before any one had time to start asking awkward questions. Then he could rally his reserves and finish off what had been so well begun.

CHAPTER XVII

THE mission launch that picked Nina up at Waigonda deposited her at the district headquarters of the mission at Makalu; as she possessed nothing but what she stood up in, the two lady missionaries, who ran the training school for coloured girls, equipped her with a brush and comb and underwear such as were issued to their charges. They knew her story, as did all the Coast, and were sorry for her until they discovered that she had been fond of her bandit husband. They had thought at first that she might, out of gratitude and to earn her daily bread, lend a hand with the mission work, but as soon as they realized that Nina had loved Cassalis they decided that she was unsuitable and ceased their efforts to draw her in. What to do with her became a problem. Exhausted by recurring bouts of fever and the strain she had undergone, Nina was apathetic. One thing and one thing only she knew: she would cling to Africa while the slightest chance of Cassalis's survival remained. The mission ladies asked for the address of her parents in order that they might get in touch with them and make arrangements for her return. Nina refused to give it, and relations became strained.

The mission's supporters had subscribed money for the saving of black souls, not for the support of stubborn white girls who wouldn't face facts; yet they could hardly turn Nina out and strand her among the beachcombers. Finally they agreed to let her stop on until it was known for certain whether Cassalis was alive or dead.

This agreement had been reached, and the dragging days were going by one after the other, enlivened only by rumours of the native disturbances, in which the monkey Messiah was variously reported to be Cassalis, Ibrahim, and the genuine article, when the native girl whose turn it was to act as parlourmaid announced a caller for Mrs. Cassalis.

Nina went to the parlour, her heart beating in her throat, wondering if her visitor would prove to be Lewis, to find there the cadaverous Willis, looking more unpleasant than ever, having been drinking arrack for the last fortnight for want of whisky. His manner of greeting her was that of an undertaker, unctuously commiserating, but all in the day's work. Without any preamble he offered his condolences on her widowhood and told her he had called to get her to sign certain papers so that whatever there might prove to be of Cassalis's estate could be handed over to her.

"There may not be very much," he said, "for your late husband hid everything so securely that we cannot lay our hands on the bulk of it; but there is sure to be something— the proceeds of the sale of the launch, for instance. As there is no will, you are sole beneficiary, and if you would be good enough to give me your signature to certain documents I can proceed with the business."

Nina hardly heard what he was saying. Her mind could take in only one thing—that she had got to face the fact that Lewis was dead, and she could no longer hope even against hope.

"Is—is it certain my husband is dead?" she asked, oblivious of the explanations with which Willis was furnishing her.

"Er—yes, Mrs. Cassalis, I am afraid it is. The—er—remains were definitely identified, you know. I am applying to the court for leave to presume his death; it is for that I want your signature as next of kin."

He put a paper in front of her. She glanced through the legal wording, saw that it was to that purpose, and signed her name where indicated. Willis then put before her another paper. She saw that it authorized him to act as her representative. She hesitated. If there was one person in the world that she disliked and distrusted more than another, it was Willis.

"I think I shall leave my affairs in the hands of Mr. Hallett, our family lawyer," she said, pushing aside the paper.

He replaced it in front of her. "Mr. Hallett may be your choice as a legal adviser, my dear young lady, but I was your late husband's choice, and it is I who have to clear up his affairs as instructed. If you will be good enough to sign this document, I shall be able to get on with my work. You can still remain in the hands of Mr. Hallett so far as your independent estate may be concerned."

Nina had no independent estate, and had no idea what he meant in any case. She signed as bidden: there was nothing else she could do.

This business concluded, he offered her a cigarette, lit one himself, and settled down for a chat. Nina wondered how long he would stick it without a drink, and concluded that she would not have to endure him unduly.

He tried to probe her as to her family affairs, and drawing blank, for Nina had no mind to confide in him, began to tell her about his own. He had, apparently, a wife in the Old Country who had been a mistake from the beginning. Nina was relieved to hear he had a wife, as she had feared he was going to propose to her. But it gradually dawned on her that though Willis could hardly be said to be proposing, he was certainly suggesting something, and she gave him her attention, which had previously wandered, in order to find out what it was. She discovered that he was suggesting she should become his mistress. Willis would risk a lot, but he wouldn't

244

risk a prosecution for bigamy.

He was mentioning a pleasant little bungalow in the neighbourhood where she should have every luxury, and where she could withdraw discreetly, safe from prying eyes, until he had wound up his affairs and was ready to retire, and then she could return to England with him and pass as his wife and no one would ever be the wiser. He considered that he was making her, under the circumstances, a most honourable and advantageous offer. He did not choose to remember that the proceeds on which he proposed to retire were Cassalis's savings, which Nina's signature would enable him to get into his hands as soon as Cassalis should be genuinely dead—an eventuality that could not be long delayed now as he had arranged with Ibrahim that it should happen if all hope of getting Cassalis to return to the fold of African Tammany had to be abandoned.

Consequently he was genuinely surprised to see Nina get up and hold open the door for him without a word.

"My dear girl, don't take it like that. Think it over," he said.

Nina did not reply, but continued to hold the door open.

Willis waved an airy hand.

"Do not take it to heart, dear child. I merely suggested an arrangement that might have been to our mutual convenience. We don't take these things very seriously in tropical countries, you know— 'East of Suez, the best is like the worst'. Think no more about it."

Nina gazed at him in surprise, not knowing what to make of this complete *volte face*. She could not understand how a man who was sufficiently in love to propose could take his dismissal so lightly. She felt suspicious, but his next move made her wonder whether her suspicions were justified.

"If you will not consider my offer, then the next best thing will be to see about sending you home to your family."

Nina had to admit that this was the only thing to do. There was nothing she had dreaded more than this, but it was inevitable in the circumstances. As she had realized when she was stranded at Pedro's hotel, a woman could not maintain herself alone in Africa. If she would not accept Willis's protection, there was nothing for it but to return home.

"There is a boat due in the roadstead this evening," continued Willis, "and if it would be a convenience to you, I should be prepared to advance the money for your passage against the proceeds of the estate."

Nina made one last desperate bid for liberty. "Do you know where Lady Piercy is?" she asked.

"Still touring, I believe. But in any case, you are no longer in favour since they could not get what they wanted in the way of information out of you."

Nina remembered the open exasperation of Mr. Grigson and the quiet reserve of Sir Robert, and acquiesced hopelessly. There was nothing for it. She must haul down her colours and return home. She thought of the grey Northern skies and muddy lanes, and the days that followed one another in an endless and unchanging succession. Unable to speak, she nodded her head in acquiescence. Her lover was dead and her African adventure was over.

Willis took his departure, renewing his protestations of disinterested friendship and promising to make the necessary arrangements with the shipping company, and in a short time the shipping company rang through to say that the arrangements had been made. Nina was to be at their offices on the quay at eight o'clock that evening, and the company's launch would take her out to the ship in the roadstead.

She set to work to pack her scanty belongings, most of them mission stock as issued to the converts. She wanted to make some return to the missionary ladies; they had done their best to be kind, though it had been up-hill work for

246

both parties. There was only one possible thing she could give them—the miniature revolver that Cassalis had given her the time he had left her alone in his eyrie; it was a tiny American shooting-iron that could be concealed in the palm of a man's hand. It had gone everywhere with her in her under-arm bag—to the hotel with Willis, the ju-ju house, everywhere—and it had the curious personality that weapons and sporting gear develop. She looked at it lovingly as it lay in her hand, but it would be of no use to her in England, and very useful indeed to the missionary women when they went on their trips up country, so she made up her mind to the sacrifice.

"I have a little keepsake I should like to leave with you," she said as she thanked them half-heartedly for their half-hearted hospitality, and proffered them the little gun. There was an embarrassing silence while they gazed at it as if it were a scorpion.

"Er—thank you very much, Mrs. Cassalis, it is very kind of you to offer it, but—er—I don't think we should care to have it."

Nina returned the little gun to her bag, greatly relieved at having done the handsome thing so cheaply. With her scanty belongings in a native-made basket carried by a youthful convert, she set out for the shipping company's offices at the appointed time. It was the hour of the evening meal for both whites and blacks, and the sordid and dusty alleys were deserted. The shipping company's offices, too, were shut when she arrived, but a man in the company's uniform was there to meet her. He was not a very prepossessing specimen, looking more like a beachcomber than a seaman, but she had no option but to give him her belongings and follow him through the gathering dusk down the quay. It was reassuring to see the steamer lights out in the roads, and a good-sized launch, not a surf-boat, drawn in to the steps.

She entered the small but brightly lit cabin; the dead lights were over the windows, and it was intolerably stuffy. She asked her escort if the windows could not be opened, but he said no, it would be rough crossing the bar. Nina, remembering her arrival in Africa, shuddered, and accepted the inevitable. The door was shut on her and she settled down to endure as best she might. It would not last long. The steamer was only a couple of miles out, and launches are fast.

The engine started up. She felt the launch get under way, and settled herself in a corner of a settee with her feet braced against what looked like a cocktail-cabinet, to await the tumble on the bar.

But time went on, and time went on, and the water still remained smooth. She could not see out of the windows owing to the deadlights, but she could tell by the way the launch was quivering that it was being driven all out. She concluded that the bar had not been as rough as was expected; and yet it was difficult to believe that they had passed out of the shelter of the estuary without encountering any swell. Perhaps she had not realized how far out the steamer lay. It was easy for a landsman, and still more a landswoman, to miscalculate a thing like that. She must possess her soul in patience. It was no use getting nervous and imagining things.

But anyway it was intolerably stuffy in the shut-up cabin. If there were not going to be any rough water, she might as well have some ventilation. She turned the handle of the door that led aft, knowing that there she would find whatever there was in the way of a crew, but the handle refused to yield. She went forward, and tried the door opening into the cockpit, but that too was immovable. It dawned upon Nina that she was securely shut up in the cabin of a launch with deadlights over the windows, and that the reason the water was calm was that the launch was not going down-stream, but up. So this was the explanation of Willis's readiness to

248

take no for an answer!

Nina sat down on the settee and pressed her feet against the cocktail-cabinet again in an effort to keep herself from trembling. Had she fallen into the hands of Willis, who wanted to keep her, or of Ibrahim, who wanted to get rid of her? It was difficult to know which would be the least unpleasant. It would probably be easier to come to some sort of an understanding with the Arab, who was a gentleman according to his lights, than with the sodden and besotted solicitor. Her bag slipped from her trembling knees and fell to the floor with a thud that reminded her of what it contained, and she breathed a prayer of thankfulness for the care of Cassalis that still overshadowed her and that had not left her entirely defenceless. Some such tight corner as this is always a possibility for a woman in an uncivilized land, and his first care had been to protect her against it.

She examined the little gun, practising releasing the safety-catch as Lewis had taught her, until she could be sure of doing it quickly, even in the dark. Then she returned her weapon to her bag, along with her powder-compactum and the little tube of solidified eau-de-Cologne that Lady Piercy had given her, and sat still to await eventualities. She did not suppose she stood much chance if it were Ibrahim's hands into which she had fallen, but Willis was not going to get any change out of her.

She had hardly settled herself when she felt the launch slow up, and a shuddering bump told that it had been brought alongside a wooden wharf none too skilfully. She wondered what Cassalis would have said if anyone had bumped his launch like that. The door forward opened, and the individual who appeared to be in charge of the expedition put his head in and announced politely that she must be good enough to step ashore here for a little while. He added the gratuitous information that the tide was not yet high enough

249

for them to cross the bar, and that they were to wait here for a bit. Nina accepted the shallow lie without demur, and allowed him to help her out on to a tumble-down jetty that stuck out over the sluggish surface of a narrow backwater. A musky smell advertised the proximity of crocodiles, and as always when she smelt that smell, she thought of the horrible end of Lewis and sickened at the picture that rose before her imagination, do what she would to turn her thoughts away.

She followed her escort up a winding path through thick undergrowth, and saw ahead the gleam of lamp light. They passed through a narrow gate that stood open in a stout stockade, and came upon a good-sized bungalow, much out of repair, its fly-screens hanging askew by their rusting hinges, guttering sagging from the eaves, planks rotting in the verandah. It had all the look of having been hastily put into commission after being long abandoned. Nina's escort stood aside for her to enter by a french window, and she found herself in a fair sized room, in the centre of which was a table laid for two with all the tinned delicacies of the season. So it was the infatuated solicitor whose prisoner she might consider herself to be; Ibrahim would never have risen to a cocktail shaker. She sat down on a new but cheap cane settee and waited. She did not have to wait long. In came Willis. He was got up in the cleanest white ducks she had ever seen him in, his face looking all the yellower and his nose all the redder for the contrast. In repose, his face had a kind of cadaverous dignity derived from his large hook nose and high forehead; but when he smiled it looked like one of the masks that unfold from Christmas crackers, the gap left by the loss of a front tooth showing black amid the grog-blossoms. He was smiling at the present moment.

He swept her an elaborate bow. Even her eyes, inexperienced in gauging inebriety, could see that he was as full as a tick.

"This is the little bungalow I told you of, dear child," he said, speaking with the careful articulation of the tipsy.

Nina looked at him, and the dour blood of Mr. Barnet was very apparent in the set of her mouth. She opened her bag and groped about inside. Willis thought she was feeling for her handkerchief preliminary to bursting into tears, and concluding that everything was going according to plan, smiled still more widely, revealing a missing molar; but out of Nina's bag came, not a handkerchief, but a very serviceable little revolver. His visitor raised the safety-catch as if she knew how to handle it, and Willis recognized that it was a case for parley, not force, and began to gather his arguments together; but before he could make any use of them he saw Nina shut her eyes.

"I am going to shoot," she said, and pressed the trigger. A shattering crash and a tinkle of broken glass followed, and Nina opened her eyes to see Willis, too flabbergasted to move, standing with his mouth wide open, gazing at the wreckage of the cocktail-shaker. She took careful aim at his widest part, shut her eyes again, and pressed the trigger once more. This time a howl followed the crash, and she saw Willis hopping on one leg while a broad stain of red spread rapidly over his white canvas shoe. She had shot him through the foot. He turned, took a mighty hop through the door by which he had entered, and disappeared, leaving a trail of blood-spots behind him.

Tense with excitement at her own daring, her mouth shut like a rat-trap, Nina walked out of the window by which she had entered, and found herself face to face with the man who had brought her to the launch. He was grinning widely.

"Keerful with that gun, lidy," he said.

"You keep off," said Nina, turning the muzzle more or less in his direction. He backed away hastily.

" Keerful, now, marm, it might go off without your mean-ing it. Better put the safety-catch down."

"I prefer it up," said Nina, following him with a wavering barrel.

He stood still and considered her.

"You gone and plugged the boss good and proper," he vouchsafed. He was wondering what in the world they were going to do with their prisoner. A man who has been shot through the foot has got to have medical attention quickly in Africa if he wants to keep his leg. If they fetched a doctor to Willis, how were they going to explain the girl? And she might start loosing off that revolver again if the fancy took her. She had got another four shots in it anyway, and ap-peared to have nerve enough for anything. He too decided to parley.

"Now see here, marm," he said, "I ain't got no grudge agin you, an' I hope you ain't got none agin me."

As he had been responsible for the kidnapping of her, this was rather a forlorn hope, and Nina's grim silence was not encouraging, but he struggled on.

"Now see here, marm, I'll make you an offer. I'll put you on board the *Biafra*, if she ain't gone, provided you'll let by-gorns be bygorns and not make no trouble for nobody. The boss, 'e's out of the running. It's me you've got to deal with now, and I don't want no trouble, see? That's fair, ain't it?"

It certainly was fair if he carried out his offer in good faith. She followed him down to the launch, ignoring his re-peated admonitions to be careful with the gun, and took her seat in the cockpit, declining to re-enter the cabin in spite of his entreaties. You cannot argue with a lady with a gun, so he left her outside to get bitten by mosquitoes and soaked on the bar if she had a mind to, and by the time he delivered her at the accommodation ladder of the *Biafra* the revolver had slipped from her helpless hand and she was in no state to

252

make trouble for anybody.

On the *Biafra* she found the young ship's doctor who had given her champagne on her voyage out, and he had his hands full, for she was down with malaria again by the morning.

Now Dr. Martin had been rather taken with Nina when he had first met her, but as she was going out to be married had refrained from poaching on another man's preserves; but since she was going home a disillusioned widow, his hopes revived, and he succeeded in discovering Nina's home address in the course of making arrangements for her transfer from ship to hospital in Liverpool, and determined that he would present himself after a decent interval in the hope that she might not prove inconsolable.

The return to the moorland vicarage was all that could be expected of the return of a prodigal daughter. Reduced to a shadow by the drastic treatment that had been necessary to eliminate the malaria, she crept home like a wounded animal. Her mother was kindness itself to the sick girl, but had a kind of congratulatory air, as if Nina had come extraordinarily well out of a painful experience; like the mission ladies, she could not understand that Nina had been genuinely fond of Cassalis, and that his death was a shattering blow to her, or that she had loved the adventurous tropical life and hardly knew how to breathe in the narrow confines of the moorland village. Nina's father had sufficient sense not to rub things in, but she knew that he felt that, as usual, God was on his side.

Under the circumstances Nina's health picked up slowly, and the deadly depression that follows malaria lay heavy upon her. She had always kicked against the pricks of parish work, and she made her health the excuse for refusing to undertake any of the hundred and one odd jobs that fall to the lot of a clergyman's womenfolk.

There was no local society that they could meet on a level footing, for the county was above them and the country below them. Lacking the physical strength to battle with the moorland winds and take the dog for a walk as of old, Nina seldom went outside the vicarage garden, and convalescence seemed as if it would be prolonged indefinitely and she would never recover her health. The only diversion was afforded by the visits of the young doctor between voyages; but although she liked him and enjoyed his visits, she told him frankly that her heart was buried with Cassalis in whatever African grave he occupied. He, however, having heard that story before, declined to give up hope, and continued his visits, which, needless to say, were encouraged by the vicarage.

It was, in fact, through him that Nina set forth on the next stage of her life's journey. An elderly lady had approached him on board ship and asked him if he knew of any nice young girl whom she could engage as companion. His mind at once leapt to Nina, and although the old dame was not everybody's money, he felt that anything was better for Nina than moping at home any longer, and put the lady in touch with her. It was not till after Nina had left for Paris with her employer that he learnt from the horrified purser that she was the notorious keeper of a house of ill repute in Georgetown. He also learnt from the same source that Nina was by no means a widow, Cassalis having turned up again, very much alive. The wretched lad did not know what to do, and, being on the high seas, could not have done it if he had. He sent a long and involved cablegram to Mr. Barnet, warning him as to the record of Nina's employer, and set to work to mend a broken heart with whisky till the captain put his foot down.

CHAPTER XVIII

THE bottom had fallen out of African Tammany with a vengeance, and the authorities had no further anxiety from that quarter. There appeared to be a good deal of disorganization of local black-and-tan society, and a number of public characters faded away like morning dew and were never heard of again. Several minor officials in the Telegraphs and the Customs sent in their papers on account of health, and one senior official in the Customs shot himself; then everything quieted down till the coast was like the Garden of Eden before the serpent. Cassalis had vanished and African Tammany was no more. The weeks went by. Sir Robert settled down to his routine, replacing the resignees with men of his own choosing. Grigson reported crime down by fifty per cent, and Lady Piercy bore her share of the burden of Empire by constant entertaining at Government House, as was her duty.

A cruising liner lay off in the roadstead, her human cargo swarming all over the town, weirdly got up in what they imagined to be tropical kit. Lady Piercy, who knew her job, gave a garden party to all who had signed their names in the book at Government House, thus forwarding the cause of our Colonial Empire to the best of her ability.

The tourists had heard all about the native rising and African Tammany from the organizer of the trip, who had beguiled the dark hours in Northern waters with lectures on

African history. Everyone was therefore all agog to see the heroines who had been kidnapped into the heart of the forest and rescued so dramatically by the villain of the piece, the legend of the monkey Messiah losing nothing in the telling. By the time the lecturer had finished, it was the Indian Mutiny on a small scale and Cassalis was a cross between Tarzan of the Apes and Nana Sahib.

But although Government House, protected by no more than a garden wall, did not look as if it ever had stood, or ever would stand, a siege, and silver-haired Lady Piercy and dumpy Mrs. Grigson were not exactly figures of romance, nevertheless, the tourists made the best of it, and their friends were not to know that the one was no longer young and the other no longer slim when the tales came to be told when the cruise was over. Everybody walked about the grounds and admired the tropical flowers, and those that had the energy danced, and all went merry as a marriage bell.

All the local residents were in snowy white, the dress clothes of the tropics, so that visitors glanced in some surprise at a man in khaki shirt and shorts, a cartridge belt round his waist, and a heavy revolver on his hip, who passed quietly among them and went up to where Sir Robert was receiving his guests, unbuckled his belt, and held belt and gun out to Sir Robert without a word. The drama of the two men standing silently, the handsome, urbane Governor shaken out of his poise and rendered speechless, and the other man, in bush kit among all the guests, silently tendering a weapon which the other would not take, caught the eyes of those around. They saw the red-haired chief of police, who was there with his wife, go up to the two silent men and put out his hand for the revolver; but the man who held it immediately put it behind him. The policeman put his hand in his pocket; the other man slipped the revolver half out of its holster. Sir Robert laid a hand on the shoulder of either man and spoke to them in a low voice. The policeman took his hand out of his pocket. The stranger handed over his belt and gun to the Governor, who took it this time. Lady Piercy hastened across the room to join the group, took the stranger's hand in hers, and held it for quite a long time while she spoke to him; then the police-officer and the man in bush kit went off together towards the door.

But the drama was not over yet. At the door Grigson made an error of tact and tactics—he laid his hand on Cassalis's arm. Immediately Cassalis drove his elbow into his ribs and knocked the wind out of him. The native troopers on duty in the hall closed round the pair of them, and someone tactfully shut the door on the ensuing scuffle. The visiting tourists gaped—here was something indeed to talk about for ever and a day when the cruise was a thing of the past—they had seen the famous bandit, Cassalis, come in and give himself up to justice!

When Cassalis found himself in the cell of the local lockup with handcuffs on his wrists—for Grigson, having had the wind knocked out of him, had had no compunction about putting his prisoner in irons—he was surprised to find he felt no emotion whatever, save a fierce resentment at having been handcuffed. He had accepted his conviction and execution as a foregone conclusion, and for all practical purposes considered himself as good as dead. In the complete abandonment of hope there was peace, perhaps more peace than he had ever known in his lawless life and he realized for the first time the weight of the strain he had carried so long that it had become habitual. He knew that Nina—and her child—would be well provided for, and the only thing that remained to him to do was to get hold of Willis and make the necessary arrangements for the transference of his secret caches into her name.

He intended to plead guilty at his trial, so there was no need to bother about a defence. As soon as he was convicted, all facilities would be given him to arrange his affairs. He kicked off his boots and lay down on the narrow wooden bunk to sleep the sleep of the just. Being without hope, he was without anxiety.

He arose in the morning in the same tranquil state of mind. As if taking part in some rather boring formality he walked between his guards to the courthouse and took his place in the dock. He listened to the formal evidence of arrest by Grigson, and then suddenly sat up in his chair when the Crown prosecutor arose and said he did not propose to offer any evidence, no witnesses being now available; the negro interpreter had disappeared completely, the gunnery expert had returned to England, and the prosecution had no intention of re-importing him.

There were only two people in court who appeared in the least surprised at the turn things had taken: one of them was the prisoner, and the other was his legal adviser, who had been listening to the proceedings from the back of the gallery reserved for the general public. Once again Willis had to consider hastily which side his bread was buttered. Having made sure of Cassalis's execution, he had been getting on with the disposal of the estate; but if Cassalis were not going to be executed, then he must be cultivated. There were affairs in which he could be very useful, for Willis had not allowed African Tammany to fall into complete desuetude, and most of the pieces were available for picking up when the right time came.

So Willis took his client by the arm as he came dazedly out of the courthouse, a free man, and led him to the mean room in a broken-down hotel which was serving him at the moment as bedroom, sitting-room, office, and what looked like a bonded warehouse for whisky. There he sounded Cassalis carefully to see which way the wind blew, and laid his plans accordingly.

As he suspected, Cassalis's one idea was to get in touch with Nina, and for this he was prepared. Before the news of Cassalis's surrender to his parole had taken him by surprise— for the idea of such a thing had never crossed his mind as a possibility—he had carefully prepared a siding into which his client could be shunted if he showed any inclination to let his wife lead him into the paths of virtue, and Cassalis was confronted with a complete set of papers relative to divorce proceedings. Willis's skill as a lightning artist had not deserted him, and there was Nina's signature, most legible and convincing. Willis was also well informed of certain developments with regard to a young ship's doctor, and Cassalis was given to understand that the divorce proceedings were being brought by Nina in order that she might be free to marry him. Before Cassalis were also laid copies of assorted affidavits by various of his nigger mistresses, who for a consideration had been quite willing to post-date their affairs a trifle. Cassalis, staring at the evidence, and hearing the poison that Willis was distilling into his ears, felt all his good resolutions crumble into dust, and there came upon him the old evil mood of the killer, and African Tammany woke again.

Willis, rubbing his hands in triumph, was entirely contented. But presently a new worry developed as the days went by; for although Cassalis was diligently picking up the threads of African Tammany, he would not consider any of the schemes laid before him, and would not reveal what schemes were in his own mind. It was very inconvenient for the intriguers not to know what Cassalis was up to; moreover Willis resented not being confided in as a slur on his professional honour.

For Cassalis was picking up the threads of African Tammany for purposes of his own, and these did not include the enrichment of Willis. He had spoken the truth when he had warned Nina on the launch that she must never make him jealous or he would not be responsible for his actions. Willis, knowing this trait in Cassalis's nature, had regarded the affair of the ship's doctor as the most effective weapon he possessed. But it had proved too effective, and had unleashed forces with which he had no power to cope. He had reckoned upon Cassalis going completely berserk in rage and pain, but he had never reckoned up on this cold, controlled, long-distance scheming. Gradually it dawned upon him why African Tammany was being reorganized—Cassalis was out for revenge! Willis dithered in terror, wondering on whom the vengeance would fall. Did Cassalis suspect anything? And if so, what—and whom?

He knew that Cassalis and Ibrahim had been openly hostile and their men shooting each other up. He himself had not forgotten the interview when Cassalis had threatened him with a cutting-whip and ant-hills if he did not reveal the truth about Nina. Those are the kind of things that no one really forgives, and the more they smile the more dangerous they usually are; for a man suffers from ingrowing *amour propre* till such a debt is settled, and he does not smile until he has the wherewithal to meet it safe in the bank.

Willis, judging others by himself, did not like Cassalis's readiness to let bygones be bygones, Christian charity being no part of the frontier code on any frontier.

But on the other hand, when rogues work together, they have perforce to overlook a lot that would not be tolerated by decent men. Willis took heart of hope that since Cassalis evidently had a use for African Tammany he had really put the incidents that had led up to the strained relations behind him now that the *casus belli* had returned to her family. He was certain that they had been on the right track when they had set to work to disillusion Cassalis with regard to his wife, and had refrained their hands from anything so crude

260

as murder.

He determined, however, to make assurance doubly sure, and, after taking a quantity of aspirin to steady his shaking hand, got down to work, burning the midnight oil till pretty late, and next morning Cassalis found in his mail a letter bearing an English stamp duly postmarked, though the postmark was, as it not infrequently is, indecipherable. He had no means of knowing what can be done to an old envelope with a stain remover.

Inside was a letter from Nina. He could not bring himself to read that letter with Willis watching him as they sat at their belated breakfast, so to the disappointment of that worthy, who had hoped to be able to observe reactions, he placed it unopened in his pocket and stolidly ate his food, though Willis observed that he did not eat much, and gulped his coffee scalding hot, oblivious of burns.

The meal over, Cassalis went out. Willis sneaked after him at a safe distance, but Cassalis went too far and fast for his legal adviser, who was still suffering from the after-effects of having a jigger cut out of his foot, or so he said; anyway, he was suffering from a bad foot.

Having reached a spot far enough from the town to be safe from intrusive native children, Cassalis seated himself in the shade on the twisted roots of a tree and stared out over the sunlit ocean, his ears full of the thundering roar of the ceaseless surf. He dreaded opening that letter. The fact that Nina was writing to him personally after divorce proceedings had been begun, and not through her lawyers, looked as if there might be a chance of a reconciliation. Dare he hope for this? As long as the envelope remained unopened it was a messenger of hope, but its contents, once known, might be the end of everything; for even if he defended the divorce suit successfully, and for once in his life he was entirely guiltless of that with which he was being charged, the breach between them would still remain—the breach between the outlaw and the daughter of the manse.

Finally Cassalis broke the seal. It was a pityWillis had not been able to stay the pace, for he would have been amply rewarded.

"Dear Lewis," the letter ran. Willis had worried a good deal over that opening. Were there pet names in use between them? He had no means of knowing; but anyway their use would not be in good taste in a letter of this nature, so it did not really matter.

Cassalis read on, seeing the words through a scarlet mist.

"This is to appeal to you to let my divorce go through undefended. I can never return to you, for I know you to be a murderer." ("That will stop him showing it to anyone," thought Willis as he penned the words with laborious care, sketching them, not writing them.)

"Your ways are not my ways, so it is useless for us to try and live together. I do not think it would be right for me to forgive you, as you are a criminal, and never likely to be anything else. If I had known all I now know about you, I would never have married you. It has been a painful experience that I wish to forget.

"I dare say you would like to know that things went wrong with me, and there is not going to be a child after all, but I am all right again now.

"Nina."

"That ought to do it," Willis had thought, and it did.

He did not quite know what to make of Cassalis when he turned up in the evening, after having been absent all day. Cassalis always had an enigmatic countenance at the best of times, but today it was like stone. Anguish? Tantrums? Vengeance? Acceptance of the inevitable? It might have indicated any of these, and there was no more means of knowing which than there is of knowing what is on the dark side of the moon. Willis knew that he had got results, and only hoped to God they were the results he aimed at. When he saw Cassalis go out again after the evening meal, and wend his way to a certain house whose reputation was not even doubtful, being a dead cert, he breathed a sigh of relief, concluding that all was well.

But if he had known what manner of bargain was struck at the interview that took place behind the red light, he might not have been quite so well pleased.

To say that Cassalis was quite unknown to the lady of the house would have been untrue, but it would be equally untrue to say that he had ever been near her tawdry premises since he had known Nina.

He greeted pleasantly such of his old friends as had not died since his last visit, for the life of a prostitute is that of a butterfly at the best of times, but in the coastal towns of West Africa it is that of a mayfly if she has much white blood in her.

The madam herself, raddled and jewelled and wearing an auburn toupee in spite of the heat, received him most affably, for was he not the uncrowned king of their little world of vice and crime? He hated with a bitter hatred that welcome, with its ready assumption of unclean sympathy; for even though Nina had thrown him over, he could never go back again to what he had been before he knew her. Nevertheless, he put his pride in his pocket, and exchanged the usual gallantries that were expected of him, the neglect of which would have given offence, for prostitutes have their pride in these matters, the same as other folk; then he got down to business, and the madam, looking more than ever like an evil old parrot, cackled till her false teeth clacked like castanets.

Yes, she could do what was wanted, provided, of course, it were made worth her while, for she would be put to more

263

than travelling expenses by her absence; the girls would never hand over their tips in full to the *tronc* if only the eye of her aide-de-camp were on them. Cassalis told her to name her price. She did, and gasped when he agreed to it. Worked as he proposed to work the job, there was very little risk attached to it. Violence would not be necessary, unless, of course, the police recognized her and got suspicious at her travelling with a young girl. But, if that happened, she could always slip through into the underworld. Cassalis said that he did not wish her to do that if it could possibly be avoided, and if she did, she must let the girl go and only use the channels of the underworld for her own get-away, and they would have another shot later. But as he could provide her with a really good passport, it was unlikely that she would have any trouble with the police once she was clear of the Coast. So all was settled to everybody's satisfaction, and he had a drink with her and the girls, which she actually would not let him pay for, and went home to Willis, who made no secret of his surprise at seeing him back so soon.

When Cassalis told him that he wanted a passport for the madam of the red-light house, who was to pass as the widow of a missionary, he nearly fell over backwards. There were no technical difficulties in the way, Willis having produced notes on the Bank of Engraving in his time, but he absolutely declined to put pen to paper until he knew what a passport was wanted for. So Cassalis had to tell him.

"She said she was finished with me because I was a criminal, so I thought, all right, I'll damned well be as criminal as I know how. There's only one kind of crime I've never tried my hand at, and that's white slaving, but it's never too late to learn, and she can teach me. If she won't be ornamental, she can damn' well be useful."

"Good Lord!" exclaimed Willis, genuinely horrified for once. "Are you going to hand her over to old Mother Montmorency?"

"Not until I've finished with her."

"My heavens!" said Willis, completely sober for the moment. "You can't do that, Lewis. What have you come to?"

"Oh, can't I?" said Cassalis. "You watch me." Willis groaned and clutched his head.

"I'd better get to work on the passport," he said, "since you want her to get off by the *Biafra*," and took the occasion to escape from the presence of the man he had turned into a devil.

He sought Ibrahim, who was at home at the moment with a new wife, and told him the agitating news. Ibrahim, however, was delighted. If Cassalis was taking things in that spirit, he had no choice but to stick to African Tammany, for nothing and no one else would have him.

"You don't know white men," said Willis agitatedly. "We shall have trouble, and bad trouble, as surely as the sun will rise."

"Then," said Ibrahim, smoothing out the folds of his robes, "it will be for the last time, for I am weary to the depths of my heart of the white sheik and his ingratitude. If he will serve as heretofore, well and good, I will forget; but if he lifts one little finger without my bidding, he dies, and dies quickly."

"I guess you are right," said Willis, his agile brain lighting up at the prospects opened up by this attitude of Ibrahim's. If, as soon as Nina was safely landed in Africa, and before Cassalis had time to get her out of the clutches of Mother Montmorency, Ibrahim were stirred up with tales of plotted treacheries, Cassalis would be put out of the way with the minimum of mess and the maximum of expedition, and Nina would become available for his own advances in the ordinary course of business. That passport would be a masterpiece, he would see to that.

Peace restored to his worried soul by the rosy prospect opening before him, and his conscience never being one to give trouble, he went home and turned out the masterpiece as promised, pushed it under Cassalis's bedroom door, then locked his own and settled down to drink till the rats ran about. Then they removed him to hospital and kept him there for three weeks.

CHAPTER XIX

NINA, meanwhile, was "doing" Paris in the company of the good-natured but terribly vulgar old dame who was her employer. She had been a Gaiety Girl in the palmy days of that institution, and her anecdotes of the peerage and the beer-age would have been beyond price if she had not kept on pulling herself up out of respect for her hearer. Nina thought that their relations were the oddest variant of employer and employee she had ever come across.

After a few days in Paris the old lady announced that they would proceed to the Riviera; but although they boarded the Sud Express, the place they ended up at was Marseilles. Then the old dame had another sudden change of plan— she would go to Madeira instead of the Côte d'Azur, as she had heard that the mistral was blowing very badly. So they packed on board an Italian cargo-boat with accommodation for passengers, upon which they were the only passengers.

Nina could not speak Italian, and the ships' officers could not speak English, so communication was limited, and Nina had no notion where they were on the earth's surface till she saw away to port a coast-line that reminded her of Africa, and bore not the remotest likeness to what she had always understood to be the shape of those mountainous islands. She asked her employer where they were, and was relieved to learn that no mystery existed. Madeira had been in quarantine for smallpox, and so they were going on with the boat for the sake of the trip; she was sorry she had omitted to mention it to Nina, but she had forgotten that her companion could not follow the conversation in which the matter had been discussed. Nina was quite contented; she had no reason to be otherwise, geography not being her strong suit. The food was excellent, the cabins comfortable, and the weather delightful, so it was a very natural decision to make. She gazed over the rail at the coast-line to port, and felt desperately homesick for her lost romance. How strange it was, she thought, that fate was once again taking her in the direction of Africa! Perhaps there was something in astrology after all.

But in a day or two the old lady cheerfully announced that she had changed her plans again. The captain had told her that the season was excellent for sightseeing, so he was going to land them at his next port of call, and pick them up on his return trip. To Nina it was like visiting the grave of all her hopes and happiness, a bitter and sorrowful pilgrimage. But she had no choice save to acquiesce with such pretence of cheerfulness as she could muster. Was she not an employ-ee and a dependent? Not even the price of Cassalis's launch had come her way in the winding-up of the estate of which she was nominally the sole beneficiary.

So in due course she and her employer put off in a surf boat, just such another as had taken her to Okiki in the open-ing chapter of her African adventure. Mindful of her previ-ous experience of the climate, she wrapped the camel-hair cloak about herself over a thin frock her employer had given her for the abortive trip to the Riviera. She saw the old dame stare hard at this cloak, the one Lewis had always worn, with its funny little red tassel swinging from the point of the hood, but she offered no comment, and Nina offered no explana-tion. Then they came to the bar, just such another as guarded the estuary at Okiki, and conversation ceased to be possible for the next few minutes.

268

Then, her heart sinking within her, it dawned upon Nina that it was Okiki they were coming in to. She saw the squat white Custom House where Harold had worked, and Pedro's dreadful hotel where he had lodged, and the low stone jetty where she had landed. But this time the surf-boat did not draw in to the jetty, but continued on up-stream and presently entered a backwater.

They progressed up the backwater for some time, and then pulled in alongside a large launch tied up to a tumble-down jetty, and their belongings began to be handed across to the half-caste crew. Then they were helped across themselves, and Nina looked round in disgust at the frowzy cabin as she contrasted its threadbare, paint-less grime with that other launch she had known so well, and watched an outsize in cockroaches stroll across the torn matting of the floor.

To her surprise, when the launch came out of the back water into the main stream, it swung sharp about and made for the estuary. She turned to speak to her companion, but the old lady was having a nap, with a large silk handkerchief over her face to cover her open mouth, from which snores already came, and from which Nina knew from past experience the dentures might slip at any moment.

Back past Okiki they went, through the tumble on the bar into the open sea, and turned north up the coast. The *Biafra* was already bull-down on the horizon, the low launch, of course, invisible from her decks.

All afternoon they ran up the coast at a good speed, and as it grew dark they saw the lights of a large town come up over the skyline. They travelled on until each separate lamp on the water-front could be seen, and even the riding-lights of the boats at anchor, and then they turned and, not without difficulty, entered a creek that led straight into the primeval forest that stood up on either hand like a railway cutting. Nina expected to see the big headlight switched on, but the

269

unlit launch felt its way inch by inch unaided. Finally they saw the dim light of a hurricane lantern being waved on the bank ahead, and drew in to one of the rotting timber jetties that are everywhere on that coast, where the waterways are the only feasible means of travel and so many enterprises are abandoned owing to the death of the owner.

Nina asked her employer, who had wakened up by now and was disposed to be chatty, though she kept the conversation in her own hands, if she knew where they were going, and was assured that she did. They were going to a place belonging to a friend of her girlhood, who had also been in the chorus at the Gaiety till she had married and done very well for herself. They were now going to the country house where she lived with her husband, who was a big man in these parts. She had already been communicated with by wireless, and would be delighted to see them. That lantern was probably being waved by her butler, or of course it might be a footman, she couldn't tell at that distance. As a matter of fact it was being waved by a dilapidated darky afflicted with elephantiasis.

Nothing dashed by this revolting welcome, the old dame hopped on to the jetty as if she had spent a lifetime getting in and out of African launches on to slimy timbers at all states of the tide. Nina struggled after her unaided rather than let the revolting darky touch her, slipped on the slime, felt her foot catch in the rotting boards, heard two sharp snaps one after the other, like breaking sticks, and sat down helplessly.

"Good God, what's the matter?" cried Mrs. Montmorency, hearing her fall. "Sprained your ankle?"

Nina felt her foot, that had fallen sideways at a queer, unnatural angle from the leg. It did not pain her but she felt very sick and faint.

The old lady seized the lantern from the diseased horror of a hand that held it, and threw the light over the prostrate girl.

"Pott's fracture," said she, with the knowledge begotten of her ghastly trade. "Seen one before. Now we're for it. God only knows what we'll do about it. Anyway, it's not for me to say. I've done my bit and I'm finished."

She spoke to the negro in his own language. Nina was too far gone with shock, though she felt no pain as yet, to realize the discrepancy of this, and when the negro returned with two others and an improvised stretcher, she had other things to think about, for the broken bones jarred one against another as her bearers stumbled over the rough forest path.

Luckily for her, they had not far to go, and in a few minutes they were sidling the stretcher through the back gate of the compound of a large house that stood on the edge of the town. They carried her in through a long french window to a spacious room on the ground floor, and laid her down, stretcher and all, on the big double bed which was the only furniture it contained.

Nina heard a tremendous cackling of female voices in another part of the house, and then her employer came back accompanied by just such another as herself, though crowned with a blonde toupee instead of a chestnut one. This, she concluded, was the other Gaiety girl who had married so well; Nina thought she had not worn as well as she had married, for she had never seen such a parody of womanhood as the raddled old wreck that padded clucking up to the bedside, an old pair of bedroom slippers showing under all her finery. Round the door, however, two pretty half-caste girls peeped in, whose looks more than made up for the unsightliness of the lady of the house. Nina supposed that the excellence of the marriage had been marred by more than a touch of the tar-brush.

"Are you in pain, deary?" asked the newcomer, all of a twitter, much more of a twitter than Nina thought there was any need to be.

"Not if I keep still," she replied.

"Well, you soon will be. You'd better swallow these, they'll help to keep you going till we can get a doctor to you," and she held out in the palm of her withered hand four tiny white pellets.

"Gawd!" said Mrs. Montmorency, upon whose lips the name of God was as frequent as all godliness was absent from her life, "you can't give her all those! She'll die on us," and picked up one of the four.

"I think I could do with this meself," she said, and swallowed it.

Nina thankfully took up the other three as a red-hot pain ran up her leg, and in a few minutes felt the world slipping away and peace descending upon her like a cotton-wool cloud.

When the doctor arrived at the brothel he was called upon to set the leg of a girl who could neither ask nor answer questions.

CHAPTER XX

GOVERNMENT HOUSE was keeping a close eye on Cassalis, wondering which way the cat was going to jump now that he had been set at liberty. The decision not to press the case against him had led to very strained relations in official circles, Mr. Grigson being particularly embittered; for he had signed on for another spell of service in the belief that, Cassalis being disposed of, the Coast was going to be a bed of roses and he could reap the reward of his labours. Sir Robert, however, had resisted local pressure, and backed his own judgment, and turned the bane of the Coast loose once more, and everyone was prophesying woe.

But even Sir Robert was beginning to have his doubts as the days went by and repeated invitations to Cassalis to present himself at Government House for an interview were evaded or ignored. He even went so far as to write him a personal letter hinting at the possibility of Government employment, for he was exceedingly anxious that Cassalis should not slip back into his old ways again; but it received no answer, and he became more and more uneasy as to the wisdom of his decision when reports began to come in from all sides that Cassalis was associating with his old friends again.

"If only the girl had stuck to him!" he said to his wife. "But I suppose with the baby pending it was an impossibility."

"I wonder why she never told me she was expecting a baby," said Lady Piercy. "I don't understand it at all. And I don't understand her going off like that, without a word to anybody, either."

" Well, she's done it, anyway, and the fat is in the fire with Cassalis, I am afraid. He is reverting to type. Grigson looks like being justified of his wisdom."

Sir Robert was more anxious than he chose to admit, even to himself; for he knew better than anyone what Cassalis's capacities were, and what he would have to contend with if that able renegade set to work once more to reorganize African Tammany, as it looked very much as if he were doing. How was Sir Robert to know that Cassalis was feeling Nina's treatment of him too bitterly to care to face her friends and their questions, even if their questioning was sympathetic— though several times he had been on the verge of going to Lady Piercy and pouring out the whole bitter story for the sake of comfort and consolation?

Sir Robert sent him a chit inviting him to meet a visiting magnate who was interested in copper and would like particulars of the deposits of which he had spoken that night on the river. Cassalis was desperately tempted to accept the offer and cut loose once and for all from African Tammany and know the happiness of being able to run straight; but when he remembered the plot that was steadily taking shape in the experienced hands of Mother Montmorency, he knew that the friendship of people like the Piercys was not for him.

Once Lady Piercy, going into the post-office, met Cassalis coming out, and tried to corner him and talk to him, but found him sullen, embittered and rude. Being wise in human nature, she knew that his savagery was that of a man in torment, and barred his path so effectually that, short of physical violence, he could not pass her. Brought to bay thus, he shot at her the information that Nina was divorcing him.

Lady Piercy was amazed.

"She must have had pressure brought to bear on her by her family," she said. "Why don't you go home and see her?

You can do so much more by talking than you can by writing. I believe if you talked to her she would come back to you. Do go home and see her, Mr. Cassalis."

Cassalis laughed harshly. "I know a trick worth two of that," he said.

His bloodshot eyes and excitable manner gave the impression of a man in the mid-tide of a debauch, but there was no smell of alcohol about him. Lady Piercy, accustomed to mothering subalterns, made one last bid to save the renegade.

"Won't you come and see me one evening when I shall be alone?" she said.

"No," said Cassalis, "I will not."

She stood aside and let him go. It was no good trying to do anything with him in this mood. He raised his hand to his sun-helmet in the curt salute of the tropics, where a man bares his head at peril of his life, and strode hastily off through the parti-coloured crowd, looking neither to right nor left, as if the one thing he wanted was to get out of her sight. She, watching him go, thought of the waste of all that fine manhood, and of the girl who had failed to stand by him at the parting of the ways. Why, oh why had Nina not had the courage to stick to him? She had presented the government of the colony with an awkward problem in breaking with him, for Cassalis had turned nasty in his grief and disillusionment. The bigger the man, the uglier the handful in such circumstances.

Suddenly, as she watched his retreating back, something caught her eye, and she noticed that he was not the only person who was making a bee-line through the crowd, regardless of whom he hustled: three Arabs were doing the same thing, strung out as inconspicuously as possible in his wake, but nevertheless obviously following him. Were they a bodyguard, or were they shadowing him? There was none of the truculent swagger of a bodyguard, whose best weapon is advertisement, and they were evidently bent on not letting Cassalis out of their sight, no matter whom they capsized, as the cursings that followed them indicated. What was the significance of the shadowing of Cassalis by the Arabs? Was African Tammany a house divided against itself?

"Looks like it," said Sir Robert when she told him. "And if that is so, it may be troublesome, with its big organization and all the rest of it, but it won't be dangerous. All the same, Cassalis himself is a dangerous brute; about as dangerous as a mad dog in the mood he is in at the moment."

The presence of the three shadowing Arabs was due to the activities of Willis, who was keeping Ibrahim posted as to the secret negotiations he was supposed to be conducting between Cassalis and the Governor. His fertile brain, that whipped round like a snake at every turn of events, had conceived the masterly idea of working up Ibrahim till he bumped Cassalis off; then working up Government House till it bumped Ibrahim off; squaring Mother Montmorency in the matter of Nina, and himself collecting Cassalis's secret funds. It all fitted in admirably—in theory, anyway. He had already interviewed Mother Monty's second in command, the peroxided, parrot-like creature who had been left in charge of the staff—or should it be called the stock?—during the absence of the head of the firm, and she had vouched for her partner's compliance in the matter as soon as it could be explained to her. Cassalis would be told that she had had to relinquish her grip on Nina owing to police activities; she would collect payment for her attempt from Cassalis, and payment for Nina from Willis, thus making a double profit. It was that simple, naive, short-sighted rascality that passes for normal in the underworld and prevents it from ever being organized for a war on society.

Consequently Nina lay quietly in the comfortable bed in the house on the outskirts of the town that was known to its frequenters as the Ash-can, the Dust-hole, and various other titles, the rest of which are unprintable.

Nina was no longer in any pain, though with her leg hung up by pulleys from the beam of the ceiling she was, of course, absolutely helpless. An old darky mammy looked after her solicitously, and the two old parrots cackled in and out in their tawdry finery and toupees and were very kind and pleasant. Nina had expected her employer to be at least upset at being deprived of her services and put to expense in the matter for weeks on end, but she did not appear to be in the least put out; Nina was treated as if she were a guest in an hotel. The only person, in fact, who was at all inconvenienced by the contretemps was Willis, who was being charged through the nose for Nina's keep; Cassalis had no suspicion she was in Africa, believing she had been sent home from Marseilles by the consul. The worst hardship Nina suffered from was lack of books, which were conspicuous by their absence in that house, the few there were being battered and bloodthirsty, and she soon got to the end of them.

"Do you read French, dearie?" the peroxide parrot had said to her once when she was clamoring for reading matter, but had been snubbed into silence by the auburn one before Nina could reply. She was sorry that she was never visited by the pretty young half-caste daughters and their lively friends, whom she could hear making merry at most hours of the twenty-four except the morning ones. Apparently Mrs. Lascelles kept open house. Nina knew that the household was very vulgar, and very Bohemian, but she had not the slightest suspicion that it was of ill repute. She considered that the two old parrots, though common, were very kind, and was thanking heaven that she had so lenient an employer. She had not yet seen Mother Monty when she was crossed!

277

Through the long hot afternoon Nina lay, her hair dank with perspiration, listening languidly to the sounds of Africa coming through the swinging gauze screens that guarded the wide-open french windows against flies. Across the ever-open door of her room a bead curtain hung for the sake of such privacy as is possible in the tropics, where life is unendurable unless the air is on the move.

Just behind the wall of the large garden was a native hamlet, the noise from which arose all day and far into the night; but as the noise from the house was both louder and later, this was no great matter, and Nina lay listening to the sounds of native life and thinking of the days when Africa was her home and she was happy with Cassalis. There came over her a great wave of misery as she thought of her home and her man, both taken from her after so brief a happiness. She had never dared to allow herself to dwell on the memories of her lost happiness, for they always ended in the picture of Lewis being torn to pieces by crocodiles, which made her physically ill.

Today, however, the long empty hours lying listening to the random sounds of village life wakened all her memories, and they rose in a flood that overwhelmed her. She gave herself up to her grief, whatever price it might demand in payment, and all her life with Lewis rose before her eyes; she could see him, his walk, his ways, as clearly as if he were with her in the room. The gold wrist-watch that looked so incongruous on the muscular red-brown arm. The loose mesh shirt that fluttered in the wind, the close-fitting shorts that showed off the spare lines of hips that always seemed to her so unexpectedly slim for the shoulders, accustomed as she was to a less stream-lined type of male, in whom the proportions were reversed. Lewis's voice, deep, abrupt, with the chuckling laugh that was never let right out—the laugh, had she known it, that is typical of men outside the law who are always on their guard. The short, light-brown hair that Mammy Jonah clipped with clippers evenly all over his head when it got too long between his visits to more orthodox barbers, giving his head the look of a small boy's, in queer contrast to his rather lined face. Cut thus, unsoftened by any long hair left on the forehead, for it was beyond Mammy Jonah's power to achieve a quiff, the broad, high forehead that held Cassalis's brains rose like a cliff over the deep-set, light-hazel eyes that shifted from green to grey as his mood changed. He had had a curious trick of always keeping the lids half lowered over his eyes, a trick acquired originally to prevent the colour from being seen when he was in disguise, and eventually becoming habitual. Cassalis never opened his eyes fully unless he was laughing, and as he seldom laughed except when he was with Nina, he had acquired that curious look of a basking lizard that she had noticed at their first meeting.

She saw him so clearly that she seemed to re-create him, and there went out from her an intense longing for her man, a longing that seemed as if it must draw him back to her even from the grave, it was so powerful. For a moment she felt as if she were in touch with him, that he had heard her voiceless call and had answered. Then she dropped back helpless on the tumbled pillows from which she had raised herself in the intensity of her emotion, scolding herself for the folly that could only make her suffer, and trying to turn her mind to other things before her imagination presented to her the last horrible scene, as muddy waters churned to foam and a sunburnt arm with a gold wrist-watch rose for a moment above them, and more and more and yet more crocodiles came from every direction until far as eye could reach there was a heaving surface of scaly, squirming bodies.

She concentrated her attention on the braying and bleating of a gramophone that some mechanical genius had put into reverse so that the tunes were coming out backwards; this was a very popular game at Mother Montmorency's, and visitors tried to guess the tunes and betted on their guesses, considerable sums of money changing hands; the quality of the music, being modern, was surprisingly unaffected.

As she listened, a loud but jocular dispute about a bet broke out, someone, who denied the charge with squeals and giggles, being accused of welching; there was a sound of breaking glass and a perfect hurricane of squeals as rough horse-play started, and the screens of Nina's window suddenly burst open and in shot a mulatto girl without a stitch on her, who vanished through the bead curtain of the door with a hop and a skip and a wiggle of her mauve behind—evidently the welcher. Hard on her heels came a heavier step, the fly-screens flew open again, and in came a man, who stopped in amazement as he saw Nina lying hung up by the heels to a kind of gallows. To her amazement and delight she recognized Leary, the raffish but decent newspaper-man who had entertained her during Lewis's trial.

She spoke his name, and he came up to the bedside and stood gazing down at her in speechless amazement, his choolate charmer forgotten.

"In the name of God, Mrs. Cassalis, what are ye doing here?"

"Lying in bed getting over a broken leg," said Nina, delighted to see him.

"But in this house, Mrs. Cassalis? What are ye doing in this house? Lewis wants his neck breaking."

"He is dead," said Nina, the smile vanishing from her face. "Didn't you know that."

"Dead? Lewis dead? Not him. Not till the Day of Judgment, if then. No use telling that story to me. Truth is my trade, though I don't always tell ut."

"He is, though. They—they identified the remains. I

signed all the papers."

"What papers?"

"Why, for clearing up his estate."

"With Willis?"

"Yes, with Mr. Willis."

"Hmm, that explains a lot. Look here, I daren't stop talking to you, this looks like deep water. If I'm caught here, I mayn't get out alive. Don't say you've seen me, for the love of God, and I'll look into matters." And he, too, vanished through the bead curtain as precipitately as his lady friend.

He was not a moment too soon, for right on his heels came Mrs. Lascelles, rather breathless.

"Sorry you've been disturbed, deary," she said.

"It doesn't matter," answered Nina, "I wasn't asleep."

"What was it that happened, deary?"

"I don't know, they just charged through."

"Ah, I expect they had been surprised while they were sun-bathing," said Mrs. Lascelles, looking relieved, and padded out again on the dropped arches that had given way on the pavements of Piccadilly.

CHAPTER XXI

IN answer to an urgent telephone-message to his hotel, Cassalis went round with a very ill grace to the offices of the local paper, that was now edited by his old acquaintance Leary, vice a succession of better men who had not stood the climate. In fact, he would probably not have gone at all if Willis had not advised against going, for he was in that mood when his hand was against every man and he imagined in consequence that every man's hand was against him, for Mother Monty had broken it to him that her mission had ended in failure; the Marseilles police having got suspicious, she had had to drop Nina, but nevertheless she claimed expenses. So far she hadn't got them, Cassalis being a true son of the underworld.

He was stopping at Willis's hotel and sharing his sitting-room, since that worthy, released from hospital nominally convalescent, was still too jittery to be left to his own devices. It was an unpleasant menage; Willis, ringing the changes on sedatives and tonics, for he dared not drink, was by no means pleasant company; and Cassalis, his plans gone astray and not seeing how a second attempt of the same sort could hope for success, was little better.

He arrived at the offices of the local paper, which was also the local printery, was shown into the editorial sanctum, slammed his helmet down on top of Leary's raffle of papers, and scowled at him.

Leary scowled back with interest.

"Lewis Cassalis, ye're a dhirty dog, and if ye weren't so large and me so fat, I'd kick ye for ut."

"What's the matter now?" asked Cassalis. Leary was one of the few people who weren't afraid of him, and he liked him for it. He would have shot any other man for the half of that.

"What is your wife doing in ould Mother Monty's Dusthole?"

"What!" cried Cassalis.

"Didn't ye know she was there?"

"No! My God, no, I swear I didn't!"

Leary, who prided himself on his discernment, could not make out whether Cassalis was telling the truth or lying. He appeared to be genuinely astonished, but not as astonished as might have been expected at such news. Cassalis's next question puzzled him still more.

"How long has she been there?" he asked. Leary looked at him through narrowing eyes.

"When ye say ye did not know she was there, I believe ye. But if ye tell me ye know nothing about her being there, I shall not believe ye. I don't know how long she has been there, me going through her room on the run accidental-like, as ye might say, and your affairs being too explosive to be meddled with by family men like me; but some time, I should say, for she was strung up by the leg for a broken bone but otherwise thrivin', so far as I could judge during me hasty interview. Now will ye explain her presence, or shall I go to Lady Piercy with me story?"

Cassalis's hand went to his hip.

"Leave ut alone," said Leary. "Ye won't want ut. I'm by way of bein' a friend to both of ye. Now, Lewis, me lad, what is the meanin' of this onpleasant situation? For I take ut it has a meanin' and is not fortuitous."

"It means," said Cassalis, contriving to look exactly like a thoroughbred horse with flattened ears, "that my lady wife has started a divorce action against me, and I don't see the fun of it."

"So Mother Monty picked her up for ye, did she? I saw she had no suspicion where she had landed herself. But I'm puzzled about the divorce, Lewis, for she's convinced she's a widow."

Cassalis pulled a letter from the pocket of his shorts and flung it in front of Leary, who drew his spectacles down from his eyebrows to his eyes and studied it.

"That looks pretty conclusive," he said. "Harris, Harris, and Kimmins, of Clifford's Inn: now, what are me associations with that name? Wait a minute an' I'll get ut; I've a memory that has never failed me yet. Harris, Harris, and Kimmins, of Clifford's Inn ..." He held the paper up to the light and studied the watermark. "Well, I'll be—wait, wait, Lewis, I think I've got it!"

He disappeared in the direction of the printing-house at a remarkable speed for one so fat, for he had put on weight rapidly since he had ceased reporting.

Cassalis's heart was beating hard. He thanked his savage gods that Nina was indeed safely in the Dust-hole, but he also prayed to them to help him get her safely out, for that might not be very easy if Mother Monty were bent on double-crossing. He had a momentary thought of going to the authorities, but he saw at once he was hardly in a position to do that, especially if Nina were resentful and obdurate, as she had every cause to be. No, he had best rely on his reputation for ruthlessness. He did not think even Mother Monty would face what she must know would be coming to her if any harm came to Nina.

Leary returned with a small and dirty piece of metal in his hand.

284

"Here's the key to the situation," he said. "I came across this in the composing-room the other day, and nobody could tell me whose it was or how it came there."

He rubbed the little plate on the pad belonging to the rubber stamps, turned it over, and slammed it smartly down on top of a plain quarto follower, picked it off carefully with his long, neglected finger-nails, that came in handy for a job like that, and pushed the result over to Cassalis, who saw before him another headed sheet of note-paper such as Nina's solicitors had used.

"I don't know who Messrs. Harris, Harris, and Stick-in-the-mud, of Clifford's Inn, may be when they're at home," said Leary, "but they have their stationery printed in this office."

"I don't understand. What do you mean?" said Cassalis.

"You know Willis is a damn good engraver?" said Leary. "It's pretty certain he was the source of the ten-shilling 'lils' that have been passed to the niggers all up and down the Coast. If I hunted a bit further, I don't believe I'd be long in finding the plates from which all the forms you've had to fill in for your divorce were printed."

"But what's he playing at?"

"What's he playing at? Same thing he was playing at when he got her to put up at his hotel during the trial for some reason or other."

"Did she do that?" asked Lewis sharply and suspiciously, his mind ready to leap to any evil conclusion in the mood he was in.

"She did that, for about ten minutes. Then off she went back to the launch and left him to pay for the fun he hadn't had. She picked up fever there, though, and damn nearly died on Ngumba's hands. I got wind of it, and put Lady Piercy on to her. That's how she came to get in with Government House."

285

Cassalis sat staring into space, trying to piece together the significance of the things he was now learning for the first time.

"But I had a letter from her in her own writing, and with an English postmark."

"Let's have a look at ut."

Cassalis hesitated.

"No, I'm not interested in its contents, I only want to examine the handwriting. I suppose you know why Willis came to the Coast?"

"Lord Chancellor jealous of his brains, so *he* says."

"So I've heard every time the subject comes up for discussion. Let me see the letter, Lewis; fold it anyway ye like."

"Oh, I don't mind. Read the damn thing. I've got past caring."

Leary picked up the grimy sheet that was flung at him, stained and sticky as paper gets that is carried next the skin in hot countries. He handled it carefully, for it was on the point of falling to pieces in the folds. Holding a powerful reading-glass over it, he made Cassalis examine the writing letter by letter, and he saw that instead of being formed of the single line made by a pen gliding over the paper, it consisted of a series of tiny strokes, so minute, so delicately adjusted, as to be invisible to the naked eye and look like a continuous line, but nevertheless clearly revealed by the powerful glass.

"Forgery," said Leary succinctly. "What he ought to have done time for originally if he had had his rights." He turned over the page and read the letter through. "A nice thing to send a fellow," was his only comment. "But you're a damn fool, Lewis, you ought to have known this was a put-up job on the face of it. No woman ever gives a man the go-by because he's a criminal. That's the sort they always like the best."

Cassalis rose slowly to his feet and put on his helmet.

"Where are you going?" said Leary.

"To see Willis," said Cassalis.

"No, ye aren't. You're a respectable citizen and a family man these days. You'll telephone him. He's done a lot of your dirty work for you in his time; he'll do this job, too, for you if you handle him properly. At least, I should if I were Willis."

Cassalis nodded and sat down again. Leary pushed the desk telephone over to him.

He asked for, and got, the hotel. He asked for, and got, Willis.

"I want you to make a note of what I'm going to tell you, Willis," he said into the mouthpiece, and waited patiently while Willis apparently got pencil and paper.

"I don't like your sense of humour," said Leary. Cassalis paid no attention. A murmur from the other end showed that Willis was at the post of duty.

"Never mind where I'm speaking from," he heard Cassalis say. "But I've got in my hand one of the blocks you used to print the forms in my divorce case. The one for the solicitors' note-paper, if you want details. I also hear that my wife is at the Dust-hole, laid up with a broken leg, and has been there for some time. Have you got anything to say? No, I thought you hadn't. Good-bye."

"So that's that," said Cassalis. He and Leary sat and looked at each other. They hadn't long to wait. The sharp crack of a revolver-shot disturbed the afternoon stillness a few blocks away.

"That also is that," said Leary. "Much better to let'm do it than to do it yourself. Tuppence for a telephone-call works out cheaper than squaring juries, even if you get a reduction on a number. No, damn it, I don't want your tuppence, I was only being romantic. Come and have a drink. I should think even you could do with one on this occasion. As for me—well, it's a part, and a very integral part, of me profession."

Over the drinks they laid out the next phase of the campaign. Cassalis was too old a campaigner to rush straight up to an establishment like the Ash-can, ring the bell, and ask for Nina. They were used to that sort of thing, and prepared for it.

But Leary would allow no finesse.

"Lewis, you go straight to Lady Piercy and make a clean breast of the whole business. You want somebody to put you right with the authorities, and you want somebody to put you right with your wife. You're a dhirty dog, and ye know ut."

Cassalis agreed.

People did not usually call on the Governor's wife in shirt and shorts, or, if they did, were not received, but Cassalis was passed straight through to Lady Piercy's drawing-room with the very minimum of delay, and Lady Piercy welcomed him by taking both his hands in hers and shaking them.

Very embarrassed, blushing scarlet to the ears, he told of his excursion into white-slave trading. He wasn't sure that Lady Piercy would know what he was referring to, and stumbled in laborious and ambiguous circles, but she knew all right.

"I've never had anything to do with the trade before, at least—er—not as a trader," he said, getting redder and redder. She believed him. She had never seen anything so hot and bothered in her life.

She made him sit down and have tea with her while they waited for Sir Robert to come out of a conference. The wide windows opened upon a terrace below which the lovely gardens stretched to a retaining-wall over-hanging the main road to the interior, and as they sat at their tea they could

288

hear the trade of Empire rumbling and hooting and crashing its gears below them.

"By the way," said Lady Piercy, "there is something I have been wanting to tell you, but I daren't venture, after you were so cross with me out side the post-office."

"I say, Lady Piercy, I'm frightfully sorry for that piece of oafishness. It's no use trying to apologize for it. All I can do is to tell you the explanation—I'd just had a code wire to say that Mrs. Montmorency had bagged Nina. So you can judge the sort of cad you made me feel when you spoke to me so kindly."

"Is Mrs. Montmorency the same as Ma Monty?"

"Yes, that's the creature. But how do you come to know these things?"

"I know lots of things," said Lady Piercy, laughing.

"I don't know what women are coming to nowadays," said Cassalis, quite seriously.

Lady Piercy laughed more than ever.

"But let me tell you my bit of information before my husband comes, as there may not be a chance after that. As you went across the square outside the post-office, I saw quite unmistakably that you were being followed by three Arabs."

Cassalis sat up.

"Can you describe them?"

She did her best. One man of any pure breed is very like any other of the same age. It is only we Anglo-Saxon mongrels who show sufficient diversity to enable anyone to be recognized from a verbal description. A reference to the boil-scarred back of a neck glimpsed under a tarboush in passing, however, enabled Cassalis to place his pursuers with certainty. Boils in that situation are not common among Arabs. That could only have been Yussuf ben Ibrahim, who had had the advantages of education forced upon him by his father, among them being a stiff collar for a time.

Afar off in the sultry air they heard the sound of a fire-bell drawing nearer. At Lady Piercy's suggestion they went down to the terrace overhanging the road to watch it go by, for the darky crew were intensely proud of their outfit, and the driving was a marvel.

Down came the red engine, going hell for leather, all the black faces agrin with eager anticipation under the brass helmets, traffic scattering before this municipal Juggernaut far quicker than any police could have cleared a way for it, for there was nothing to do but scatter or be scattered. Cassalis and Lady Piercy stood laughing at the panic-stricken dive for the ditches by everything on the road.

"It will be well worth while to stop and see the escape go by," said Lady Piercy. "They never allow for its length. I wonder where the fire is?"

Cassalis cast his keen hunter's eye over the low-lying ground that stretched away from the slight rise where stood Government House towards a creek, that wound sluggishly inland after the manner of African rivers to furnish an extra mouth for the main stream whose estuary formed the harbour. Just beyond the last of the houses, and just before the first of the huts, a large bungalow stood in its own grounds; from it rose an unmistakable column of smoke on which a red glare was already reflected, for the bungalow was of wood, and was burning like tinder.

" God!" cried Cassalis. "It's the Dust-hole!"

Both their minds leapt to Nina, lying there helpless in her splints and slings.

The clangour of a second fire-bell was heard coming down the hill.

"I'll jump the escape as it slows up for the bend," cried Cassalis, throwing his leg over the low wall that guarded the terrace on the garden side.

"It won't slow up for the bend!" shrieked Lady Piercy

as he hung by his hands for the ten-foot drop. Nor did it. It swung wide with a terrific lurch over the rough ground, striking a cart piled with native produce with its overhanging ladders and sending a fountain of vegetables high in the air.

Cassalis ran out towards it as it lurched back on to the road. Lady Piercy watched him terror-stricken as he judged his time. It seemed inevitable that he would be run down by the crazy crew with their lurching contraption half out of control, but he judged it to a nicety, and with one spring was up among the indignant darkies, who seemed about to throw him off forthwith. Lady Piercy gazed after the flying trolley in horror to see whether they would succeed. She saw Cassalis's sun-helmet fly off and go bowling down the road, but he appeared to retain his hold, and as the escape swung broadside on in a skid she saw that they had made a place for him in their crowded ranks, and he was hanging on with the best. Everyone connected with the fire station and any of their relatives that were handy always got on the escape.

The few brief minutes of that desperate joy-ride had served to establish Cassalis in command of the outfit, and when they arrived outside the Dust-hole, now well alight, he shouted to the driver, who did not need telling twice, to drive through the fence to save argument. Through they went with a magnificent crash of splintered timbers, the escape turning over on its side as it met the soft earth of a vegetable patch and throwing them all off among the mealies. Cassalis, scrambling to his feet, found himself face to face with Yusuf ben Ibrahim.

Hardly thinking what he was doing, for there was no Leary to counsel caution, Cassalis, berserk-mad, seized his old enemy round the hips in a Rugby tackle and hurled him clean through the nearest window to sample his own handiwork. He must have struck some supporting timber as he landed for down came the blazing roof forthwith.

A chorus of yells warned Cassalis of a new danger, and he swung round to see old Ibrahim levelling a rifle at him.

There was no cover, and to dodge at that distance was useless. He stood stock still, for it is not easy to shoot a man who looks at you and does not stir. For one brief second Ibrahim hesitated, and in that second a fire-hatchet came flying through the air, flung with deadly aim, and took the old Arab where neck joins shoulder, practically cutting his head off. He sank to the ground in a shapeless heap of blood-stained draperies.

Cassalis tore round the corner of the bungalow, the crowd of darkies streaming in his wake, some in gorgeous brass-bound uniforms, some in little more than they were born with. From Leary's description he had no difficulty in finding the room where Nina had lain. It was a mass of flames. He stood staring into the inferno through the gap that had been a window, till someone pulled him back as the walls fell in.

Sir Robert Piercy came quickly round what had once been the corner of the building but was now a column of flame. He spoke to Cassalis and laid his hand on his shoulder. Cassalis took not the slightest notice but continued to gaze into the heart of the fire, his face blistering unobserved with the heat. Sir Robert took him by the arm and led him away.

As they made their way out by the gate at the back to avoid the crowd gathered in front, they heard a faint cry—a woman's voice calling, the voice of a white woman. Cassalis shook off Sir Robert's hand from his arm and was off like a hound in pursuit of the sound. Down to the bank of the creek he went with a sure instinct, and saw below him a native canoe just pushing off, with Nina lying on a stretcher among the rowers. Cassalis jumped. He lit on the decked-in stern, rocking the frail craft so violently it shipped water over either gunnel alternately, threatening to swamp at any moment.

292

From the bows Ibrahim's headman rose with a flutter of draperies, a heavy, native-made Arab gun in his hand, levelled it at Cassalis, and pressed the trigger. The bullet just tipped the lobe of Cassalis's ear. The report, reverberating in the hollow channel of the stream, was like the report of a cannon. The recoil must have been like one too, for as in a slow-motion picture Cassalis saw the Arab's draperies go up in the air as he turned over in a back somersault out of the cranky craft and landed with a splash in the water.

Instantly the quiet pool was alive with action. From every shoal and bar what had seemed to be rotting timber galvanized into life, and Nina, lying helplessly on her stretcher, saw her nightmare materialize as more crocodiles came, and more, and more, and more—and fainted at the sight.

In a white airy room on the upper floor of Government House, Nina lay in bed under a "cradle". She had had a bad time. Her leg, clumsily splinted after being hastily taken down from the pulleys that supported it prior to her removal, had come unset, and she had been in agony, and an operation had been necessary before it could be reset.

Through the drugs that had deadened her pain, and the aftermath of the anaesthetic, she had seen the face of Cassalis coming and going; but she had also seen, with equal vividness, the crocodiles swarming all round her in thick dark water that never ceased churning.

Now, however, her mind was clear and everything had faded together. The cleaned-up wound gave no pain and she lay at rest, watching the boats moving over the glassy surface of the harbour stretched out below the window beside which her bed was drawn.

Lady Piercy had been to see her earlier in the day, and also the previous evening. She remembered these two visits though she remembered no others. But she had come out

293

of the mists now, and her mind was clear, and she must think of both the present and the future. She had broached the subject to Lady Piercy that morning, and had been firmly squashed. But she would try again next time her hostess came, for she could not be easy in her mind till she had talked things out. There was so much that was like a bad dream that she could not tell what was real or what wasn't.

The door opened softly and the starched blue-and white nurse came in and smiled at her.

"So you are awake at last?" she said. "I must make you tidy, for I think you are going to have visitors this afternoon."

She brushed and dressed the fair curling hair that had got lank and draggled under the sketchy care of the old black mammy at the Dust-hole, and with her own compactum powdered Nina's slightly tip-tilted nose. Then she put about her shoulders Lady Piercy's very best négligé in shell-pink silken swathes, propped her up as high as she would go among the frilled pillows, and left her.

The door opened softly again, and Lady Piercy came in. She sat down at Nina's side and took her hand in hers.

"I have come to talk to you," she said, "on behalf of a man who is so afraid of what you will say to him that he daren't come himself."

Nina began to laugh.

"Yes, I know. It was too funny. I wonder what Mr. Leary's wife would say if she knew. I can still see that girl shimmying through the window with him after her."

"You know, then, what kind of a house it was you were in?"

"Yes, I realized at the end, when I heard Mrs. Montmorency quarrelling with Sheik Ibrahim about what she was to be paid for allowing her house to be burnt. Hadn't they got marvellous names, that pair? Montmorency and Lascelles! I wonder what their real names were? Buggins and Muggins, I expect. All the same, they were very kind to me."

"Do you know why you had been brought to that house?"

"Well, I suppose I was a white slave, only I hadn't noticed it."

"No, you weren't that. All the same, the white-slave organization had been used to kidnap you. I have been asked to be absolutely frank with you, that is why I am telling you all this." She paused. "There was a man who loved you once, wasn't there, Nina?"

"Yes," said Nina, her eyes filling with tears.

"I expect you knew him better than I did, though I got to know him quite well in the end. Can you realize what an extraordinary mixture a man can be, especially a man out in a wild country among wild races?"

"Yes," said Nina, "I always knew that. And the trouble was that I could never remember he was a mixture for more than a few minutes at a time, but only knew I cared for him and how happy we were together." The tears in Nina's eyes threatened to overflow, and Lady Piercy went on hastily.

"What made you decide to leave Africa so suddenly, Nina, without saying good-bye to any of us?"

Nina told her the story of Willis and his dreadful bungalow.

"There wasn't anything else to do," she said. "Lewis was dead, and I was penniless, and you were still on tour, goodness knows where, and the mission was getting ready to show me the door. Beggars cannot be choosers. I had meant to write you, but I was deadly ill all the way home, and after I got home; and then so depressed and miserable I simply hadn't the courage. I should have had to explain so many things if I had written to you, and it was all too sore."

"How do you feel about things now, Nina?"

Nina sighed. "I don't know; it has all been like a bad dream. Especially the crocodiles. I always see crocodiles just as I am going off to sleep. It is beastly."

"It will soon wear off now."

"It has been going on for months, and hasn't shown any signs of wearing off."

"You know Lewis wasn't eaten by crocodiles, don't you?"

"No? Wasn't he? Then how did he die?" asked Nina apathetically .

"Are you sure he is dead, Nina?"

"Yes, quite sure. I saw all the papers in connection with his death when I had to sign things for Mr. Willis."

"Are you sure Mr. Willis is to be trusted?"

"Oh no, quite sure he isn't. But he couldn't very well be mistaken in a thing like that, could he?"

"Do you know that Mr. Willis—he's dead now, I don't suppose you will be sorry to hear—"

"Oh, is he? What did he die of?"

"He blew his brains out."

"Why?"

"I am coming to that. Mr. Willis was the cleverest forger we ever had on the Coast. Do you know that he forged a set of papers that made it look as if you were trying to divorce Lewis, and even forged letters in your handwriting?"

"How perfectly rotten! Whatever did he do that for? Surely there was no need to go on blacking Lewis's character after he was dead."

"He did it for the same reason that he forged certain other papers that I am coming to in a moment. Now do you see who was at the bottom of the kidnapping of you, and why it was done?"

"Willis?"

"No, Lewis, Nina. The papers that made you think Lewis was dead were just as much forged as those that made Lewis think you were trying to divorce him. It was Lewis had you kidnapped, Nina, not Willis."

"O-oh !" said Nina, and dropped back on her pillows. Lady Piercy looked at her closely.

"I don't think you've taken too much harm," she said. "I will send Lewis along to talk to you himself presently."

Later in the afternoon Nina had more visitors despite the protesting nurse.

"Better get it over and then they will settle down," said Lady Piercy, as she and her husband bearded her where she blocked the passage, defending her charge.

As they entered the room where Nina lay, Cassalis rose hastily from where he had been sitting on the edge of the bed. He had been turned off repeatedly by the nurse, but somehow he always seemed to get back there again. Seeing it was not that dragon, he cautiously reseated himself, taking infinite care not to jar Nina. But Nina did not mind how much she was jarred by her Lewis.

Nina had not seen Sir Robert since she had come to the house, and he chaffed her gently to relieve the tension.

Then he turned to Cassalis, who, though he still watched everybody about him, had lost much of the look of the outlaw that had marked him and set him apart.

"Well, have you settled with Sir Leopold?" he asked. "I've squared up all right with him. He'll pay what you said I was to ask."

"Good Lord, man, that was the price at which I told you to start bargaining! If he's paying that, you've been spoiling the Israelites. Are you going to have a job with him?"

" No, don't want it. I'd be no use in a job like that. I know my limitations. I'd kill somebody the first time they hauled me up for not clocking in on the tick."

"Well, would you like a job with me?"

"Very much—provided I work directly under you. I've no use for intermediaries."

Sir Robert repressed a smile.

"Nothing sticks to people's palms in the Civil Service. You must break your habits of thought," he said.

" 'Tisn't that—though you're wrong about their palms not being sticky—but I'm a one-man dog. I'll work for you, but I won't work for anyone else."

"Well, will you work alongside Grigson? He's stopping on after all."

"In the police? Does that mean brass buttons and drill?"

"No, in the secret police, on the political side."

"Now you're talking. Yes, that's just about my fighting-weight. That would suit me fine. But fancy my ending up in double harness with Grigson! Doesn't that strike you as humorous? How does he like the idea?"

"It was his suggestion."

"Well, I'm damned!"

"Yes, I dare say you are, but we don't like you any the less on that account."

THE END

Made in the USA
Columbia, SC
30 December 2017